Aman da

(CALTER CREEK 1)

LizAnn Carson

Amanda (Calter Creek 1)
© 2015 Elizabeth Carson

ISBN: 978-0-9939790-5-7

Cover photos used under license from:
Shutterstock.com, Deposit Photos
"Amanda" font: Stalemate, ©2012 by Jim Lyles for Astigmatic

Thank You

To the wonderful, supportive women of the critique loop in the From the Heart chapter of the Romance Writers of America. Your varied and insightful comments helped me make *Amanda* a better book.

Chapter 1

Pink.

Amanda Sinclair hated pink.

Hot pink. Dusty pink. Baby pink.

"You're lovely in pink, with those dark curls of yours," her mother had assured her, way back when.

Amanda was thirty-nine years old now, not seven, and she'd come to terms with the curls. She'd never been able to overcome her aversion to pink.

Her inner dialogue taunted her as she made her way to the Floor.

You've chosen to stock the stuff. It's good quality, in demand, reasonably priced.

It's not tasteful.

Ah, but you're not the mother of a seven-year-old princess.

But she *was* president of Sinclair Imports. Nothing mattered more to Amanda than keeping her customers happy and her bottom line healthy, so she made a point of checking out new merchandise as soon as it hit the Floor.

Sinclair Imports, or SI, occupied a bright, modern warehouse in an office park on the western outskirts of Calter Creek, Ohio. Offices and meeting rooms lined corridors along the south and west sides. The warehouse, known as the Floor, took up the rest of the building. Merchandise from the Floor shipped to retail outlets throughout the Midwest.

Amanda spotted Charlie, her Floor supervisor, talking to one of the forklift operators. He signaled that he'd get there as soon as he could, so she made herself at home in the Inventory Control Office, propped against a desk. This unscheduled down time was a small bonus in a busy day. She'd always loved the Floor, with its exotic atmosphere of wooden shipping crates, packing materials, and merchandise from faraway lands. She took the opportunity to be a fly on the wall and watch her company at work.

Charlie came into the office a few minutes later. "Sorry to keep you waiting, Amanda. Had to get a misfile sorted out ASAP, or something would have shipped wrong. You're here to see the new girls' line?" He removed his hard hat and ran a hand through his short, blondish hair.

She pushed off the desk. "Mel's ecstatic. Just what she wants to give her nieces for Christmas." Her mouth quirked when she thought about her executive assistant's enthusiasm.

The Floor team had set up a display in the little viewing room, adjacent to the Inventory Control Office. She'd expected it, but faced with the reality of the items on the tables when she entered the room, she pinched her eyes closed for a moment. Right in her face were a desk lamp with a bubble gum colored shade, a cell phone pouch in pink paisleys, pale pink bookends with a ballerina frieze, and a pen and pencil set in a dusty rose leather-like sleeve. A peachy-pink clock radio clashed with a mauve-pink wall poster showing a girl in a tiara absorbed in a book.

Charlie shook his head in sympathy. "The idea seems to be that even princesses have to go to school and learn stuff. Here's the current comparables." He picked up a sheet of paper with pictures of similar items and handed it to her. She scanned the sheet, noting that most of the items listed were higher priced.

With half her mind Amanda followed Charlie's discussion of schedules and market demand. With the other half, she studied articles spread out in front of her, trying to get into the thoughts of the girl whose life presumably would be complete if she found these things under the tree on Christmas Day.

"... so the pre-orders are healthy. We'll be shipping this stuff starting this afternoon—Amanda?"

"Sorry, my mind wandered. All that pink's hypnotic. It's scary, frankly." She turned to the door. "Let's get the staff in here for a look."

"Will do." He escorted her through the office. "Kinda makes me glad I don't have a daughter."

Amanda laughed and waved, and headed back to her desk. She started speaking before she was fully through the outer door of the President's suite. "Mel, have you got those projections ready? I want to go over them this afternoon."

"Done. I put it in your Sharedrive folder. What did you think?" Her voice betrayed her enthusiasm, as did the elevated color in her freckled face. "Aren't they adorable?"

Amanda met her excited assistant's eyes with a small smile. In her early thirties, Mel Chesterton was a dynamo, sassy and confident. A redhead whose mid-length, sometimes frizzy hair tended to look like a halo when backlit, today she wore an emerald green pantsuit and a scarf covered with jungle animals in primary colors.

Amanda herself had dressed in tailored navy and white, and kept her hair strictly controlled by a thin black headband. Essentially, the polar opposite of Mel.

"The overall effect curdles your brain. You're the one who voted to stock them. I expect there'll be a staff viewing later today."

"Sorry, but you share the blame. You wouldn't have approved them if there wasn't a market. I'm drooling." Mel bounced in her chair.

Amanda frowned a little. "Tell me something. Did you want pink stuff when you were a girl?"

"Are you kidding? Princesses, ballerinas, a horse with pink ribbons in her mane ..." Mel clutched her hands to her chest and looked rapturously off into the distance before coming back to earth and chuckling. "Right up to the time I discovered real boys."

Amanda waved a thank you to Mel and disappeared into her office, mildly puzzled. She had *never* wanted pink. She preferred sensible. Her ideal Christmas present had been a fountain pen, not glitter, even before the time when she was fourteen and resolved that she, not her older brother James, would one day run Sinclair Imports.

Well, she ran it now, and had for eight years. SI had grown to be half again the size it had been when she took over from her father. It paid her parents, her brother, and herself a nice dividend each year. She and Sinclair Imports were doing well.

* * *

By mid-afternoon, Amanda's equanimity was long gone.

Damn headache.

A classic tension headache had wrapped itself around the back of her head like a spiked steel band. The headaches, which assaulted her every week or so, were a new development, one she couldn't figure out.

She was aware of, and cultivated, her reputation: unflappable, capable, efficient, pleasant, and fair. But at that moment she felt as brittle as cheap china.

Painkillers in hand, she headed to the break room for coffee to wash them down. Mel wasn't at her desk, which meant there would be a group gathered for afternoon coffee. She'd rather not deal with her staff just then, but she'd cope. She always coped, whatever happened. No rule said she had to be eternally affable.

As she strode along the south corridor, she glanced through the big windows overlooking the Floor. She could see her reflection in the window.

Haggard. You look like a demolition site.

She paused long enough to square her shoulders, then, drawn by the life-restoring properties of ibuprofen, she carried on to the west corridor and the break room.

The three members of the accounting team, Mel, and a man she didn't know stood chatting in the middle of the room.

"... get you set up with a password ...."

"... staff barbecue lunch next week ...."

"... protocols for when you work at home ...."

A potential new hire, then. The stranger was about her age, a little more than average height, and lanky. Dark blond hair, brownish-green eyes. He had on slacks and a tie, but he looked as if he'd been playing touch football in them. A dirt smear on the shirt, wet stains on the knees of his trousers.

She might have admitted she was in a nasty mood and looking for a target. She didn't admit anything. Holding herself stiffly upright, she joined the group and fixed her eyes on the stranger.

"Amanda, hey, you're just in time." Stan Johnson, the avuncular head of Accounting, turned to pour another cup of coffee. "Jac—"

"I gather you've applied to work here?" She addressed the newcomer, riding right over Stan.

Before he had a chance to reply, Mel spoke up. "Amanda, this is Ja—"

Her voice shot ice pellets into the room. "Is it remotely possible you're unaware that your appearance is inappropriate? Especially for an interview." His eyes met hers and a look, wary on his part, less than friendly on hers, flew between them. "You will *never* work here if this is how you choose to present yourself."

"It's not," the man said mildly.

"And that—" Words nearly failed her. A ponytail. The man had hair so long he'd pulled it back into a ponytail. Had Stan lost his mind? She gestured dismissively. "Unacceptable. I hope that's clear?"

"Perfectly clear." The still unnamed future employee's voice was cool and assessing. "However, the hair stays. It's mostly invisible under a jacket. But it stays."

"Most unfortunate, Mr. — whoever you are. I'm sure there are other applicants. Good day to you." She tore her eyes away, took the cup of coffee from Stan's hand, and turned, giving them an excellent view of her ramrod-straight back as she made for the door. She heard someone mutter, "Whew!" when she'd gone a few steps along the west corridor.

Mel's presence in the break room meant Amanda had a temporary respite. She needed the time to … *to what? Cool off? Regroup?* She used the coffee to swallow the painkillers, then put her head down on her desk, cradled in her arms.

As she fully expected, Mel stormed into the suite well before the pain subsided. She closed the outer door none too gently and stomped through her own office to Amanda's. Amanda didn't look up.

"Overreact some?" Mel demanded. "Do you have any idea what you've done?"

"My head's splitting open. Stop yelling, Mel, it hurts."

"Can't help that. Maybe if it splits enough you'll have room in it for one more fact. That's Jacob McKinnon in the break room. Stan's been doing happy dances for days at the thought of bringing him on board." Mel plopped down on a guest chair. "He's the best potential new hire we've seen in ages, especially in Accounting. And now Jacob McKinnon isn't so sure he wants to work for us after all. Thanks a bunch."

Amanda slowly raised her head. She didn't even try to bring Mel into focus. "Jacob McKinnon," she repeated blankly.

"The same Jacob McKinnon Stan's been trying to recruit for months. Furthermore," Mel continued, on a roll of her own now, "I expect you'll think this is irrelevant, but I bet you only saw his clothes and the hair. You didn't even notice what was *in* the clothes, did you? That sun-bleached streak in his hair, and he looks kind of tired and sad, as if he needs someone to take care of him? And no wedding ring." She produced the last piece of information like a trump card.

"I *saw* that his shirt wasn't properly tucked and there was a stain on it. The lack of a ring is relevant how?"

A comment like that wasn't enough to discourage Mel. "His eyes are hazel, did you notice? His mouth, the whole package … if he doesn't join SI, we're deprived, that's all I can say."

Notice his eyes, when he'd virtually skewered her with them? Amanda wasn't about to admit it. She put her head back down on her folded arms. "Even if he's God himself, he can't work here looking like that."

Mel returned to business. "Hasn't anyone told you what happened? There was an accident out in the parking lot. A car sideswiped a woman from one of the other buildings. He stayed with her until the ambulance got there. Didn't you hear the sirens?" Amanda shook her head on her arms. "Rattled him, I think. But that's why the stains. And as for the ponytail—"

The anger resurfaced. "Before we know it he'll be selling marijuana out of the Accounting suite."

"With his credentials? Give me a break. We can't expect everyone to be as conservative as you are. Lots of perfectly ordinary men have ponytails these days. In fact, Marco has one." Marco was one of the forklift operators on the Floor.

Mel was right, and Amanda knew it.

The railway spike had become a finishing nail. She could have wept with relief. She raised her head again. "I'll go talk to Stan."

"May be too late for that. This McKinnon guy's in enough demand that it wasn't only us interviewing him. He was interviewing us as well. Seems he prefers a peaceful environment and doesn't take stressful contracts. We'd been doing fine until your tirade, but the last thing he said to Stan was he's going to have to think it over. Sounds like a brush-off to me. Stan agreed, but his language was more colorful."

"And we need him specifically?"

"Or similar, but he's got a first-rate reputation. And we've been looking for someone in accounting forever."

Less than an hour southwest of Columbus, Calter Creek was large enough to provide all amenities, small enough to be safe and family-oriented. All of which was important to Sinclair Imports since most of the staff were married with families.

It wasn't large enough to offer a decent selection of available CPAs.

Amanda reached for her coffee mug. Caffeine wasn't a sure bet where the headaches were concerned, but it might help finish this one off. She circled the desk to sit in the other visitor's chair and sighed. "I don't understand this. I don't go around insulting people. It's just lately …"

Mel was the one person at SI she could actually talk to regarding the scene in the break room. Mel spoke her mind, guarded the portal, and as the central repository of SI gossip, kept her abreast of what was going on. They enjoyed each other's company and respected each other's capabilities. She was a companion, if not a friend exactly, in a life in which close companions were in short supply. Amanda sometimes thought Mel could run SI as well as she did, but Mel willingly affirmed that she wouldn't have Amanda's job for all the tea in China. Or rather, for all the imported tea, in fancy canisters, they had in stock now. They'd brought in an expert to be sure the quality of the tea was equal to the beauty of the canister. Mel's idea, and like most of her ideas, it had paid off.

So Mel showed no qualms in reporting, "On the Floor they say you need to get laid." At Amanda's glare she waved a hand. "Hey, don't shoot the messenger. I'm just telling you what I heard, after the incident when the forklift sent the pile of picture frames flying, and you went out there with guns blazing."

"And it turned out the driver had blacked out. How's he doing, by the way?"

"Better. They've got him on some medication and told him not to drive. Charlie assigned him to inventory control, so at least he's working. Wife, two kids. Scary time."

"My head just … I was ready to kill someone. The same as today."

"It's four o'clock, Amanda. Go home."

"I still have to finish—"

"Take it with you. I'll run interference here. But tomorrow you're going to have some crow to eat."

Mel was right. Her presence here, at her own company, wasn't doing anyone any good this afternoon. Time enough tomorrow to face her staff. Again.

"You're right. I'll figure out what I need and go away."

Mel left the room and opened the suite's outer door before settling at her desk. Amanda sorted through the work she'd been doing before the headache struck, stacked it in her attaché case, and headed out.

At the outer door she paused and looked back at Mel. "You kept Stan away from here this afternoon, didn't you?"

"He would have eaten you for dinner. I thought that might not be the best management plan." Mel winked at her, then grinned and flapped her hands at the door.

Amanda nodded and left.

* * *

That evening, the man who had brought on the wrath of Amanda Sinclair tiptoed into a darkened bedroom and kissed the cheek of the child sleeping there. They'd already had a story, hugs and kisses, and the quiet time together that made up their post-bath bedtime routine. This was a small ritual of his own, a plea to the universe to keep his daughter safe and teach her how to be happy again.

Norah was now six, but her room held a lingering scent of powder and lavender from her babyhood. For Jacob McKinnon, this translated to protection, blessing pretty much everything that mattered in his world. He pulled her door partly closed, then headed downstairs to his favorite chair near the living room fireplace.

A small fire sent out the occasional spark against the screen. He queued up Internet radio on his tablet. New Age music floated through the room while he sank deeper into the chair, closed his eyes, and sat completely still for the next twenty minutes or so. Meditation had kept him sane over the last couple of years, and despite his pal Dave's teasing, he wasn't about to stop now.

Coming out of the meditation, he stretched his arms toward the ceiling. *Better.* Better than relying on alcohol or drugs to survive the evenings. While he enjoyed a beer as much as the next man, he'd made a resolution not to rely on alcohol as a crutch to get through the bad days.

Not that this had been a particularly bad day. Just one worthy of consideration.

He was starting to come alive again after the numbness following the loss of his wife, two interminable years ago. Norah remembered Debbie, although for her — for them both — those memories were fading. Including memories of the crash that had killed her mother before her eyes.

Norah had regressed after her mother's death, so much that it had been like having a baby to take care of again. Only recently, and with professional help, had she begun to return to her expected level. She'd been a deeply wounded child, with him the only stability in her short life. Add the need to keep them both fed and housed … yes, nights could be tough. Dave came over regularly to share a beer and some guy talk, but that was the sum total of his social life.

Now he had this new complication to deal with. The scene at Sinclair Imports had rattled him, but not for the reasons the others present probably thought.

The word on the street was that Amanda Sinclair, SI's president, was an excellent manager and employer. But according to the internal scuttlebutt, in the last few months she'd become more and more irritable.

"It's a controlled explosion, cutting you down with words. And that look, like you're a mutant. We can't figure it out," Jim Murdoch, one of the bookkeepers, had told him after Stan and Mel left them alone in the break room. "Business is good, but she can't seem to relax and let it flow." Jim shook his head. "She's logical to a fault. She listens, believe it or not, and she's willing to delegate. So don't ask me to explain that scene. Shakes you up some when she strikes."

But the attack on his appearance wasn't what had shaken him. He didn't need her approbation for staying in the parking lot with the injured woman, however challenging it had been for him to be anywhere near a car accident. No, it was her eyes. Blue as a deep glacier, framed by dark lashes. Icy, yet flashing fire.

And a pale face, that dark, curly hair. Lips that drew your eyes to her mouth, that made you want to ….

Oh, he'd noticed. And his reaction was one he hadn't experienced in over two years, and not from a woman other than Deb in more than ten. He wanted his hands in her hair. He wanted their mouths growing closer, wanted to see those ice-blue eyes closing ….

"Oh, boy," he muttered.

Not that there's any harm in being attracted to her. You're forty-two. And single. It's okay for you to notice women.

But some things hadn't been a part of his life for so long, it was as if he'd forgotten how.

As had become Jacob's habit when he was turning something over in his mind, he tugged on the end of his ponytail. The ponytail that reminded Norah of her mother, that she went hysterical over every time he suggested cutting it off. Sometimes he wondered if he should just do it, get rid of the thing. But he wasn't about to put Norah's recovery at risk.

The scene earlier. What was he going to do about that? He hadn't quite said no to the job at Sinclair Imports. He'd told Stan he'd call in a day or two with his decision. But he was more ambivalent about the position than he'd been prior to the interview.

Scene or no scene, the work was straightforward, and the perks were good. He could do a lot from home if he needed to, and the warehouse was only a ten-minute jog from his house. He stayed close to Norah these days. She was easing into first grade, working with the psychologist in the afternoon, but sometimes it boiled up in her, and he had to be there.

He loved his daughter more than life. But life was showing signs of growing complicated.

He heaved himself out of his chair and headed for his home gym tucked in the attached garage. He might be a slender guy, but he'd rather know there was muscle beneath the packaging.

Chapter 2

The next morning, Amanda was back at SI early. Before settling into her workday, she followed the south, then west corridors to the Accounting suite.

Stan looked anything but pleased to see her and didn't waste time on preliminaries. "Thanks a lot, Amanda. McKinnon isn't the kind of guy you interview, he's the kind of guy you court. He has his pick, and he knows it. We had him and we lost him. I wish I knew where we'll find anyone his equal." He slapped his glasses down on the desk and ran his hands over his head, barely disturbing the short gray brush cut.

To her, Stan seemed eternal and unchanging, though today his face looked older than his sixty years. He was the grand old man of SI, the only one who'd been with the company from its beginnings. She'd always liked and respected Stan, and now she had to apologize and placate.

"I hate this," she began. "I messed up, and I'm sorry. I need you to tell me how to fix it. If it's fixable."

"Sit down, you're making me nervous." Stan gestured at his guest chair.

Uneasy, she perched on the edge.

"It's not fixable by me," he continued. "McKinnon told me, very politely, that he wasn't sure he'd be a good fit here, but he'd mull it over. He's going to phone today and turn the job down. Maybe he'll be able to recommend someone." Stan made a hopeless gesture with his hand.

"Would it help if I talked to him?"

Stan shot her a look of flat disbelief. "In case you didn't notice, you insulted him, even though he had the manners not to show it."

Amanda winced. "So you don't want me to try?"

Stan leaned forward, forearms on his desk. "You've done a lot to be proud of at SI, but at the moment I'm royally pissed off with you. But if you can get McKinnon to give us another chance to win him, I'll buy you a throne and crown you queen of the miracle workers. Now go away. We have October month end to get through; it's gonna be a zoo. And you wanted the sales stats in the Christmas lead-up."

"It's always a zoo at the end of the month. Somehow you always come out on top of it." She stood. "Give me his phone number. I'll do my best."

Stan looked up the number in a folder and scribbled it on a pink sticky note. "I wish you luck."

Back in her office, Amanda studied the sticky note. When she'd taken it from Stan, she'd had a weird reaction, a little hitch in her stomach. She called out to Mel, "If your insides kind of twitch, does it mean someone walked over your grave?"

Mel, fully restored from her rant the previous day, laughed. "No, it means you've fallen in love. What happened?"

"I don't know. It's probably just nerves. Keep the vultures away for a while, would you? I have to call the highly regarded Mister McKinnon."

"Whew. And I thought those eyes hadn't got through to you."

"Business, remember? I prefer to grovel in private, if you don't mind."

"Grovel with grace." Mel closed the connecting door between their offices.

Amanda settled at her desk, somehow not quite ready to deal with the number in her hand. She didn't get it. She'd smoothed over numerous confrontations during her years at SI. It came with the job, and she'd never been one to put off the less pleasant aspects of her position. But the phone number on the sticky note made her uneasy.

Amanda cleared her inbox and reviewed a memo from Paul, the head of the search team, regarding a possible new line of lamps from Korea. She opened her office door long enough to walk down to the break room with Mel for coffee. She stared out the window for a while at the shrubbery and trees, becoming barren under the onslaught of rain but not yet softened by the first snow. She wondered why she was so hesitant to make this call.

Then she took herself in hand, as she'd done in various circumstances over the years, and punched in a number. But not Jacob McKinnon's.

"Pat, it's Friday. Come over tonight. I'll order pizza."

The woman on the other end of the line laughed. "Good morning to you, too. Throw some beer in with the pizza and you've got me. What's up?"

Amanda could picture her oldest and closest friend, Pat Fraser, probably in sweats, probably still at breakfast. She would have tied her reddish blond hair back at the nape of her neck. A nest of early laugh lines surrounded her brown eyes, and Pat didn't even mind. She had the ability to take herself as she was, without a lot of care and tending in the mix. They'd been best friends since college.

"Don't know. It's the temper thing again." She paused. "I'm not happy about this."

"Look for me between five thirty and six. I've got a kid this afternoon, and I'll need to clean up." A child psychologist, Pat worked part time with private clients, part time for the county Social Services Department.

"Pizza at six. Now, invoke the gods in my name, please. I have to call a potential contractor I royally offended yesterday. We need him, so it's got to be done."

"Should be done anyway, builds character. Karma and all. Talk to you later."

Finally, Amanda picked up the sticky note — and again noticed the funny little hiccup in her middle. She dialed the number. Jacob McKinnon answered on the second ring.

"Mr. McKinnon, this is Amanda Sinclair."

"Ms. Sinclair." His voice betrayed nothing.

Amanda took a breath. "I'm calling to apologize. I was completely out of line yesterday. I hadn't talked to Stan, and I didn't know what happened before your interview. But irrespective of that, I should never have attacked you for your appearance the way I did. There's always a reason, and I didn't take the time to find out yours. I'm sorry."

There was a pause. "That's okay, Ms. Sinclair. We all have bad days sometimes. Apology accepted." His voice remained neutral, neither friendly nor annoyed.

"Thank you. I'm asking you to give us another chance. I don't want my company to suffer for my behavior. I want to make this right."

There was a silence before he said, "I'm willing to meet. Perhaps we can get a sense of whether we could work together. Are you agreeable?"

"Yes, I'd be willing. Can you come into SI?"

"Not in the next few days. Not before the date Stan wanted me to start, anyway, and I want to be able to give him an answer as soon as possible. What we might do … I have to pick up my daughter at Fremont Park, at the picnic tables, at five o'clock. Could you be there at four thirty? I'm finishing a contract, so I can't get away today any earlier. And after five, I'll have Norah with me. Do you know the place?"

He wants to meet you at picnic tables in a park? Who is this guy?

But business was business. She squared her shoulders. "I'm sure I can find it. Should I expect it to be muddy?"

"Bark chips. There might be a soggy patch here and there, but no mud. I hope you understand, if I take this contract, it's likely you and I will be thrown together occasionally. One on one, we can both see if it's feasible."

"Fair enough. I'll see you later."

Amanda studied the receiver in her hand, then put it back into its cradle. She rose and opened the door to the outer office. "Mel, would you clear my schedule from four o'clock on? I'm going to meet your Mr. McKinnon."

Mel grinned. "Stan will be pleased."

"At a park. At the picnic tables."

Mel's grin widened. "Do you still have sneakers here? I haven't seen them in a while."

"In my closet. You think I should wear sneakers? With this?" She gestured at her slim below-the-knee black skirt, tailored white shirt, and black blazer.

"They're white, aren't they? They'd go. Except ..." Mel dove into a desk drawer, always a miracle of found objects. "How about this?" She held up a bright red pendant necklace. "This was from that jewelry shipment from Bangladesh six months ago. I haven't had a chance to wear it yet, but it'd be dynamite with your suit."

"I don't need to dress up for him, you know." There was an edge in Amanda's voice.

"Are you sure?"

Amanda sighed and went back into her office, sure she'd find the red pendant on her desk sometime that afternoon.

* * *

Jacob put down the phone and wondered what had happened. Whatever his views about yesterday's confrontation, his background and instincts had kicked in and he'd immediately tried to ease the situation. But why on earth had he suggested that she meet him at the park?

And whom exactly are you kidding?

It was nothing to do with work. It was the attractive face, the shapely lips that made the apology. It didn't sound rehearsed, and Ms. Amanda Sinclair, President, was a little off balance. Not nervous, but not comfortable either.

"You idiot," he muttered. But it would be a test for both of them. How gracefully could she handle a venue that was, to say the least, unconventional? How well could he withstand those eyes?

He hoped they could finish their business before Norah turned up. That would be a meeting of female minds he wasn't ready for.

* * *

Just before lunch Amanda's private phone line rang. She noted the number and grimaced. Colin, SI's founder and her father, was checking up on her again. Amanda loved her family and had a great relationship with her mother. Her father, not so much. He loved her, but he still resented being forced into retirement after years of stress, overwork, and doughnuts in the break room had caught up with him.

She picked up. "Hi, Dad."

"Glad I caught you. How's things?"

"Fine. Everything's going well."

"It's been a while since you last checked in, and your mother wants to be sure you'll be over for Thanksgiving."

"Dad, first of all Thanksgiving's weeks away, and second of all where else would I be? Tell Mom I'll be there and ask her to let me know what I should I bring, okay? How are you both?"

Her dad snorted. "Your mom's fine. Stan tells me you're branching out into clothing."

So that was the reason for the phone call.

"Not deeply. It's an ethnic line from Vietnam, the kind of thing you might find in a gift store." Amanda didn't get her back up over her father's passive-aggressive attempts to control her anymore. "We're looking at having a great Christmas season, based on current sales. You should come in one day, poke around."

"You're right, I should. Next week, perhaps."

"Always welcome."

She settled back in her chair, chatting with her father, catching up on family gossip while she fed him enough information about the business he'd founded to keep him happy. Family, she thought. Family, and the family company. She could spend a few minutes being the daughter instead of the company president. Her father wasn't going to change, so she'd roll with it.

Chapter 3

Amanda walked toward the picnic area, the damp cold penetrating to her bones. Despite the bark chips, water from two days' rain stood in puddles. She'd thank Mel tomorrow for suggesting the trainers. Years ago, she'd tucked them in the back of her office closet when she'd given up on an ill-fated idea of taking up jogging at lunchtime. There'd been a crisis, and that had ended the jogging. It seemed a crisis, or a crunch, or *something*, always kept her chained to her desk—

Amanda stopped in her tracks.

Chained to her desk? Where had that come from? For one thing, she *liked* being at her desk, a Scandinavian rosewood design, fronting her ergonomic chair upholstered in gold leather.

Anyway, working for the company was hardly chained. She loved her work.

Chained? Once she'd thought the word, she couldn't seem to un-think it. Pat the psychologist would have a field day with this one.

Amanda stared at the wet picnic tables and benches. With nowhere to sit, she paced, mildly annoyed.

You didn't have to agree to this ridiculous meeting place.

She'd arrived a few minutes early, so she couldn't expect Jacob McKinnon to be here yet, but a trickle of annoyance worked its way into her mind. The picnic tables hadn't been her idea. He might have had the courtesy …

Get a grip, Amanda.

She caught sight of Jacob McKinnon on the path from the parking lot. He walked quickly, weaving through the tables. She noted his pressed khaki slacks and conservative winter jacket.

Neither of them smiled.

"Thanks for coming," he said. "I'm sorry I couldn't come up with a better venue."

"We're both here now."

"Then, if it's okay with you, shall we start over?" He held out his hand. "I'm Jacob McKinnon. I'm pleased to meet you."

"Amanda Sinclair." She accepted his hand and the brief shake that followed. And registered another jolt, faint, but real. The same as when she'd taken the sticky note from Stan.

He frowned when they shook hands, but went straight to business. "Here's the thing, Ms. Sinclair. I like the look and feel of this contract. I enjoyed meeting the staff, the work sounds interesting, and the location's perfect. Stan agreed to my requests to work at home or take time out of the day when I need to. My daughter's settling down now, but if I get an emergency call, I'm going. That's my reality." He kept his voice uninflected, presenting facts without emotion. He still hadn't smiled.

Nor had she, although she appreciated his unemotional delivery. "Almost everyone on staff has a family. Crises happen, and no one can work well when they do. It's better to deal with them up front."

He nodded in acknowledgment. "Another thing. I do my best to choose contracts in companies without a lot of discord. SI obviously qualifies, but after you reamed me out yesterday, I didn't know what to think."

She began another apology—and inconveniently remembered Mel's comments about his eyes and the rest. So she noticed. Given the unlikelihood of this meeting, the last thing she needed was to become aware of him as a good-looking man. For a moment she forgot her well-rehearsed speech.

You're a company president. You can handle this.

She hauled her mind back on track. "About my outburst yesterday, it's not a common occurrence. Most people say I'm easy to work with. I'm not in the habit of second-guessing Stan's hires, so I hope you'll accept the position." She'd hit her stride now. Amanda was a master at promoting Sinclair Imports. "It's a good workplace, we have excellent employee retention and a first-rate benefits package if you ever decide to come on staff instead of contract."

His eyes hadn't left her face. "Your coming out here today says a lot about your commitment to your company. I appreciate it. But you need to understand that I don't take well to temper. I'm not much of a fighter myself, but if something like yesterday were to happen again, you'd have a really unhappy person on the payroll. As I'm sure you know, that kind of thing can be contagious."

Amanda heard the threat in the words, however mild. He was setting out the terms, defining the ground rules. To her. She looked down for a moment. Maple and beech leaves covered the bark chips, sodden and forlorn. Then she raised her eyes and met his. "I hear what you're saying. You can always speak to Stan or directly to me. It's a mistake to let things fester."

"I agree." He nodded and looked away, pinching his lips together. Then he returned his attention to her. "Very well. I'd tentatively arranged to start on Wednesday next week. Stan wanted to wait until the company's through month end, which seems sensible to me."

"I'll notify Stan. He'll be pleased."

For the first time a half smile touched his face. He shrugged. "I'll confirm with him directly, as well. We discussed a six-month contract. That'll give us a chance to see if it works out. One other thing you need to understand. For personal reasons, I'm stuck with the hair for the foreseeable future."

It shouldn't be a big deal. It wasn't as if other, perfectly normal men didn't choose to wear their hair long. But for some reason, accepting the ponytail felt like a major concession. "If it's tidy, I can't object."

"Good." His smile widened, although it still didn't convey much warmth. In keeping, she supposed, with the chilly afternoon and the general bleakness of the park.

"Stan told you that we're on a first name basis at SI?"

"He did. I'll try for Amanda, but it may take some practice. Did you drive? Could I drop you anywhere? Norah should be here any minute."

"My car's in the lot, but thank you. I'll probably see you Wednesday."

He nodded.

They'd maintained a polite, cool conversation, and they had a deal. She'd accomplished what she set out to do. "Have a good weekend." She turned in the direction of the parking lot.

"Oh—" he said, just as someone shrieked, "Daddy!" Amanda turned to see a little girl in a pink coat and hat charge across the playing field and hurl herself at Jacob.

Behind the child came Amanda's best friend.

Jacob's face relaxed from the formal look he'd given her to a smile that made the skin around his eyes crinkle. He swung the child up into his arms. She launched into a nonstop report. "We've been into town to Pat's office, and Pat said you said I need new shoes and maybe a new coat and we can go shopping and—"

"Hi, Amanda," Pat said. "Fancy meeting you here."

"Business. Hard to schedule."

"Pizza's going to be more interesting than I expected." Pat gave her a quick shoulder hug. "So, Miss Norah, I'll see you Wednesday and we'll look into those shoes. You have a good weekend."

"Do you know her?" Norah's stream of chatter broke off to ask this one important question. She studied Amanda from under blonde eyelashes, then looked from her father to Pat and back.

"A little," Jacob said.

Amanda noted the way Jacob's face had relaxed, as if he'd left his work persona behind in favor of fatherhood.

"I do though," Pat said. "Amanda, Norah. Norah, Amanda."

"How do you do." Norah studied Amanda. The child had been taught her manners.

Amanda was probably the least family oriented person in the whole company, but since she'd been promoting the family values of SI to Jacob, she'd have to demonstrate them. She was, after all, also the person most willing to go the extra mile for SI. She returned the little girl's greeting formally. "Very well, thank you. How do you do?"

She'd piqued Norah's interest. "Oh. I didn't know there was an answer. I thought it was just something people said, and then other people said it back. Is it a real question? I'm not sure what it means though. I've had fun this afternoon. You're lucky if you're Pat's friend. We always have fun, even when she makes me work."

"And Amanda has to go on home now," Pat said, "because she's promised me pizza tonight, and I want to be sure it's ready when I get there."

"We could have pizza, Daddy. Couldn't we?" Norah took her father's face between her hands, peering at him.

"As long as there're lots of veggies on it."

"Oh. Yuck."

This cozy conversation got on Amanda's nerves. Pat worked with kids; she didn't. "Goodbye," she said to Jacob and Norah. She glanced at Pat, said, "See you later," and turned to walk toward the parking lot.

She heard three distinct voices echoing some variation on goodbye. She waved a hand behind her but didn't turn around.

* * *

At home in her modern two-story townhome, Amanda changed into casual slacks and a tailored shirt, ordered the pizzas, vegetarian for her, all dressed — *even anchovies, how could she* eat *those things?* — for Pat, and poured a glass of wine.

And found herself pointedly *not* remembering hazel eyes

...

Don't be ridiculous.

She sipped the Sauvignon Blanc.

So Pat was working with Jacob McKinnon's daughter. Why? The kids Pat worked with had been wounded in some way, facing challenges no child should have to face. Jacob McKinnon was single, his application to SI told her that much. She wondered how Pat fit into this limited set of facts, but wouldn't ask, respecting the need for client and employee confidentiality.

She heard the double rap that preceded Pat's key in the lock. Amanda got to the door as Pat opened it. She met a barrage. "Mandy, how'd you link up with Jacob? You've been holding out on me." Pat tossed her coat onto a chair, kicked off her shoes, and headed for the kitchen. "Food first, please, I'm starving. But I admit I'm dying to hear how Jacob McKinnon found his way into your life."

"How was I supposed to know he's in yours? I mean, it was just a conversation. To establish whether he'd be happy at SI."

"Apologies and karma? Got it. Thanks for putting me in the picture. I don't smell food." Pat raided the fridge and pulled out a beer.

"Not here yet. Should be soon."

The two women stood in Amanda's pale yellow kitchen, leaning against the counters. "Do *you* think there's any chance we can discuss Jacob McKinnon like sensible adults?" Pat asked. "Speaking for myself, he reminds me of what it was like to be a swooning teenager." She tipped back her beer bottle, Amanda sipped her wine. Their eyes met, and they both grinned.

"Do you really think he's all that special?"

"Your senses have dulled. Yes, he's a heck of a nice guy, and he's one fine looking man, in my not so humble opinion. Not conventional-sports-hero gorgeous, more in-shape-accountant gorgeous, but still. Unfortunately, he's also widowed not so long ago, and his daughter's all he sees. My radar's been on the alert, but nothing. Nothing at all until I saw the two of you. Then the radar went nuts. One or both of you are living in serious lust."

Widowed. One question answered.

Amanda laughed again. "Oh, come on. But I have to admit, when we shook hands there was this jolt—"

"Better elaborate."

"Well, my insides kind of skipped a beat. It's probably nerves."

"Uh huh. Tell yourself whatever lies you must. There's our dinner." Pat broke off when the doorbell rang. Between them they collected the pizzas and loaded their plates, stowing the rest in the oven to stay hot.

Pat ate her first slice and retrieved another. "Okay, tell me about flying off the handle."

Amanda recounted her day yesterday. "Headaches, rages ... I never lose it like that. Never. Mel tells me the staff think I need to get laid."

"Probably true. You do hire intelligent staff, with a great command of the English language."

"Hang on." Amanda retrieved another slice of pizza and pulled the wine bottle out of the fridge. "I'm confused. One minute I'm in control, the next I wig out."

"I've been worried lately." Pat reached out across the table and drummed a finger on the back of Amanda's hand. "You really are a classic case of all work, no play. It isn't enough anymore, is it? You need more variety in your life, more fun."

"You're going to tell me I need a man?"

"Have you considered that you're in your fortieth year?"

"Not that again. We waded into those waters on my birthday. On *both* our birthdays."

"Waded, didn't plunge. Are you prepared to go into your dotage manless?"

"From where I stand there isn't an option."

Pat shook her head. "Look harder. I see at least one."

Amanda sighed, exasperated. "Not possible, even if I were interested. Which I'm not, by the way. He's going to be working for SI. You know I can't go there."

"He would."

Amanda's gaze popped to her friend. "He would?" she blurted before she had time to edit the thought. "I mean, really?"

"Really. Those eyes couldn't unglue themselves. I suspect he's come to terms with losing his wife, and he's gearing up to start again. And he has no vibrations for me at all, worse luck. So it's over to you."

"You do agree with the guys on the Floor. You think I need to get laid."

"Sure, but that applies to every single woman, myself included. What's more to the point is, you need a life. You need other things to do. A man worthy of you. A family, two or three kids to teach you what a *real* management challenge is."

Amanda swallowed a bite of her pizza. "Well. Here I expected you to say it's biological clock. As if looking at those pink things in the viewing room started my heart going pitter-pat."

"Pink?"

"Little girl line."

"Not your style, but some perfectly normal people love it. And you can't escape the biological clock thing. We're both approaching the last hurrah. I'm willing to take another chance, but I'm not sure you are. I want a kid, Mandy."

Amanda looked at her friend thoughtfully. "Shawn dumped you and disappeared, and took most of your savings with him. And you'd try again."

"Shawn was a creep. When you're twenty-one you don't recognize a creep when he oozes under your door. When you're forty, you do. Yeah, I'd try again. If the right guy came along, I'd jump at it." Pat helped herself to another two slices of her pizza. "Your problem is you don't like pepperoni. How do you expect to score a lusty guy without pepperoni?"

"Scotch," Amanda stated succinctly. "Works every time."

But later, when Pat had gone home, with the kitchen extractor fan removing any trace of pizza from the air, she took out a pad of paper and a pen and tried to figure out what had unsettled her. What made her so snappy at work? What about being chained to her desk, which somehow she'd never discussed with Pat? How could she explain Jacob McKinnon and the jolt? Was this one picture or two? And how was she supposed to handle it?

* * *

Jacob settled down in front of his fire, his thoughts going rogue on him.

Well, aren't you the smooth one.

His meditation stood no chance against the memory of his conversation with Amanda earlier.

So very formal, it was almost robotic.

He was clearly a cretin, deranged by the first pair of eyes he'd noticed since Deb.

Although the rest was good, too, even inside her winter coat, a slim tweed thing that hugged her figure before it flared out around her knees. He could sense her slender shape, and the right height to be a good fit—

"Stop it!" he snapped, then looked at the stairs and listened, to be sure he hadn't wakened Norah. More quietly, he stated, "The wrong part of your anatomy, McKinnon. Get over it."

But getting over it didn't seem to be in the cards any time soon. He'd pump some iron later to work it out of his system. In the meantime, he settled into his chair and tried to bring logical thought to the problem. He wanted the woman who was his new boss's boss, the *big* boss. Based on her frosty demeanor, she didn't want anything to do with him. Not to mention needing to keep things professional.

So what did you expect, dragging her to a picnic table in a soggy park at the end of October?

He realized when he turned it over in his mind that there was more to the conundrum of Amanda than desire. He couldn't pinpoint it, but there was something unsettling about her. Sure, she could take Fremont Park and turn it into a boardroom, then conduct a meeting with complete formality. She'd proven it. So what was the missing piece?

By all accounts she was determined to run the best import business in the Midwest, if not the country. As far as he knew, she didn't have a husband or kids. That fit. Sinclair Imports was her baby.

And the reaction he had to her? The idea of great passion, or even great lust, had its allure, and in a way it was a relief after the last two years. Maybe he could be a—what? An escort? A boy toy? Outrageous, but his mood perked up. She'd never, ever be that casual, even if he were interested in going that route, so uncommitted sex wasn't on offer. No getting his hands around her tidy waist, no tipping her pale face up to his, no kissing off the lipstick ....

No nothing. *Find something else to fill your mind with,* he ordered himself, and switched on the evening news. "Anyway," he muttered, "I'd give any odds she's never chased a Frisbee."

Chapter 4

Amanda received a text from Pat right after she arrived at work Monday morning.

"My place. Straight from work. 5:30 latest."

She replied immediately. *"Sorry, can't, end of month. Problem?"*

Pat must have had her phone in her hand, the reply was almost instant. *"Chicken tarragon stew."*

When Pat cooked Amanda's favorite stew, she had a reason. Amanda could be there by five thirty. She realized with a little kick of surprise that month end didn't need her attention. She was using it as an excuse.

Excuse for what? To dodge having a life? With your best friend?

Most weeknights, she didn't do anything after work except go home, make supper. It had become a habit. Still, chicken tarragon stew? A little negotiation was in order.

"Dumplings?"

"Cheese dumplings. Come."

"Tell me why?"

"No."

Amanda sighed and punched at the keys. *"You aren't trying to set me up with someone, are you?"*

"Hear my laughter. No. Get yourself over here."

"Will this require wine?"

"Probably."

"I'll pick some up. See you 5:30."

So now, to go along with a new pink line of girls' accessories and the weirdness of that meeting in the park, she had whatever Pat had planned to look forward to. Amanda settled in and got to work.

* * *

"Oh, good grief," Amanda said. Pat met her at the door dressed as a witch, with full regalia, including a hooked nose.

"I wouldn't say 'good grief' exactly. It's in keeping with the season. Trick or Treat tonight, remember?"

"I remember." Amanda barely suppressed a groan. She handed over a chilled bottle of Pinot Grigio. "This is fun, I suppose."

"It will be. You need to get ready." Pat moved behind Amanda, closed the door, and locked it with a finality that suggested it wasn't coming unlocked in a hurry. "I figure you for the princess type." Amanda winced. "You're going to love your costume."

Usually Amanda was comfortable in Pat's house, a small bungalow in a neighborhood of older homes on large lots. While it retained its charm from the 1940s, it didn't lack in the kitchen and bathroom department.

At the moment, however, Amanda was anything but comfortable.

Pat propelled her toward the bedroom. "Relax, no one will see you but me and a bunch of five-year-olds." She thrust a new cake of green eye shadow into Amanda's hand. "I found this gorgeous number at the Thrift Store on Superior." She gestured at a frothy, green, full-length formal gown lying on the bed. "I wanted pink, but this was the most romantic I could find. The little girls are going to die of envy. I'm assuming you have your own lipstick. Your tiara's in the paper bag—whoops, there's the door." She disappeared to welcome the first of the trick-or-treaters.

People in neighborhood houses get in costume to receive the kids?

At her townhome, she didn't get any trick-or-treaters anyway, and left her outside light off to be sure everyone knew she wasn't interested.

Left alone with the pile of froth, and figuring it wasn't worth arguing, Amanda peeled out of her suit and dropped the dress over her head. Took it off again when she saw that the neckline was cut too low for her plain, white sports bra. She'd have to be braless for this adventure. Once she had the dress zipped, she turned and studied herself in the mirror. It fit fairly well, and was so far from her usual attire she hardly recognized herself. She used the eye shadow more liberally than she would normally dream of doing, applied lipstick, then whipped off her black plastic headband and tucked the tiara into her curls.

She figured barefoot would be better than the no-nonsense loafers she'd worn to Pat's, so she took off her shoes and wandered out to the entry. "What do you think?" she asked, twirling.

Pat made an excellent witch. Her smile was a little evil, and a lot smug. "Gorgeous. If Jacob McKinnon could see you now, I'd have to fight him off to keep him from ravishing you, even though I expect it'd do both of you good. Too bad they don't live around here."

Heat flooded Amanda's face. "I told you, Pat—"

"Your turn to answer the door. I'm going to pour wine and start making dumplings." She left Amanda to play princess, thrill the kids who rang the doorbell, and not think about Jacob McKinnon, once again. Pat joined her after a while and they dealt with the doorbell, nonstop it seemed, for the next hour and a half.

As the rush eased up, Pat said, "Now, wasn't that worth leaving your great piles of work a little early?" She flopped down on a kitchen chair.

Amanda pushed the layers of froth out of the way and perched on another chair. "I haven't put on a dress like this since junior prom in high school," she grumbled.

"Oh, no, you don't. No complaints allowed. You've been the most romantic character in Calter Creek this evening. Have some wine, perk yourself up." Pat pushed Amanda's glass across the table. "Remind me to learn from you and be a barefoot witch next year. My feet are killing me." She toed off the pointy black boots and propped them on a chair, then sipped her own wine. "The thing is, the more I thought, the more I realized that my friend here, the one I adore like the little sister I wish I'd had, my little sister's stopped having fun. She's stopped laughing and enjoying life."

Pat heaved back onto her feet and headed for the slow cooker, where she ladled the tarragon-laced stew into bowls. "We sure earned this," she spoke over her shoulder, then returned to her main theme. "So I decided. The best thing I can do for you is guarantee you have opportunities to get away from work. Incidentally, you did great at having fun tonight. You really got into those kids. Definitely a better princess than I'd be. Though I can't help but think you'd make a first-rate witch." She brought the bowls to the table.

"Oh, thanks. Just what I needed." She took a mouthful of stew. "Mmm."

"And you've been laughing. Few and far between lately."

"Have I really become so grim? Fabulous stew."

"Thanks, and yes, you have, but you've passed today's test. Finish your supper and you can go get out of that thing." Pat waved her hand at the dress billowing out around Amanda's chair. "I'll see if they'll let me sell it back to them."

"Or we could keep it for next year."

"Words I never dreamed I'd hear you say." Pat grinned. And the doorbell rang again.

By the time they'd handed out some hundred and fifty candy bars, scrubbed off the makeup and climbed into their regular clothes, and helped themselves to second helpings of the stew, Amanda had had enough. "And I do have to work tomorrow. Don't you?"

"Some report writing, the usual home visits. I've got the little McKinnon girl Wednesday afternoon. I gather her dad the hunk is starting at SI."

"One more thing to thrill me. Don't you start." She pointed a finger at Pat. "I'm heading home. And before you ask, yes, I guess I did learn something. I enjoyed tonight. I didn't expect to, but I did."

"I thought you would, once you didn't have any option, so you could relax into it. Drive safely."

Amanda rescued her discarded shoes, shrugged into her coat, and headed out the door. She paused before she stepped outside. "Do I get a veto over these fun things you're planning?"

"Not a chance."

Chapter 5

Amanda rose from her desk and stretched. It had been a good week. Friday, six o'clock, and for once she had no work to take home with her. SI had cleared October month end without a glitch, sales figures and the balance sheet were encouraging, and everything in Amanda's world looked positive.

She wondered how the week had gone in Accounting.

She shrugged into her coat. Accounting would be what it would be. She didn't poke around in Stan's domain.

Mel had brought Jacob McKinnon up in conversation over afternoon coffee. "What gets me right here," she had said, with a dramatic thump on her chest, "is that he looks tired, or a little stressed. I expect he takes his solo parenting role seriously. I'd be curious to meet the kid."

"I met her at the park. Seems like a bright enough girl, blonde, cute. There's no question he's crazy about her."

"There's something about him. Almost makes me maternal."

Amanda had chuckled, but for some reason she wasn't happy with the idea that Mel might be interested in Jacob McKinnon. He didn't bring out the maternal in *her*. Not at all. But that was neither here nor there.

She'd put her hand on the door to pull it shut for the weekend when her phone rang. She went back to her desk and answered.

"Thought you'd want to know," Stan said, as usual without preliminary. "Jacob's going to fit right in. Nice guy, reserved. And sharp. You did good work there, Amanda."

"Thanks, and I'm glad to hear it."

"He's a little curious about you."

"Don't go matchmaking, Stan."

"Aw, hon, why not? I'm your surrogate dad, aren't I? You've gotta let me poke fun sometimes."

"Yes, Daddy." She let the affection show in her voice. "Good weekend coming up?"

"Not much planned. Sue has a get-together with some girlfriends. I'll be doing the popcorn and college football routine. Last chance to kick back before we hit the Christmas crazies for real."

"It's not going to be that bad. Not with the systems we have in place."

"No system in the world can help the volume. Be grateful."

"Very grateful."

As Amanda locked up, she thought about the upcoming weekend without work. It had lost its appeal. Because she didn't have anything to replace the work with? Stan had his football. Pat was out of town at a conference somewhere. Jacob had his daughter—

Wait a minute. Jacob—Mr. McKinnon—doesn't figure into this equation.

Dissatisfied, she headed for the grocery, stocking up for a weekend with no plans.

* * *

Comfortable in battered jeans and an old gray sweatshirt, Jacob sprawled on the broad front steps of his friend Dave's house and listened to the shrieks coming from Norah and Sammy, Dave's youngest, over to his left. He and Dave had been raking leaves that afternoon—their sweat, the kids' joy. Worth it, he supposed. For a Saturday in early November, the weather couldn't be better, crisp and sunny. He and Norah had spent most of the day at the Carters', having lunch, doing yard work. Jacob felt more alive than he had in a long time.

He'd been friends with the Carters for years. The four of them, with their collected offspring, had picnicked and partied together, camped, shared barbecues and Thanksgiving dinners. Dave was the best pal a man could have, and Nancy was like a sister. Dave and Nancy had stuck by him after Deb's death, when many of Deb's and his friends had melted away.

"Next week, my place," he said hopefully.

Dave's enthusiasm wasn't evident. "Yeah, right."

The door opened behind them, and Nancy came out with mugs on a tray. She handed them each a mug, then squatted to wrap an arm around Jacob's neck and kiss his cheek. "Mmm. You smell good."

"Sweaty male? Your husband's lowered your standards."

"You're elevating them again." She gave him a gentle punch and settled down between the two men.

"It's a territory thing," Dave growled at her, and pulled her up next to him. Then he raised his mug. "To autumn. Turn of the seasons."

"New beginnings," Jacob said.

Both Carters looked at him. "Share," Dave said.

"Well, there's Norah, first of all. Listen." He paused while the squeals continued from the leaf pile. "She's always had a good time with Sammy, but we haven't heard that in a long time. She's turned a corner."

Nancy fought off her husband to lean forward and put a hand on Jacob's arm. "It's good to see. You're looking better, too, I'd say."

He put his hand on top of hers. "You've got way more leaves than is healthy. Tell your man to cut down a tree or two." He sipped. She'd made a hot concoction of apple juice and — rum? "Never mind. This counts as payment."

Nancy leaned back against Dave and studied him. "How's SI working out?"

"People are nice, location couldn't be better. Not much pressure now, but that could change as we get into year end."

"Well, it seems to be good for you. *Something* is. You're different." Nancy batted her husband's roaming hands aside and got to her feet. "I'm going to make some of this for the kids, non-spiked. I get my hug before you leave, remember." She gathered her tray and disappeared.

"Nancy's right though." Dave said. "There's a change. You're not so restless. It's been below the surface, simmering. If

I had to guess, I'd say you're getting suited up for a gloomy castle and a fair maiden to rescue."

"I wish, but your analogy isn't working. I'm too worn out to rescue a maiden, fair or not. Sometimes it's like a long slog through a bog with no solid ground in sight. There's always so much." He leaned against the post supporting the porch railing, gazing into the sky and breathing in the autumn-scented air.

"That's the first time you've admitted to that. Old Jacob will see it through. Take it all on and get Norah through college. Any idiot can see you're tired. Norah could stay with the in-laws for a week, couldn't she? Give you a break?"

"I wouldn't relax. I'd end up mowing the lawn or sanding floors. Laundry."

"You've wandered off topic. I'm guessing you've found a fair maid, even if you aren't up to rescuing her."

Jacob paid attention to his mug; he wanted reinforcement before going anywhere near that one. "First things first. I want some real opinion here, not your wiseass cracks. Do you think I'm ready?"

"To get back out there? How should I know? The question is, do *you* think you're ready?"

"Far as that goes, yeah. There's a definite response. She's got the eyes, the body, the smarts. Something's spooking her, I can't figure that part out, so tough but vulnerable, but doesn't let it show. She's in my head."

"So, there's point one. Points two and three both involve Norah. Are you okay with getting a babysitter occasionally? And how would she react to a sitter and a new woman in her dad's life?"

"Talk about jumping the gun. Said lady is not interested, as near as I can figure. Her baby's the company. Her lover, her daddy and mommy, her life."

"Aha!" Dave sat up, leaned forward. "You're speaking of the inscrutable and lovely Amanda Sinclair."

Jacob frowned at his friend, surprised. "You know her?"

"Slightly. Chamber of Commerce meetings." Dave owned a local U-brew beer-making establishment in town. "I had an idea I might sniff in that direction, a helluva long time ago, before Nancy. But you're right. If she's looking, she's not showing it. Never say never, but that may be the wrong tree to go barking up."

"I'm not barking. I'm just aware." Jacob paused to think it over. "Truth to tell, it's good to be aware again. It's been like I'd died, too. This woman wanders into my line of sight and I'm seeing things again, noticing things. Like how ratty my house looks. Even Norah gets on my case. Being aware of her has flipped a switch."

"And now the juices are flowing again. And you ask me if you're ready?" Dave snorted.

Jacob had almost finished the apple juice before Dave spoke again. "I've been running a business in Calter Creek for a long time."

"True. Is this going somewhere?"

Dave nodded. "Four or five years ago, after she took over the reins from daddy, she was involved with a guy named Brandon Caine. Real estate, housing developments. You may have heard of him."

"There's a billboard east of town. Great big face?"

"Good looking face, to give the devil his due."

"Trashy billboard."

"He seems to be doing well, based on how fast he's throwing up subdivisions. But I never liked him. Always thought he was little sleazy. Too slick, too full of himself. He hasn't been at Chamber of Commerce meetings in years. I suspect it's because he doesn't reckon he needs us since most of his work's outside the town limits. Fewer rules, is my take on it."

"Amanda and Brandon Caine. Not a nice thought."

"You'd rather live in the illusion she's virginal and you'll open her eyes to the glories of love and sex, right?" He leaned over to clink his mug against Jacob's. "Sorry to burst your bubble."

"You've fed my fantasies." Jacob chuckled. "Thanks for the input. This is theoretical though. I have another girl in my life to consider first."

They both looked toward the leaf pile. "Norah seems great to me. The way she tore into the nachos over lunch, chattering away like she hasn't in—well, you know how long."

"Too long. Seeing her like this, well, thank God."

"Then, time to try a babysitter, I'd say. Ohio State football tomorrow night. Come over."

"Not yet. I have to find someone I'd trust with Norah, and that could take a while."

"You've been out of action so long you're stalling, hiding out in your quiet living room with meditation music. Aren't you meant to be finding deep meanings and living in the moment and stuff?"

"God, Dave. Be real."

"I'm real, Jake. You're the one with lust in your heart."

"It's just ..." Jacob slumped back against the post, downed the last of the apple drink, and stared out over the lawn, wondering how on earth he could explain Amanda's lure to Dave.

"Stop analyzing so much. It's lust, like I said. Good place to start."

After that salvo, Dave let the silence happen. Jacob readily accepted the conversational pause. Sure, he agreed that desire was a primary component of what he was experiencing. It had been a long time. But there was that little niggle of something more, that hint of curiosity about what made Amanda tick. He wasn't ready to dismiss that.

Finally, after some time just relaxing into the autumn day, he faced Dave. "Okay. I'll talk to Norah's psychologist. She'll be able to recommend a babysitter. Then we'll see. But with starting the new job, there's no way for this weekend. I'd be a drag."

Dave got to his feet, clapped his friend on the shoulder, and headed down into the yard.

Chapter 6

Late afternoon Saturday, Amanda had just pulled a frozen chicken scaloppini out of the freezer for dinner when the phone rang. She picked up, frowning at the unfamiliar number.

"Amanda, it's Susan Johnson." Stan's wife, and in some kind of distress. She struggled to get words out.

"Susan, what's wrong?"

"It's Stan. They say he's had a heart attack. A bad one. When I got home I found him. He's—" Susan choked up.

Amanda's heart sagged in her chest.

A new voice came on the line. "Ms. Sinclair, it's Fran here, Stan's daughter. Dad would want you to know as soon as possible. He's in Sunnybrook Hospital. The prognosis is cautiously good, but he's not out of danger. I'm here with Mom, my sister will be here in the morning." She heard Fran take a deep breath. "We'll be at the hospital till he's stable."

Amanda had regrouped while she listened. "Thanks for calling. Stan means a lot to SI, and to me personally. If there's any support we can give you, don't hesitate."

"Yes, we will, thanks. I have to go. Good night, Ms. Sinclair."

Amanda abandoned the idea of supper and went to her office. Even at home, it seemed she did her best thinking at a desk. Facing a disaster in the making, the desk reinforced her confidence that she'd get through it.

Stan held so many reins at SI. Where financial matters were concerned, he was their rock. Now the rock had shattered. Her mind blanked, unable to process for a moment.

As the first shock of the news wore off, she faced the reality that neither of their bookkeepers could handle Stan's job, so that left her little option. She'd already copied the number from the sticky note into her cell phone. She bought herself a little time by nuking and eating the chicken, then returned to her desk and called Jacob McKinnon.

* * *

And doesn't that change things.

Jacob studied the phone for a minute before returning it to its cradle. Amanda had sounded utterly businesslike, but he had heard the upset under the calm voice.

So, not an ice maiden after all.

Amanda, needing him.

No. SI needing you. There's a difference, McKinnon.

He hoped she'd appreciate that he was only human. SI needed one full-time and one part-time accountant, and they'd hired him for the part-time role. With Stan out of commission, Jacob found himself staring uphill at a short, steep learning curve.

He picked up his phone and punched in a number. "Pat, do you have a minute? I need your help."

"Hi, Jacob. What's up?"

"Nothing about us, we're fine, but there's a crisis at SI. I have to work tomorrow. Is Norah ready for a babysitter? And can you recommend someone she'd trust? Who'd fix her lunch and make it seem fun?"

"Sure, I have a roster of sitters. They're not teenagers, so they're not cheap, but they check out. Have you told Norah?"

"Just that it's work stuff. She was almost ready to go to bed when Amanda called. I thought I'd wait till tomorrow morning."

"Fair enough, but don't put it off. She's a canny kid. She'll want to know the story. I'll email you my list, it has names, numbers, and a little background information, plus I'll give you some recommendations. Pick three and book one. We'll get Norah used to several, so in any given crisis you'll have options. Can you tell me what's going on?"

"Stan, the guy I report to, he's had a heart attack. I've hardly got my feet in the door, and I'm the only one who can do half of what he does, so I'm it."

"Whew That's big. Is Amanda okay?"

"I think so. A little off balance."

"Not surprising. She and Stan go back to when she was a kid. Look for the email."

He ended the call and wandered into the living room.

The next couple of weeks would be insane, but he trusted himself to master Stan's system without much difficulty. Keeping up with the workload—well, good thing he liked challenges. He'd have to set some priorities. Once he fully understood the systems, he'd be able to determine where he could risk getting behind, what was immediate and urgent, what he could delegate.

He could handle that. He'd straightened out worse messes.

The bigger challenge was that he wouldn't be staying quietly in the Accounting suite doing background work anymore. He'd be in daily contact with, in Dave's words, the inscrutable and lovely Amanda Sinclair.

He tapped his fingers on the arm of his chair.

Admit it. You're looking forward to it.

* * *

Sunday morning, Jacob arrived at SI to find Amanda unlocking the front door. "Do you have a key?" she asked him.

"No. Since I'm a contractor, I'll have a key on an as-needed basis."

"I'd like you to come on board as an employee."

He pulled the door open and gestured for her to precede him. They turned left down the west corridor, heading for the Accounting suite.

"I usually work on contract. Other businesses have been fine with that."

"It's about accountability. If we're going to entrust SI's financial integrity to you, I'd prefer a tighter relationship."

He mulled it over, then shrugged. "Okay. I'm an employee. I'll talk to Marcia tomorrow." Marcia, a dynamo of a fifty-year-old, constituted the entire personnel department. "It still won't be full time. I can't get here until after school starts, and I'm not willing to stay later than four thirty. Even that's assuming the babysitter thing works out."

"I'm not happy about it." At the Accounting suite Amanda unlocked the door and let them in. "We're talking Stan's job as well as what we hired you to do. Are you sure you can manage?"

They hung up their coats. "No, I'm not, to be honest. Everyone agrees there's too much work for one person." He closed the closet and faced her. "I'll need to make some decisions around priorities and workload. I'll run it by you when I have some kind of plan. If things start backing up you'll be the first to know, and we'll come up with a strategy. I can work over lunch or from home at night occasionally. Unless you see some other option."

"Very well," she said, grudgingly accepting the reality of SI's staffing situation. She went into Stan's office and switched on the computer. "I'll give you a quick overview of what we're up against."

Jacob followed her. "Do you have a background in finance?"

"Business degree. I didn't get to where I am by smiling sweetly." Amanda looked a little affronted, and every inch the company president, for all that she had on casual slacks and a pale blue sweater that failed to cling, but still somehow hinted at curves.

Mind on your work, McKinnon.

"It's almost all computerized now. I'm sure Stan's already shown you most of it. But you'll also be responsible for tax filing, among other things. Turn away, please."

"What?"

"Password. You aren't getting Stan's password until you really are an employee."

Facing the door, he heard her type in a string of keystrokes, and shrugged off his momentary exasperation. SI was her company.

"There. Come and look." He pulled another chair over to the desk. Amanda launched into a description of Stan's job.

Jacob listened, questioned, took notes, and surreptitiously watched her. It was more an elemental force than a conscious choice, the way she drew his eyes. The animation in her face when she discussed the ins and outs of running her company. The affection that lit her eyes when she mentioned Stan. That sweater, the blue setting off those eyes ....

Did she watch him as well? Maybe he was deluding himself, but he was pretty certain she had noticed him, and not just as a useful employee.

After an hour of intensive information exchange, he stood and stretched. "It's noon. We never planned for lunch."

"I brought a sandwich."

"No way. If we don't get out of here for a while I'll be brain dead by mid-afternoon."

She didn't like it. She pinched her lips together, but finally said, "I guess we could go over to the pizza place across the street."

"Closed Sundays, remember? Let's go further afield. I was thinking Monet's Garden, downtown. It's not that far, and it's getting a good reputation. Aren't women into salad bars and that kind of thing? Quiches?"

"Don't stereotype." She stood. "We'll take some sample reports with us, so we can get some work done while we eat."

"Not if you want to do anything efficient this afternoon. Come on, I'll drive."

They collected their coats and headed down the corridor toward the main exit. In the lobby they reached for the outer door at the same time, and her hand landed on top of his. His heart leapt into his throat, then dropped down into his stomach before settling uneasily in his chest. The electricity between them was so strong it might have been visible.

Amanda snatched her hand away.

So she felt it, too. So that's how it is.

After she'd locked the door behind them, he put his hand on the tweed coat covering—*defending?*—her arm. "What are we going to do about that?"

"I—I don't understand what you mean."

He let his hand drop. "Sure you do. You jerked your hand away. That was the second time, actually, but the first one, the one at the park, wasn't this strong. It was like nothing I've ever experienced." He held his hand up, studied it a moment, and shook his head.

Then, unexpectedly, their eyes met. In hers he saw distress, while he felt like singing, dancing in the street. She looked down. Jacob could almost see the steel in her spine. "You mean the static electricity? It surprised me. I'll see if maintenance has anti-static spray. Or something."

Or something. Fixing his eyes on her face, Jacob reached his hand over to brush hers. When she jumped a little, he said, "That wasn't static."

At least she didn't deny she'd felt it, even if she denied everything else.

"Our hands brushed, it's not that unusual. This is business. It stays that way."

"Your call, but this does sort of go past 'just business'. You're in the driver's seat, Amanda. I won't make you uneasy." He turned, then, and took her arm for the walk to the parking lot.

* * *

Amanda, like many residents of Calter Creek, didn't go downtown often, but enjoyed it when she did. Calter Creek had its share of modern subdivisions, shopping malls, and up-to-date office buildings, but it was the heritage touches that drew people and convinced them to stay. The town took pride in its downtown core, with old-fashioned streetlights and hanging baskets heavy with flowers all summer.

The hostess at Monet's Garden led them to a table near a window, a little way from an outdoor-style fireplace that radiated a welcoming warmth. The waitress left, and self-consciousness struck. She was alone at the table. With Jacob McKinnon. When the Jolt nudged at her, she resolutely pushed it away and fumbled for a conversational topic. "It's like a garden." *Neutral. Safe.* The bright room featured large flower arrangements and terra cotta floors. Cheerful floral tablecloths covered the well-spaced tables. She'd expected Monet prints on the walls, but instead they were bare, rough stucco in a pale gold. The place managed to look sunny, even on this overcast day. "Your spirits can't help but perk up in a place like this."

He grinned. "Always assuming the food's good. I'm famished. Balancing diets for a grown man and a six-year-old girl isn't easy."

"That wouldn't have occurred to me." She thought about it now, fleshing out the dimensions of this man she barely knew, his home life, raising a daughter.

"You've known Pat for a long time?"

"We shared an apartment for my last two years at Ohio State. She's like family."

"Siblings?"

He was doing the same thing, coloring in his picture of her. "James, big brother. He went to college in Colorado and never came back, except for visits. What about you? What route brought you to Calter Creek?"

He toyed with his water glass. "I grew up in Indiana, only child. You know I'm widowed?"

She nodded.

"Deb came from Columbus. From everything we heard, Calter Creek's a great place to raise kids. Found a house in an older neighborhood, and we were on the way to everyone's dream. Home, two cars, perfect kids. We hadn't quite made it to the dog and cat. Deb's parents take Norah for the weekend once a month, so she's still got grandparents close. It's weird, being in touch with them, but it'd be rotten to cut them off from her." He picked up his menu. "Better read through these."

"I'll just have a salad."

He studied the menu for a moment, then looked up, his eyes twinkling. "Ah. On the special sheet. Smoked salmon quiche."

She grinned at his self-deprecating humor. "We women love quiches?"

45

"What's a guy to do? I like my eggs."

The waitress came back, and they placed their orders.

"So, you haven't been here before?" he asked. "I assumed you'd know every restaurant in town."

"I don't go out much. Pat and I sometimes grab a meal, but we're more inclined to order in. Or sometimes she cooks. She's good at it, which I'm not. I guess you're the cook in your household."

"Yeah." Jacob shrugged. "Frankly, my life these days is work and Norah, so cooking's part of the package, but I'm way too inclined to use shortcuts. Too much take-out pizza, too much frozen fish. I just can't quite think of cooking as fun to do."

"Have you heard Pat's plan to drag me into the world of extracurricular activities?" Amanda told him about Halloween night. "And she's threatening to sign us up for art classes in January. The funny thing is, she may be right. I work hard, and perhaps I'd forgotten what it was like to do things for no good reason. I've enjoyed SI for so long, the challenges ...."

"Not as much fun anymore?"

"I don't know. Nothing's changed." *But something has.*

For one thing, she never, ever talked like this to anyone except Pat.

* * *

Jacob's quiche arrived, and Amanda excused herself to visit the salad bar. He watched her go while he absentmindedly buttered a roll. She's a queen, he thought, the way she signals inaccessibility. A woman who knows where she is and what she wants.

Unlike you. Starting to want a woman in your life again.

To hold a woman again. To act on the need to be close.

You know how it works. You're just nervous.

He didn't speak until after they'd begun their meals. "What happened earlier." Her eyes went to her plate. "Hey. It's not the end of the world. It happens. I wasn't looking for it, and I'm sure you weren't either. The idea of a new ..." He sifted through his vocabulary. "What should we call it? Involvement? Is that too much?"

She looked up, her eyes narrowed. "Definitely."

"Whatever, you've made it clear you don't want anything to happen between us, and I'm not sure I do, either, but it's going to be a challenge to keep things neutral. Eat your salad."

Amanda could put distance between herself and another person like no one he'd ever met. "You're quite right about my expectations, even if you're presuming something that's not there. If you find it awkward to be around me, I'm sure we can limit our contact."

Nice one. Talk about closing doors.

He took a bite of quiche and watched her move her fork mechanically from plate to mouth. She was controlled and unemotional—and faking it.

Things aren't getting easier, that's for sure.

This could prove to be a long afternoon.

* * *

The trip home from the western suburbs to the eastern edge of Calter Creek was far too short. It would take more than a twelve-minute drive in light Sunday traffic to figure out how, and why, a day spent with Jacob McKinnon had twisted tangles in her mind and set her nerves quivering.

She had one priority, first, last, and always: Sinclair Imports. SI needed him, and she fervently hoped he had the competence to take on Stan's job. Would he be a team player? Could SI work with him? Could she?

They'd reviewed Stan's job and discussed how it integrated with the business flow at SI. He grasped the work quickly. His reputation might well be justified.

But the Jolt—when had she started capitalizing it in her mind? This time it had been worse. Much worse. When their hands touched, then when he had the *nerve* to brush her hand again. And then he had to start talking in that quiet voice of his, telling her he knew, he *knew* she'd responded to his touch. Her thoughts tumbled around in her mind. The Jolt was a living being, a gremlin inhabiting her and sending awareness to parts of her body that hadn't had any attention in a while.

She couldn't let him get to her. He seemed convinced he *had* gotten to her, and that wasn't good. That couldn't be good. It was past time she got herself under control.

On the other hand, being with him hadn't put her guard up, in spite of the threat he posed to her peace of mind.

And then there was lunch.

He'd felt warm and solid next to her, at Stan's desk, holding her arm, across the lunch table. Not threatening, just comfortable, as if —

No. Don't go there.

She consciously used her position at SI as her shield and defense, the governing principle in her life. She couldn't afford to forget that. She wouldn't do anything to put SI at risk. She wouldn't have relationships with employees, especially when they had little girls and hazel eyes that —

That what? That looked at you as if they could see right into you?

You haven't obsessed like this in twenty years. Maybe never. Even to yourself.

What could she do about his refusal to recognize static electricity?

How was she going to handle this newcomer who now held a key role in the company? Nothing added up in her logical mind.

And on top of that, he looked good. Not drop-dead handsome, but …. She'd seen him at work, in suit and tie, and now in casual slacks and a sweater. A part of her approved. She wasn't supposed to approve. Surely by now she'd moved past the point of succumbing to the allure of physical attraction.

Surely Brandon taught you that much.

Oh, yes, Brandon had taught her that much. She wasn't likely to forget that lesson.

But good looks wouldn't account for the way Jacob's presence made her feel. A sense of security. Of rightness.

Admit it, you're rattled. There's something happening between you and Jacob McKinnon.

Businesslike, she determined. Formal. That's what it's going to be.

Chapter 7

Pat pulled into the parking lot. "Bowling?" Amanda asked. "I didn't even know bowling alleys still existed."

"Not many. But this one's getting more popular instead of less. You used to go bowling when you were a kid, didn't you? I checked it out earlier. There's a league that bowls here, but I reserved a lane at the other end, so we don't have to worry too much about being laughingstocks. I'm hoping I've magically gotten good at this, now that I'm old."

"But I'm not—I mean come on, it's been too long."

"You were supposed to tell me I'm not old."

Amanda laughed. "Whoops. I'm still younger than you, anyway."

"So, have you forgotten how to roll the ball? How to score?"

"I think I remember the scoring. Not sure about rolling the ball." Her voice sounded dubious, but somewhere inside she wondered if this might be fun. At least it would be different.

And somewhat to her amazement, she had a good time, from choosing a pair of rental shoes to hefting the smooth, hard balls to test the weight and fit for her fingers—*Had they always been so heavy?*—to facing the lane for the first time. In the middle of the second game, she actually bowled a strike, to their shared astonishment.

The martinis at the bowling alley's sports bar went down well, too. Amanda hadn't felt so—sort of loose and … happy?—in a long time. "You know," she reflected, playing with the stem of the martini glass, "I'm beginning to wonder if you're right.

I'd forgotten things like this. I need something like a recreation club, people who get together and do whatever."

"Does SI have a bowling league, by any chance?"

"No, and it wouldn't work anyway. When you're the president, you stifle the fun. We're a reasonably casual company, but no one's going to relax around the person who has the power to approve your raise or fire you."

"So you gave up. That's wrong. You've got to find outlets that work for you. Consider it part of a healthy adulthood."

"Sort of grit my teeth and bear it?"

"Yeah, force yourself." Pat chuckled. "This is nuts. I'm advising my best friend to force herself to have fun. You want to hear the real, underground reason I went into kids' counseling? Because I get to play. I found the same thing you are now, back in my engineering days. It was an uphill battle, constantly having to prove myself, and not always with the nicest people — especially one I could think of." She clicked Amanda's martini glass with her own and sipped. "Have fun. I dare you. For instance, you might consider having fun with the new hottie on your staff."

"Hottie!" Amanda sputtered out a laugh. "When did that word get into your vocabulary?"

"The same time I first laid eyes on Jacob McKinnon. So, how's it working out?"

Amanda went still, remembering hands brushing. "Tell me something. Why is it that sometimes someone new comes into your life, and it just doesn't matter, then another time … I told you about the Jolt. It's fortunate that I don't see him often, he's at one end of the building and I'm at the other. But this Jolt thing. It hits right here." Amanda indicated her flat midriff. "As if my stomach's giving me a warning."

"They do say your gut knows things before your brain does."

"Fight or flight. I get that. But the signal gets to the brain sooner or later. Then you have to figure out if your gut was right. And what your next steps are."

"Any idea if it's a shared experience?"

Amanda sipped her martini. "Yes," she said quietly. "It is. At least as far as the electricity." Her inner imp emerged. "I haven't asked if it's messing around with his man parts."

Pat sputtered a mouthful of martini. "Now that sounds like the Amanda of old. So, tell all. How do you know he's got your Jolt, too? And what's he doing about it?"

Amanda described the touching hands. "And nothing's being done. I made it clear that it wasn't going any further."

Pat groaned. "And he bought it."

"Yes. I think so."

"And why on God's good green earth did you tell him such a thing?"

"Be fair, Pat, you know why. He works for me, for SI. It's not a good idea."

"Against the rules?"

"Not technically. But—"

"It's threatening? I can see it might be. But I've watched Jacob McKinnon. I know what kind of father he is. SI's not going to be your forever true love."

"I wouldn't even have mentioned the Jolt if he hadn't first. He's almost as annoying as you. He actually asked me what I wanted to do, and then he tried to reassure me. I think he might want more. But maybe not. Mixed signals."

"He's been out of circulation for a long time. But he's a healthy male of a certain age, and my guess is, you're trying to stare down the inevitable. And with the finest example of single manhood I've seen in ages." Pat put her head in her hands. "Please, please tell me you might reconsider."

"I might not. I'm grown up, Pat. I know what's best for me."

Pat looked up. "No, girlfriend," she said flatly. "In this case, you most definitely do not."

* * *

Thanksgiving Day, Amanda arrived on her parents' front porch at eleven o'clock, carrying store-bought pumpkin and mincemeat pies. She and James had grown up in this older neighborhood of big yards shaded by buckeye and maple trees.

She'd had a healthy, normal childhood, and still looked forward to spending time with her parents in their family home.

"Come on in," her father bellowed. "Not locked."

She maneuvered the door open, balancing the pies in one hand. "It never is. The world's not like it used to be. Someone could walk right in."

"Have you seen the crime stats for Calter Creek?" Her father, a large, barrel-chested man who still sported a head of thick, dark hair, met her at the door. He took the pies and gave her a perfunctory hug. "You worry about yourself."

"Daughter's prerogative."

"He locks the door," her mother called from the kitchen. "Except when he knows you're coming."

"Good to know. Seems an age since I've been here." She drifted into the kitchen, her father behind her carrying the pies. Her mother already had a glass of red wine poured for her, and seductive aromas from the oven filled the room.

"We're heading out again in January. Plans aren't firm yet, but anyone with any sense makes tracks. The new motor home's in Florida. We're planning to drive across to the southwest," her father said.

"Best of all worlds," her mother chimed in. "Like a turtle, with your house right there all the time." With her curly gray bob and a thickening figure clad in a peach colored tracksuit, she looked every inch the healthy, happy senior vagabond.

"And you're having the time of your lives." At least her mother was. Her father made the right noises for her mother's sake, but even after so many years out of the workforce, he still resented the ill health that had forced his retirement.

And by extension, she thought grimly, the daughter who had taken his place. But today wasn't the day for reflections like that. Today she'd simply be glad for the blessings they'd been given.

Over a mid-afternoon Thanksgiving dinner, her mother said, "I guess you've already heard, James invited us out to spend Christmas with him and his family. But we aren't happy leaving you here on your own."

"Oh, Mom, go! You know you're dying to get your hands on those grandchildren. I won't mind at all. I did get the invitation, but, well, this time of year it's not going to happen. But you need to go."

"Are you sure you couldn't break free for a few days?"

James's undisciplined brood, with the added chaos of Christmas and your parents thrown into the mix?

"Sorry, Mom."

Her father said, "You do what you have to do, if you're going to make a success of it. Mandy knows that." It was nice to hear a note of pride in her father's voice, for once.

"Even SI's not worth killing yourself over," her mother said.

"Nothing to do with it." Her dad would never admit that his workaholic ways had led to his health challenges and early retirement.

"But it is a shame you have to miss out on a family Christmas."

"Pat's family, or as good as," Amanda said. "I'll be fine."

"I know, baby." Her mother patted her hand. "I get sentimental. And you work so hard. I wish you had a young man to spend the holidays with."

And didn't that work out well, the last time you tried it.

"Old refrain, Mom."

The conversation inevitably turned to SI.

"Always SI." Her mother groaned, then laughed and waved away the comment. "Ignore me. SI's given us a good living and a great retirement. I love it to death."

"We're going to have an excellent holiday season." At her mother's grimace she added, "Don't worry, Mom, I won't bore you with details. I have to say though, hiring the new accountant's turning out to be a godsend."

Her father looked up. "How's he working out?"

"Stan hired him, remember. No problem so far. He's around my age, has a little girl. It's the ponytail I questioned."

Her father glowered. "Ponytail? What next? When I was running SI, we'd never—"

"I know, Dad. In fact, I questioned it. But one, Stan really wanted him. Two, there don't seem to be any alternatives. Three, there's no rule that says a man can't have hair down past his shoulders."

"Amanda, promise me you'll make sure Stan stays on top of things. He's got to have more experience than this new guy does. Be sure Stan's supervising him until we're sure we can trust him."

As an old friend, her father had been among the first to hear about Stan's heart attack. "Dad, Stan's not going to be supervising anything for another month, more if his family gets their way. Right now, Jacob's what I've got. And from what I've seen of his first few weeks, I'm not worried."

"You should worry until he's proven himself. You could end up falling flat on your face."

Amanda sighed. "When was the last time I fell flat on my face?"

Since there wasn't an answer to that, her dad changed the subject. "Now, Karen, Amanda's brought pie. Shall we have some?"

"I'll whip the cream." Her mother scooped up a couple of empty plates and headed for the kitchen, while Amanda and her father continued to chat about the business, the staff, the gossip, even the pink line of girls' accessories.

The way Thanksgiving always is. Forget the Jolt. Forget Jacob. Think turkey and pie and family and all you have to be thankful for.

Chapter 8

SI made it through November month end, and the staff drew a collective sigh of relief. In the President's suite that afternoon, Mel set a coffee on Amanda's desk. "Put down your pen and I'll tell you the news."

"Is there any?"

"Always." Mel settled into a guest chair. "I had coffee yesterday with Jim. So naturally I found out all I could about his hunky new boss."

There was a little thump when Amanda's pen hit the desk harder than she'd planned. "What's happened to the female vocabulary all of a sudden? Why am I being assaulted by words like hunky and hottie? And why is every female in my world determined to apply these words to Jacob McKinnon?"

"The truth as we know it? Glad to hear others are noticing, too. He's the kind who could fly under the radar. Your basic beta male." Mel became thoughtful, focusing her eyes somewhere in space for a moment. "It's funny, isn't it? On the surface you wouldn't expect him to be that alluring. I mean, he's a little too thin, he'd look better with shorter hair. He's mild mannered to a fault, they say — hard to imagine great passion there. A basic corn-fed nice guy. But there's something about him. Like he ought to be in a park playing touch football with his pals, for a beer commercial, for instance. Beautiful people selling sex and lager."

"You've got an imagination, I'll give you that." Amanda sipped her coffee.

"Monday after Thanksgiving, we landed in the break room at the same time. Seems he and his kid got together with friends for Thanksgiving dinner, but a quiet holiday otherwise. He was worried — afraid she might have been bored. He asked me what I thought of the pink stuff, then said he couldn't bear to buy her any of it. Way too sensible, I figure. Thinks too much. And that tired thing, like the weight of the world's on his shoulders."

Amanda gave a little huff of frustration. "If parents around here won't buy the pink stuff for their children, will the public?"

"Don't worry. Doting aunts like me will buy it. That's why the kids love us best. It'll fly off the shelves."

Amanda sighed. "I suppose so. So they're a happy family in Accounting, would you say?"

"Jim says so. He says Jacob's fair and low-key and never raises his voice or slams doors or throws things."

"Good grief. Did Stan ever do any of that?"

Mel chuckled. "Not that I know of. Well, not since that first computer package, anyway. Just a bit of hyperbole. The point is, he's settling in." Mel fell silent while she sipped her coffee. "And," she added as an afterthought, "by all accounts he's good at what he does."

"Getting through month end without a hitch tells part of the tale, anyway. And that reminds me, could you give a heads-up to Legal? We're having import issues with one of the Indian firms. I want to be up to date before we have another shipment held up."

"Sure, I'll check with Legal Robert." So called to distinguish him from Warehouse Robert; Mel frequently employed internal nicknames. She stood, stretched, and headed for the door. "I suppose your Christmas shopping's all done. Me, I tried Black Friday, but it felt too much like hard work. What does the Indian firm give us?"

"Ceramics. Vases, and those odd twisty sculptures you liked so much."

"Oh, yeah, can't let Customs hold those up." Mel left Amanda twirling her fountain pen and thinking. How would things play out when Stan came back? Would Jacob McKinnon still be on the employee roster in three months' time? And did she hope he'd go, or stay?

* * *

Amanda was packing up to leave for home when her phone rang. Even if she hadn't heard his voice almost daily around SI, she'd have known who was on the other end by the way her hand tingled around the receiver—a new manifestation of the Jolt?

"Suppose I asked you out. Say for dinner, or a movie."

"I thought we understood each other."

"We do. That doesn't mean we couldn't have dinner together. Would you?"

You could. All you have to do is say yes.

"Okay," he said, "the long pause tells me you're working your way to no."

"It's not a good idea, Jacob."

"Matter of opinion."

"I'm sorry. I have to go, I'm late."

"Give me points for trying. Good night, Amanda."

Chapter 9

Jacob stood at the doorway for a moment, Norah swinging from his hand. The hotel ballroom had been decorated in elementary school chic, the noise level soared toward deafening. Piecing together what he'd learned from Jim and Mel, he expected SI's end-of-year party to be a high-spirited afternoon of cheerful if vigilant parents, hyperactive kids, and non-alcoholic punch. Everyone who possibly could turned up.

He and Norah hung up their coats and wandered into the room. An enormous ball pit of multi-colored plastic balls and a whole blow-up jungle gym contraption with tree house and slide filled one end. To his ongoing amazement, it didn't take Norah long to survey the place, size it up, and dive in. The shell his daughter had built for herself when Deb died had cracked wide open, and she was ready to take on the world.

More than you are, probably.

He stood on the sidelines as the ball pit drew his daughter like a magnetic force.

Eventually they'd have some organized activities, a visit from the Winter Elf, and a buffet, followed by dancing with a family oriented band providing the music. The staff at SI didn't number that many people, probably thirty tops, but including spouses and kids, they filled up the room.

He helped himself to a cup of punch and joined Warehouse Robert and Marcia.

"I wouldn't miss these things," Robert said. "Work can be intense, but we do appreciate each other and have fun together."

"It's a good picture," Jacob said. "Solid family values, stability. My guess is that most of you have been here for a while." He looked at Marcia.

"Average is eight years. Stan's the longest, at thirty. How's he doing, have you heard?"

Jacob grinned. "Improving daily. He'd be back in a flash if his family let him. It may not be soon though, because his wife's hoping for a tropical vacation after Christmas. He doubts he'll be able to escape."

Marcia groaned. "And only our Stan would moan about Hawaii or the Caribbean as if it was the Black Death. I hope Susan gets her vacation. She's been trying for it for five years or so."

"That could be the root of the heart attack, I suppose," Robert said. "Work, work, work, not enough exercise, the usual. And while this is a reasonably laid-back company, this time of year it's bound to be crazy, that's just the nature of the beast."

"Beasts!" Marcia executed a little dance step. "Did you see the new animal things in the little viewing room? All these make-believe what-do-you-call-'ems. They're not even monsters, because most of them aren't scary, but they're adorable. My daughter's fifteen, and I see one in her future."

"Haven't yet, but I should. Trying to come up with original ideas for a six-year-old. Could be I lack imagination."

Mel joined the group. "Oh, you do, because here we've got this really neat pink line. And you may think I'm nuts and that it's the tackiest stuff going, but you'll be her hero forever if you buy her some of it. Marcie, how's the new grandbaby?"

"Oh, Mel, you wouldn't believe. Wait a sec, I have photos on my phone." Marcia and Mel drifted away.

"Have you seen Amanda?" Robert asked Jacob.

Have you seen Amanda? Not enough.

Not outside of work since that lunch a month ago. At work he saw her frequently. They talked, always about business, but he wondered if she picked up on the subtext, the things they weren't saying. She kept her guard up in his presence. Cautious, although probably no one would notice it but him.

Wake up. That's not what Robert's asking.

"In fact, no. Shouldn't the owner have pride of place at a shindig like this? Although, from what little I know of her, I'm not sure this would be her scene."

"Her dad's better at it. Amanda keeps more to herself. She'll handle it okay though. There's not a thing you can say against her, other than those temper things. And come to think of it, it hasn't happened in a while now. Wonder if something's changed in her life." Robert gave him a look that fell somewhere between amused and shrewd.

"I know a friend of hers. I hear she's been on a campaign to get Amanda out more. And don't give me that look. I'm not the new hobby."

"Hmm. I can promise you this, the company's on alert. Like it or not, pal, you're under the microscope. And speculation is, something could be cooking there."

Jacob laughed easily. "You scare me. For that matter, Amanda scares me. Thanks for the tip."

"Merry Christmas to you." Robert tapped his arm and drifted away.

Jacob finally spotted Amanda, crossing the room toward the punch bowl. She looked less than her usual calm self. Not rattled so much as frazzled.

Mel spied her boss and charged over. "Making an entrance?"

Amanda rolled her eyes. "I went out to the garage and found a flat tire." She gestured at her gray pantsuit, the red turtleneck. "By the time I changed into scruffy clothes and got the new tire on and changed again—"

Jacob joined the conversation. "You change tires, too? If I was scared before, I'm terrified now."

"Of what, exactly?" Mel jumped on his comment lightning fast.

"Office gossip. I've just had a manly tête-à-tête with Robert. I'm told I'm being watched, in case I put moves on the lady at the helm." He noted that Amanda flushed lightly.

Mel laughed. "If you want practice, check with me, okay?" She glanced at Amanda, her eyes crinkled with humor

"Or, if said moves should prove to be unpopular, hey, I'm your girl."

"A guy'd have to be crazy to ignore an invitation like that."

"You're ignoring it perfectly well. And most gentlemanly of you, too." Mel giggled, and addressed Amanda. "This man's perfect to flirt with. Good come-back lines, and every assurance it isn't going anywhere, worse luck."

"You're incorrigible. And yes, I can change my own tires." Amanda held up her hand. "I've got the grub under my nails to prove it. No time to scrub it all out." She wrinkled her nose in distaste.

"I can't, or rather, I don't. I prefer the maiden in distress technique. See you around." Mel cheerfully left her boss and the new senior accountant standing together, alone for the moment.

"Hey, Amanda," someone called out from across the room. "Where's Colin?"

"Stomach flu," she answered. "Mom called this morning to let me know."

"He's usually here?" Jacob asked.

"Never misses. Stan's been the Winter Elf for years, too, so lots of changes this year. It's okay, I guess, but I admit I value the tradition, the stability."

"You risk stagnation though. And you have lovely hands, even if one of the nails is a little grubby."

Her eyebrows went up.

He smiled and shrugged. "A compliment, that's all. Chat, but suggesting that I don't in the least mind standing here with you." He gestured with his cup at the noisy gathering. "Most of this is a long way from my comfort zone. I'm not an extrovert, and I don't know anybody really well. Happiest here holding up the wall."

"Which you may not be for long." Amanda nodded at the small figure barreling toward them.

"Daddy, you have to come," Norah called out from fifteen feet away. "It's a race for dads and kids. You have to help me win." She grabbed Jacob's free hand and started pulling, then noticed Amanda. "Oh—hi. I remember you. Tell him to come."

"Go." Amanda received his cup from him, and Norah pulled him away.

* * *

Amanda set his cup down on the end of a table, then watched the race. She'd never understood the dynamic that would see a father make a fool of himself for the sake of a daughter. Not that the fathers out there were making fools of themselves, exactly.

Play. This is play.

But would she ever be willing to participate in something like this? She shook her head at her own foolishness. And found herself biting back an impulse to scream out encouragement as Norah bolted for the finish line.

Ten minutes later though, Norah accosted her. "Now it's the mom-and-kid race. You're the only mom without a kid. So you can race with me. Maybe?" Norah asked, as if suddenly aware that she might have overstepped.

"But I'm not a mother."

"I—but you *might* be. And I don't have anyone else."

Amanda scanned the room a little desperately for Mel or an unencumbered grandmother, but couldn't find anyone. Then she looked down at Norah, whose eyes were frankly pleading. "Does your dad know you're asking me? It might not be okay with him."

"He's gone to the restroom. Over there." Norah gestured behind her. "Pleeease?"

A whistle blew. Amanda had to make a decision. She thought about Pat and her mandate to have fun. "Come on then. But you'll have to tell me what to do. I haven't done this before."

"It's easy." They threaded their way to the start, Norah fairly dancing at her side. "I run, then you run, then I run. But you have to touch my hand before you start, or it doesn't count. And I have to touch yours. Are you a good runner?"

"No. Sorry."

"Never mind." The little girl squeezed her hand. "You'll have to do the best you can."

"How did you and your dad do?"

"Third. But he tried real hard."

Amanda shook her head in amazement at the conversation, and at finding herself at the starting line of a mother-kid race. Then the man in charge, Charlie from Warehouse, fired some kind of pop gun, and she got caught up in the relay.

* * *

Jacob sized up the situation immediately as he came out of the men's room, and watched open-mouthed as his daughter and the woman he was falling for raced together. "Hard to compute," he commented when Mel once again appeared at his side.

"You're telling me. Your daughter must be a closet witch. Go!" she shouted. Amanda made the turn and scrambled toward the finish.

"Not my doing, for sure. Mel, am I totally off base, or is it true that even at six years old, little girls know stuff?"

"You're not. You've got it exactly right. You, my friend, have female spidey senses all over you these days. You don't stand a chance."

Jacob had been grinning a lot this afternoon. "You women think I'm dangerous? I'm flattered."

"Don't get cocky. You keep your dangerous way underground, Jacob McKinnon. Naturally the females of the species are curious. The males of the species take longer to figure it out." Mel squeezed his arm and disappeared in the crowd.

He thanked Amanda when Norah dragged her over to him. The delight in his daughter's eyes spoke volumes. "How'd you do? I couldn't hear in the noise. If you did better than me, I'm not happy."

"She did her best," Norah said solemnly.

"Sixth. Out of eight. The eighth kid was three years old."

"You tried." Norah danced off.

"I managed third with her. She got a ribbon. And if it's true that the gossip mill has its collective eye on you and me, my daughter's given it some fuel, wouldn't you say?"

Something had certainly put some color in her cheeks. "That was for your daughter. Not anything that—" She broke off, then changed the topic. "Where did she learn that look? Even if I hadn't had Pat's lectures about having more fun ringing in my ears, I couldn't have resisted. Seems she couldn't find anyone else. My not being a mother didn't carry any weight at all."

"Come on, you need something to drink. A reward for valiant race-running." Jacob took her arm and steered her to the refreshment tables. "Norah's changing so quickly, I'm struggling to keep up with her nowadays. I'm starting to wonder if I should be slowing her down a little."

"You should be proud." Amanda accepted a cup of punch from him and sipped. "Young women need to be feisty and strong, and know their own minds."

"Her mind's not the problem. I'm worried about surviving until she's grown up."

Amanda laughed. They stood outside the throng of partying people, chatting — for once, not about work.

Easily. As if we could talk forever. This could get scary.

He was aware, as he suspected that Amanda, for the moment, was not, that more than one set of eyes in the room noted their standing together, their relaxed conversation.

Later, after presents from the Winter Elf and a child-friendly dinner of fried chicken, the band came out to begin the dance. They played a couple of numbers the kids all seemed familiar with.

Chickens? Where did Norah learn that?

Jacob hadn't progressed past 'I'm a Little Teapot'. Norah went into dictatorial-teacher mode, trying to show him what to do.

Then the band leader announced a parents-only dance, and the music changed tempo. And there was Amanda, so close. "So, mommy for a day." He held out his hand to her. She'd been chatting with Anne, the front desk receptionist, but—was it the shock of the request?—before he knew quite how it had happened he held her in his arms.

Jacob kept the slow dance formal. This, he thought wryly, was partly a matter of avoiding personal embarrassment; no way could he risk close and shifting contact with her, not after so long a drought. His defenses, probably emotional but definitely physical, were in danger of collapse. He was hyper-aware of her. Still, even with six inches of air between them, it felt right to hold her hand, feel her lithe back through the suit and sweater as she settled into the dance, following his lead.

"Our reward for the races and fried chicken," he murmured. "You could have caught a cab here. I'd have given you a ride home."

"True, but I rely on others all the time, especially at work. I'd rather take care of myself."

"Don't you think it's possible to be too independent?"

"No, actually I don't. Self-reliance is so important, when …" She broke off when his hand caressed her back, a restrained, experimental movement. "Be careful, Jacob," she shot at him. Quietly, but a clear warning.

He held his hand still against her back. *Good enough, for now.* "I'm careful. Just exploring that unfinished conversation we have hanging around."

She drew back and looked up at him. "I don't want—"

"I know." His words were quiet enough that no one could overhear. She looked down. "Relax, Amanda. It's been a day well beyond any hopes I had for it, so I'm not tempting fate. I was just reminded."

At least she didn't walk off the dance floor, but he could feel her muscles tense against his hand. The music ended, and she immediately broke free of him.

* * *

Jacob got them home, and somehow got his wired daughter into the tub, then into her pyjamas. It took longer than usual to settle her for bed. Reading to her finally unwound her enough that she snuggled against her pillow and stayed put.

He ran his hand over her curls and bent down to kiss her cheek, thinking, as he always did during their nighttime ritual, how blessed he was. Despite everything.

She forced her eyes back open. "Daddy?"

"What is it, Sweet Cakes?"

"I like Amanda."

"I'm glad."

"I think she's a keeper."

A *what*? Norah might be relaxed and three-quarters asleep, but she'd still managed to give him a good, solid kick.

He chose not to follow up on that one. "Sleep well, Pumpkin. See you in the morning."

"G'night, Daddy." She fell asleep almost before she got the words out.

Alone in his living room, Jacob back-burnered thoughts about Amanda and looked back on the day. He'd enjoyed himself. He'd chatted with most of the staff, and quite a few of the spouses and partners. He'd seen Norah more excited than she'd been in years, and had run a race, and danced a slow dance.

And danced a slow dance.

So much for back-burnered. He made a stab at meditating, but, predictably, without success. Amanda was taking over his mind. A keeper, Norah had said. Well, he thought so, too, but how did Norah pick up on it?

Reflecting on the party, and the last month or so, he gave up any illusions he might have had that he could avoid courting Amanda Sinclair. It was folly, because he barely knew her, but he couldn't seem to break free of the way she drew him. She kept herself aloof, but even she couldn't deny the electricity between them. Their dance had sealed the deal, as far as he was concerned. What the deal would turn out to be, he couldn't imagine.

And to complicate matters, he had to consider Norah. However much he put his own heart on the line, he had to keep her from getting hurt. Because it was far from a sure bet that Amanda would be entering their lives.

Far from sure. But a man can dream.

Chapter 10

At home, Amanda wondered what had possessed her, to run that ridiculous race. She'd probably run like an uncoordinated girl and given the staff a good laugh.

Well, she could explain that. Almost anyone would find Norah McKinnon irresistible.

And when Jacob had held out his hand for the dance, she could so easily have declined, claiming fatigue or something urgent she had to see to. She never danced at these things except with her father. What had gotten into her?

The end-of-year party always tired her out. She considered it a chore, given the noise and chaos and the necessity that she participate, but as the company president, she could never be one of the crowd. It wasn't business, that was the problem. Usually her dad took up most of the pressure. She made a mental note to phone tomorrow to see how he was and report in.

What did they think of her, those people who depended on SI for their food and mortgages and vacations? 'Doing' the end-of-year party came with the job, but it always left her a little uneasy, wondering exactly how much of herself she'd put on display. Jacob had warned her, after the races, that her staff suspected something was going on between them. Ordinary gossip? Not unexpected, all things considered.

He's like a comfortable old pair of slippers –

What?

Easy to be with, Jacob and Norah. They're a family. They do Christmases and school plays. He shops for little-girl clothes and cooks and sees to vaccinations and brushing teeth and school programs. Two people, a father and a daughter, sharing a life —

Don't go there. Just don't go there.

Oh, *what* was happening to her?

Why was everything suddenly so complicated?

* * *

Monday afternoon, Amanda was deep into a spreadsheet on her computer when Jacob entered her office and dropped a couple of sheets of paper on her desk. She looked up as he set a mug of coffee in front of her. "The pension reports you wanted, with my notes. I've already gone over them with Marcia. Take a break for a minute." He nodded in the general direction of the mug, then sat.

"I don't—"

"Yes, you do. If you don't drink the coffee now you'll waste valuable time walking down to the break room and back. Enjoy the service."

"You're being presumptuous." This was an unexpected and unexplainable situation, Jacob making himself at home like this. She had work to do. She didn't have time to linger over coffee for no good reason. She saved the spreadsheet and turned from her computer.

"Think of it as supporting your managers. I figure Jim and Bev deserve someplace where they can complain about me, so I'd rather not hang out in the break room. But I'd like someone to chat with for ten minutes."

Amanda pulled the coffee closer. "I never thought of that. Stan always treated the Accounting department like one big happy family."

"Mostly that works. But we're getting into the Christmas crazies, and I'm going to be pushing a little, so they need to be able to get away from me."

She frowned at the mug on her desk. "You know I prefer my coffee black?"

"Black and decaf in the afternoon. I'm observant."

"Clearly." She conceded defeat and picked up the mug. "How's Norah doing?"

"Wonderful. I caved in and bought her a pink princess dress for Christmas. Mel assures me that she'll adore it. I don't get it, but I'm willing to give it a try. I'd thought I might take her to meet Santa next weekend, but it's possible SI's Winter Elf filled the bill. I'll discreetly sound her out if I can."

"Does discreetly work with a six-year-old?" Amanda leaned back, cradling the mug.

She hadn't been aware of Jacob's tension until he let it go. His body visibly relaxed.

You will not notice his body.

It was the dark gray suit, she told herself. He wore a suit so well ….

She snapped her attention back where it belonged.

"She's pretty literal, so maybe not. Someone out there understands little girls. I'm not sure it's meant to be fathers though."

They chatted for another few minutes, then Jacob stood and drummed his fingers on the pages he'd put on her desk. "I've got to go. Thanks for the break, I needed it. Let me know if you have any questions."

He leaned over the desk, far enough that he could brush his fingers over her hand wrapped around her coffee mug, then left.

Mel, who couldn't have seen the touch of his hand on hers from her desk, came into her office within ten seconds. "What was that about?"

"Dropping off a report." Amanda pointedly pulled the papers he'd left toward her.

"Just a friendly, collegial chat?"

"I guess. The break room doesn't work for everyone all the time."

"Hmm. I'm heading down there now. Back in ten."

Mel disappeared. Amanda looked back on her ten minutes with Jacob and wondered what had just happened.

* * *

The thing was, it kept happening. Every afternoon in the two weeks before Christmas, Jacob appeared in her office, bringing her a coffee and sometimes a sample from the Christmas baking that filled the break room these days. Then he'd drop into a chair and they'd talk for a few minutes. She was starting to look forward to it.

And every single time, except one day when Mel joined them, he reached over and brushed her knuckles or gave her hand a quick squeeze before he left. Once, when she'd been leaning back in her chair, cradling her mug, he'd gone so far as to circle her desk. He'd brushed his fingers over hers, grinned, said, "You can't escape that easily," and left.

She phoned Pat. "I don't know what to think."

"I'd say he's upping the ante. I'd say you're in for the ride of your life."

Which did nothing to tame the Jolt or shuffle Jacob McKinnon out of her mind.

Or annihilate the lingering memories of Brandon.

Once again Amanda steeled herself and focused on work.

Chapter 11

The break room was packed, a lunchtime tradition on Christmas Eve, marking the end of the short workday. There were a couple of people still on the Floor, finishing special orders that a courier would pick up within the hour, but otherwise the SI staff had gathered to celebrate.

She tolerated the loose hugs because it had always been that way. She wished her father were there. He loved these things, but he and her mother were in Colorado with James and his family. And she missed Stan. He was as much a part of SI as her father, and his absence left a hole.

Jacob didn't come near her. That made it easier.

Mel was there though. "I hope you aren't planning on working a full day," she said, loudly enough that several others joined in the circle around Amanda.

"Someone has to while you go off to play."

"No, someone doesn't," Jim from Accounting said. "Get some rest, Amanda, you're looking tired. Make this a holiday."

"Lead by example," someone called out from another part of the room.

Charlie came in from the warehouse. "You're not working. We need you bright-eyed and bushy-tailed come Monday morning." Charlie had adopted Stan's usual role of senior uncle, taking care of her.

She caught a glimpse of Jacob chuckling at Charlie's comment. He put his eggnog mug in the dishwasher and left the break room. "I need that warehouse report, Charlie."

"You're not getting it before Monday." Charlie folded his arms and imitated a brick wall. "I'm not producing any report that you think you have to work on. Non-negotiable."

Amanda withdrew gracefully. They expected her to make some sort of formal pronouncement to mark the official beginning of the holiday, so she turned to face the room and raised her voice. "I want to say that we wouldn't be what we are, or where we are, without you. You're the best."

"And our bonuses are gonna reflect that, right?" someone called out.

She smiled. "I hope so."

She knew so. The Sinclair family didn't hoard SI profits.

She didn't stay until the end of the gathering. The heads of Purchasing and Marketing also left early.

The head of Accounting's already left.

She relied on these people, and they relied on their teams. By Monday, they'd have their departments ready for whatever the post-Christmas week might throw at them.

It had been a good year. And oh, did she have plans for next year. She'd have to start some lists, build some projections. Her fingers twitched at the thought of the new directions she could take Sinclair Imports.

* * *

It was midafternoon when Jacob finished work and shut down his computer. With four days off, including a weekend, he'd have a good break and plenty of time with Norah. The Christmases since Deb died had been pretty much a bust, so he hoped that this year it would feel like a real holiday to them both. He'd be scrambling in the short week between Christmas and New Year's, with Stan away, but he didn't want to think about work at all until then.

For now, for the next few minutes, he was a man on a mission.

Like many missions, it required planning and a fair amount of nerve.

SI was deserted. He'd heard the others calling out season's greetings as they left. Bev and Jim had both stuck their heads in his office with best wishes for him and Norah.

He finished tidying up his space, locked the door to Accounting, and headed toward the President's suite at the other end of the building.

Ah. Not quite the last one. As he reached the outer door to Amanda's suite, he collided with Mel.

Mel, characteristically, hugged him and planted a kiss on his cheek. "Merry Christmas!"

He hugged back. "And to you. Big plans?"

"Party with some pals tonight, then with my sister and nieces tomorrow. It's going to be great. She's in there. Good luck," she concluded in a whisper, tilting her head toward the door. Mel swung away from him, waved, and headed to the entrance.

Good luck?

Mel was a worthwhile barometer and knew things it was logically impossible for her to know. If that constituted her blessing, he'd take it. He crossed Mel's office and knocked on Amanda's doorframe before going in.

She'd obviously heard him coming and met his entrance with a polite smile. "You don't need to still be here. I'm sure Norah's waiting for you."

"I could say the same to you. I'll walk you to your car." Jacob sat on one of her guest chairs, dropping his coat onto the other one. "And I brought you this." He tossed an envelope on her desk. "Made especially for you, I'm told, and I got firm instructions that I'd better deliver it. Would you mind opening it so I can tell her how thrilled you are?"

"Norah?" She reached for the envelope.

"School project."

Amanda neatly slit open the envelope and studied the card inside. It reminded her of every holiday card she'd made in school, construction paper and glitter that got onto her hands. "Tell her I love it, and thank her very much. I appreciate your taking the time to deliver this, but I'm sure you want to get home."

"I'm in no particular rush. Are you trying to hustle me out the door?"

"No, I … well." Amanda gestured with a hand, a gesture that he interpreted as, look at the work on my desk, please go away.

"It's Christmas Eve, and it feels right, hanging out with you. Mostly." This was it, the moment he'd been gearing himself up for all day. "And that's why I'm here, not Norah's card."

His muscles weren't responding the way they ought to. Two years. Did he even remember how? Talk about awkward. He felt like a gawky teenager again. But he'd go nuts if this had to wait any longer.

He unfolded himself from the chair, walked around her desk, and took one of her hands. She didn't resist, and he wondered why not. He studied her face. Her lips pinched together, and her eyes shifted restlessly around the room, focusing on everything, it seemed, except him.

"Mostly we're good together," he said, "but there's this one thing that's not right between us. We need to deal with it."

She twisted, but his hand had captured hers and he didn't let go. "I'm not discussing this, Jacob."

"That's a relief. I didn't have a lot of talking on my mind." He tried for his usual light tone, but he heard the intensity in his voice and hoped he wasn't spooking her. His eyes locked on her face.

"Let me go." It was a command, not a request.

"If you promise to hear me out."

She nodded.

He freed her hand and propped himself against her desk, legs crossed at the ankle, looking down at her. She picked up her fountain pen; it began its journey from one hand to another.

"I'd much rather you go away."

"I don't believe you. I believe you wish I'd sit down and behave myself, but you can't convince me you don't like having me around."

"This isn't appropriate, and I have things to finish before I leave." The pen shuffled back and forth as she twisted it through her fingers.

"You promised, and it'll only take a minute. It's growing, this thing between us. When it first turned up, that day we had lunch, I figured we could ignore it. Dumb. Of course we can't. Every time I see you it's stronger."

He stopped and took a breath. "I'm so nervous right now my stomach's in knots, just so you know. I bet you are, too." Above all, he wanted her to believe that she still called the shots. He wasn't giving himself the right to barge into her office this way. He gambled that she wouldn't boot him out.

She didn't need to know that the cramp in his gut wasn't a figure of speech. It hurt. He hadn't been so tense and tight in years.

He watched her face. She was working on annoyed and achieving scared; he hoped she wasn't aware of it. When she didn't respond he went on. "From where I stand this isn't a problem, it isn't an executive decision. It's just you and me."

"Jacob, back off. You're crowding me."

He watched the pen go back and forth, back and forth through her fingers.

Easier than risking looking at her face, her eyes. Because you could throw up over this.

"Do me a favor. Just once, don't think. Don't talk. Don't act like it isn't happening. Don't pretend that you don't jump out of your skin if our hands touch unexpectedly, but I touch your hand every day and you don't fight me. You like my touching you." He took a breath. "The bottom line is, it's Christmas Eve and I want to kiss you. I believe you want it, too."

Her face altered from scared to panicky, but she didn't concede an inch. "Stop. I mean it, Jacob."

He shook his head. "Not this time. Not when we both know."

* * *

She watched him take the fountain pen out of her hand and place it on her desk, and twisted her empty fingers together. He put his hands on the high back of her chair, on either side of her head. To her horror, the fight went out of her.

He was going to have his way, and she couldn't do a thing about it.

She wondered fleetingly why she would want to do anything about it.

"Look at me," he murmured. Very slowly but very deliberately, he brought his mouth toward hers, his eyes on hers every moment, as if daring her to turn her head away.

She stared into those eyes, mesmerized. Noted the green flecks against the light brown. When his lips brushed her mouth, the Jolt went berserk. Her body spasmed as if she'd been electrocuted.

She couldn't have hidden it. And he responded by moving his hands to her arms, pulling her to her feet and against him, kissing her again—not a brush this time, and his eyes weren't laughing anymore. His mouth claimed hers, gently opened hers, his tongue barely touched her lips, and then his arms were tight around her, and somehow her arms were around him, too, and he shuddered under her hands, her palms fused to his back, and her eyes closed and her lips and tongue responded and why hadn't she ever known it could feel like this?

He broke the kiss and backed up a little, moved his hands to her arms and looked at her. Both of them fought for breath. Amanda stared at him, stupefied. Took in his dilated pupils, the mouth that had sent her flying, spinning. Sent her into a fireworks display against a midnight blue, star-spangled sky.

He took one final, heaving breath. "I thought you might let me kiss you." His voice was pitched for her ears alone. He was shaken, as much as she was. "But even that wasn't a sure bet. I never expected … I mean something's been happening between us, but I never dreamed …" His eyes met hers, his mouth pulled into a half smile. "Oh, boy." One of his hands moved from her arm, his finger lightly traced her lips. His eyes never freed hers.

She backed away from those fingers. "What?" she stammered. "No, I mean I don't—I have to go. I have to go home. You have to go home. I have to …." She started to turn away from him, but his hand on her arm stopped her. Gently, but he stopped her.

"Hey." He moved the hand that had traced her lips to her chin. "This isn't going any further today. Except ..." He leaned toward her, their bodies not touching. This time the kiss was gentle, not probing.

And much too short.

"No more," he said when he stopped kissing her. "That was a promise for the future. But no more today. Okay?"

Why did he stop? Why won't he go away?

Amanda broke free and sank into her chair, aware that her legs weren't stable. Aware of reactions in her body that she hadn't experienced in years, moist, swollen reactions that told her so much more than she could deal with. She ignored the signals and let her brain take over. "That shouldn't have happened. I thought we both understood." She focused her eyes on the papers on her desk, anywhere but on him.

"We're both scared of this. That's fine. I want you—as you could probably tell since that was pretty much full body contact," he added wryly. "You want me. One day we'll have to figure out what happens next." He went back around to the guest chair.

It's impossible. He has no right, you can't risk it, you can't get involved. Never again, you've learned that lesson. Trust him, trust Jacob after this?

Please, God, make him go away.

With difficulty, Amanda pulled herself together. She wouldn't go anywhere near a man who threatened her peace of mind. Her privacy, her autonomy. A man who'd want more.

But you can't ...

She placed the fountain pen in her desk drawer and closed it with a snap. Without his hands touching her she'd found her bearings again. "I'm leaving. As for this ..." She waved her hand, schooling her face to blankness. "Forget it. Put it out of your mind. I'm sure we can work together as if nothing happened."

She felt his mood shift all the way across the desk, the energy between them was so strong. He was not angry, but frustrated. "True, we can work together. We've proven it. But that's something completely aside from this. After what just happened …. It wasn't only me, it was both of us. It's not going to disappear, Amanda. I wish you wouldn't run from it."

She kept her voice curt and formal. "There's a difference between running and making decisions. I do what needs to be done. And you should probably rethink some of your own choices. I'm going home. To be honest, I'm glad we have a few days to let this cool off."

Jacob sighed. "Listen to yourself." His voice was gentle. "Weigh what you're saying against how you respond to me. See if it adds up."

Amanda got to her feet, shifting the papers from her desk to her attaché case. She prayed he wouldn't notice how her fingers fumbled with the latches on the case.

He followed her to her closet and held her coat as she shrugged into it. "I expect you won't be able to help thinking about this afternoon. It's not over. It's becoming a question of how long we keep it at bay, that's all. But I hate to see you panic."

He put on his coat while she shoved her feet into her boots, then she straightened and looked him straight in the eye. Whatever weird sparks were going on inside her, she could do this. She knew the role inside out. "I'm not panicking. Merry Christmas, Jacob." She led them through the suite and locked the door before they headed down the south corridor to the exit.

* * *

She needs to rebuild her fortifications, Jacob thought. He let it happen, even though it was the last thing he wanted.

Battles and wars. This is a long way from over.

His voice didn't quite want to behave, and his body wasn't going to return to normal for some time yet, but he managed.

They kept a formal distance between them. "Storm coming," he said when they got to the front door.

"Yes."

"Merry Christmas back to you."

She nodded.

"I'll drop by your office on Monday."

LizAnn Carson

"I'd rather you didn't." Her voice was ice water thrown on a fire.

"I'll be there."

Casual chat wasn't going to get them back to normal. He knew her better than that by now. He locked the outer door behind them, then turned to her. He took her gloved hand, squeezed, and let go. "Don't worry, Amanda. I'm sure you'll stop trembling once you're away from me."

With that parting shot, born part of frustration, part of longing, he stepped aside and let her precede him down the sidewalk to the parking lot.

80

Chapter 12

By evening, Amanda had put the whole episode with Jacob out of her mind. Of course she had. She sat on the floor by Pat's Christmas tree and ripped into her present.

They always gave each other pajamas. The only unknowns involved style and color.

"Pink," she said flatly. "I might have expected."

"I liked the bunnies. They suit you."

"Which is why I chose neon stripes for you."

"I love 'em." Pat looked toward the living room window when a blast of wind rattled the panes. "Glad you're here for the night. It's getting vicious out there. Let's try these on." They separated, emerging from their bedrooms in new pajamas under their robes. Pat led the way into the kitchen.

They both looked at the window. Amanda said, "I'm guessing by tomorrow morning no one's going anywhere."

"Always welcome." They each made regular use of the other's guest bedroom when they planned a late night, or one involving more than a minimum of alcohol. "Now, to go with those delectable bunnies, would you care for a hot chocolate?"

"I'm old but I'm not that old. Where's the wine?"

Pat laughed. "You read my mind. We could keep this for New Year's, but what the heck." She produced a bottle of Prosecco from the fridge and dug out a couple of champagne flutes from the back of one of her cabinets. "I saw this one written up in the Columbus paper, so it ought to be good. The guys from the metropolis say so." Pat's tolerance for cities in general, or anything that smacked of concrete in particular, was low.

Pat got the cork out, then poured and raised her glass in a toast. "And we have to allow for the possibility, however remote, that one of us might be busy New Year's Eve. It won't be me though."

"Good thing we love our work." Amanda returned the toast and sipped.

"I didn't say that. I said there's nothing on *my* horizon. You? Different story altogether."

"SI's on my horizon at the moment. I'm pretty sure we've broken records this year, and I've got so many ideas, but—"

"And none of that optimism's influenced by the presence of a new accountant on staff, right?"

"You don't give up, do you?" Amanda sank into a kitchen chair.

"Not often. Sometimes a strategic retreat."

"He's around. That isn't relevant though. Planning new directions for SI, it's almost a game. It's fun. But, well, sometimes I wonder if it's enough. I look at you, getting out and seeing your clients, and going to different places every day. I look at most of my staff, at home with their families, their kids. I look at Jacob—"

"I bet you do. I sure would."

Amanda swatted at Pat's arm. "That isn't what I meant. He has the freedom to move from job to job. He'll stay as long as he chooses, then he'll be gone. He has a family. He has a *life*. What did you put in this wine, anyway? I don't normally go on like this."

"I'm hearing frustration and boredom. You've been doing the same thing forever. What is it, three years since your last vacation? You're chained to your job. You've made yourself into the indispensable president, and you're bored."

Amanda frowned. "It's funny you should say that. A little while ago, I found myself thinking I was chained to my desk, and I resented it. I wondered where the thought came from, because SI is where I want to be."

"I'm heating hors d'oeuvres. I bought some of those shrimp pastry things and an artichoke dip so we'll get our vegetable content."

"One thing's for sure, no one's ordering pizza tonight."

The fierce storm outside drew their eyes to the window yet again. Amanda shuddered, watching the swirling snow. Pat turned on the oven. "Besides the storm, this is a holiday. We order pizza all the time."

"Come on, this is dinner? Shrimp pastries and artichoke dip? You're the kitchen genius around here."

"We'll save genius for tomorrow. Given your lack of affinity with kitchens, you should be grateful for anything you get." Pat dug the pastries out of the freezer and arranged them on a baking tray, poured the artichoke dip into a bowl, and shook some crackers into a breadbasket.

"To return to the subject at hand. It sounds to me like boredom and wanting a richer life. I don't suppose the advent of the delectable Mr. McKinnon has anything to do with this new restlessness?" She sat across the table from Amanda and attacked the dip.

"It's a constant theme of yours. First, he isn't that delectable."

"We should take a poll. What does Mel think?"

Amanda sighed, but it was on top of a laugh. "Okay, round one to you. I'm told he is, to most people. I'm not most people."

Pat poked her arm. "Yep, you're still human. He's delectable. Stop denying it."

"And second, I'm not interested."

"Your Jolt is."

"You keep personifying my Jolt. As if it's a pet or something."

"Pets get attention. Pets get scratched and stroked. You know what I mean." Pat used an artichoke-laden cracker as a pointer. "Your Jolt wants you to take notice of the effect he has on you. And follow through."

"He keeps dropping in. Three o'clock, there he'll be. He sits and chats for a few minutes, then he's gone."

"The man's clever. You're getting used to his being around. Oh, I like this guy."

"I try not to look forward to it." She took a sip of the wine and decided to move the conversation onto safer ground. "I don't get this. The frustration—I think frustration was at the heart of whatever made me snap those times. It seems to be gone. But let's be clear, I'm not saying it's because of Jacob." She used her own cracker to emphasize her point.

"Of course it is. It's been years since you last had anything remotely approaching a serious relationship." The stove beeped. Pat got up and put the pastries in to bake.

Amanda let out a deep sigh. "Remember how simple and exciting life was going to be? How we'd be on top of the world, invincible? Sometimes I feel so totally—vincible?"

"Point taken. However, now's a good time to stop, with four days of vacation ahead. Drink wine, stuff yourself on our incredible Christmas dinner, kick back and relax."

"Actually, I planned to work Friday."

"What on earth for? You give everyone else the day off, then work yourself into an early grave? Following in your dad's footsteps?"

"Truth? Other than some of that planning for next year, there isn't really anything pressing. Just filling up time."

"Then hang out here, and we'll dream up something. We could go fight the crowds at Creekside Mall and stand in lines and try on everything in sight and eat lunch in the food court—."

"There's fun and then there's its exact opposite. Even you can't deny that."

Pat laughed. "True. So, if what I'm seeing outdoors is real and not a figment of my Prosecco-soaked imagination, we'll stay at home and make snow angels."

"You're impossible."

"And you're intrigued. Promise me, no work on Friday."

"Okay, promise."

"To us, little sister. It'll be one to remember." Pat raised her glass.

* * *

The women were in Pat's cozy kitchen by nine o'clock on Christmas morning, once again wrapped in pajamas and robes, starting preparations for French toast. Outside, a storm to end all storms pummeled Calter Creek. It wasn't going to let up anytime soon, according to the forecast.

"It's nice to cocoon. Is there any apple butter?" Amanda said.

"In the pantry. I'm making some blueberry sauce, too."

"Not for me, thanks. Maple syrup?"

"In the fridge. Here're the eggs. Bread's in the thingy over there." She made a sideways nod at a breadbox on the counter.

"I've always admired your command of English. Thingy."

"You crack eggs, I'll heat the syrup."

The two women worked silently for a minute. "This is the smallest one I've ever seen." Amanda gestured at the turkey coming to room temperature in a roasting pan.

"It's my annual holiday challenge. I go to outrageous lengths for a nine-pounder. This year I was afraid I'd have to seduce a butcher." Pat took the bowl of eggs from Amanda and began dunking bread.

She'd just placed the first of the slices of bread into the sizzling butter in the skillet when the phone rang. They both stopped what they were doing and stared at it.

"Your parents?"

"Not likely. Only seven o'clock in Colorado. Yours?"

"They'll call this afternoon. Uh-oh," Pat grabbed the wireless phone. "I recognize this number. Keep an eye on the French toast, will you?" She disappeared into the living room, heading toward her desk.

* * *

"Whew." Jacob was on edge, hating to be making this call. "I was afraid you wouldn't be there, or the lines would be down."

"Merry Christmas, Jacob, and what's up?"

"I've got a disaster on my hands, dammit, and I'm a minute from socking something. Norah finally has a Christmas she can look forward to, and instead she's curled up on the sofa under a pile of blankets—"

"Whoa. Start from the beginning. What's going on?"

He caught his breath and commanded his nerve endings to relax. "The power's been out since three o'clock this morning. No lights on the tree, no cooked meal. With this storm, there's hardly enough light for her to unwrap her presents. It's barely warm, just the fireplace. She's sulking and crying and says it's all my fault and if her mother were here this wouldn't have happened."

"You built up a lot of expectations for this holiday."

"I'm half out of my mind, I'm so frustrated, and I can't let Norah see it. I'm really sorry to interrupt your morning, but I need ideas. I'm desperate."

"How big's the outage? And when do they expect the power to be back on?"

"This whole end of town, they say. And not till the storm blows out, tomorrow at the earliest. I wouldn't risk trying to get to the in-laws in Columbus in this weather. I thought about a hotel, but the Madison Inn's booked solid. I'd be okay driving in town but I doubt—"

"Jacob, breathe. I'm holding the space." He closed his eyes, willing the frustration and anger away. After perhaps fifteen seconds, Pat said, "You say you can get around town. Safely?"

"Yes, I think so. Plows have been out, even though they can't keep up. I've got a four wheel drive SUV, and I have chains."

"Okay, then pack up. You'll need clothes for both of you. All the presents. Food, anything associated with Christmas, special vegetables or desserts or whatever. We can cook both turkeys, so you can take yours home for leftovers. Pajamas and toothbrushes, because no one's going back to a cold house. Bring a stuffed animal or two—"

"Are you suggesting we go to your place? That isn't why I called. I don't want to impose, I just want ideas."

"If you have a better idea, speak up now. I have an inflatable air mattress, or you might end up bunking on the sofa—oh, bring sleeping bags and pillows. Get here in the next hour and we'll serve French toast with blueberry syrup. Amanda's scoffing at it but—"

"Hold it. Amanda's there?"

"Ah."

He endured Pat's silence, wondering how much more he could bear before his frayed nerves snapped. He could almost hear the thoughts buzzing in her head, and dreaded the hornet's nest he'd just opened up, today of all days, when he needed to be his calmest, most cheerful self.

"We do what we have to," she said. "She'll cope. This is the first Christmas Norah's been ready to celebrate since she lost her mother, and she deserves better than a cold house. I'm her psychologist, Jacob. I think this is important."

"Pat, you're nominated for sainthood, but I can't share space with Amanda today."

"Got a good reason why not?"

"It's complicated."

She chuckled. "No it's not. Now, did you write down the list?"

"I got it."

"Out of curiosity, why didn't you call a friend?"

"There is one person I could call, but his family goes to some kind of hockey tournament over Christmas. And he probably doesn't have power, either."

"Okay, how soon can you get here?"

Jacob did some fast mental calculations. "An hour? Or double it to be realistic. I'll keep my phone with me. Will you hold some of the French toast?"

"Happy to. Be careful out there. This is the bitchiest storm I've seen in years."

"I'm superstitious about cars. We'll be careful."

Resolute, he left his office to begin packing up for Christmas at Pat's place.

Amanda poked her head in the dining room just as Pat disconnected. "French toast's ready. Are you done?"

"Change in plans." Pat returned to the kitchen and reported the conversation.

"Oh, no." Amanda's face went pale. "Pat, there's something I didn't tell you yesterday."

"About Jacob?" At Amanda's nod Pat sat at the table, pulling Amanda with her. "Tell me now."

* * *

Jacob's worst fears didn't materialize. By six o'clock Christmas evening, the adults were exhausted and happy, the child exhausted and wired. They might have been sharing Christmas for years. "Turkey's a soporific," Pat muttered to anyone who would listen. He and Pat were in the kitchen, washing the last of the pots while the dishwasher did most of the work.

"Helped along by quantities consumed."

"Don't forget the wine," Amanda called from the living room. She and Norah were building a castle with a new set of plastic bricks.

Amanda and his daughter, building a castle.

"And the pie. Why didn't you stop me from having pie?" Pat shouted.

"Because it was *good*, silly." Norah joined the conversation.

"Norah, if all three of us go to sleep, will you tuck us in and sing 'Silent Night' for the next hour or two?" Pat finished putting away the pots, then they joined Amanda and Norah.

"That was memorable. But oh," he groaned. "I don't remember the last time I ate so much. Pat, you're a wonder woman."

"Well, wonder woman's had it. Right now, the best thing we can do is put on a video and collapse. I can't eat or drink or move or probably talk sensibly."

Amanda scooted across the living room floor to Pat's DVD collection. "Here we go." She held up a DVD cover to show Norah. Jacob watched—how could he help but watch? He'd never seen Amanda in anything other than strictly tailored business outfits. She was almost unbearably alluring in her long skirt with a sparkly holiday sweater. So far he'd managed to keep his eyes from resting on her for more than a second or two, but he'd been aware of her, every moment.

"*Shrek*! Please, can we? *I love Shrek!*" Norah jumped up, and her bare foot came down on a plastic brick. She shrieked, then dissolved in tears.

Jacob scooped up his tearful daughter and held her close, murmuring into her curls. "*Shrek* it is, if the ladies are okay with the idea—but it's time to be quiet for a few minutes first. Will you do that?"

Norah cried quietly on his shoulder, nodding against him while he rubbed her sore foot, aware of Amanda's eyes on Norah, on him. He settled into one of Pat's big, comfortable chairs and cradled his tired daughter.

It had been a day beyond imagining. The trip to Pat's house had taken him most of his doubled estimate. Norah had sulked while they inched their way across town, clearly not ready to give up her conviction that Christmas was ruined. The French toast, then the present unwrapping, had rekindled her happiness. She hadn't taken off her new pink princess gown since she'd unwrapped it.

Later, they all got involved in mixing up the stuffing, getting Pat's tiny turkey and his slightly larger one into the oven, cooking cranberries for sauce, and preparing the accompaniments. He'd never known that cranberries made little explosions when they cooked; Norah had been enchanted. He'd brought some broccoli and a big chunk of Cheddar, the only way his daughter would eat vegetables, but there'd been other things to enjoy, too, the creamed spinach Amanda contributed, the roasted yams from Pat. The meal had rounded out a near perfect holiday.

And if he'd had the sense that Pat was watching, keeping a close eye on them all, well, what did he expect?

Even Amanda relaxed, smiling at him, sharing the jokes and banter that filled Pat's little house. What wouldn't he give for them to be here together, *really* together, with presents for each other, touching hands, meeting eyes, going to the bedroom for a while ….

Stop it. You're beyond happy, and your daughter's glowing. No way in this world could it be better.

Before Christmas Eve, he could have ignored it. Then, it was potential, and might well never come to fruition. Now, he could see Amanda filling his dreams for the foreseeable future.

Outside, the storm battered the house, but inside, the three adults and his little girl settled down for a quiet evening, content at the end of an unusual, but happy, Christmas Day.

Chapter 13

As predicted, no one went home. The next morning, Amanda reached the living room, on her way to the kitchen, at the same moment Jacob started to roll out of his sleeping bag on the inflatable mattress. The sight of him startled her. She hadn't seen him before with his hair loose, falling in tangles around his shoulders like the wild hero of some medieval romance.

His bare shoulders. That bare torso. He needed a shave; her eyes drew relentlessly to his jaw. She froze, then gave an involuntary jerk. "Oh, sorry, I didn't mean—"

Jacob stopped moving. "No problem. We've been awake for a while." He flipped the hair back out of his face and gestured at Norah, in her pajamas, hypnotized by a cartoon show on the television. "I don't usually let this happen, but it seemed appropriate somehow."

Norah gave an absent-minded wave over her shoulder. He shrugged.

"But perhaps … I mean it might be better … look, I'm down to my boxers here. I'd like to make myself a little more presentable before I want you to lay eyes on me, to be honest."

She could feel her face flaming. Her hands twisted together. "I didn't think, I'll just go …" She gave up the effort and fled to the kitchen.

Later, showered, shaved, dressed, and with his hair conservatively tied back, Jacob joined her. "What are you making?"

She was still flustered. "It's a breakfast recipe my family made, I mean makes, that is, I don't know if James and his family still do it but my mother does, so she might—"

Jacob put one hand on her arm and let the other hand brush across her hair, so quickly she hardly registered it. "Amanda, whoa. I only asked what you're making."

"I … it's just …" She commanded her voice to behave, but her voice wasn't obeying orders.

He injected a note of normality. "You and Pat have given Norah the best Christmas imaginable, and I really thank you. She loved playing with you, and that means the world to me, seeing her happy. Now, what are you making?"

It's like being in some kind of alternate universe. You're at Pat's, but he's here, too, and yesterday was wonderful, and Norah's enchanting and Pat's no help at all and he's touching you and you saw him without a shirt and God, he's gorgeous. You won't cry. Why do you want to cry? Why do you want to lean against him and cry?

She moved away from Jacob and got her breath back. "It's sort of a breakfast casserole, oatmeal baked into a custard. I'll put brown sugar and currants and slivered almonds into it, and some nutmeg on top. It's good."

"It sounds it. Do you need me to squeeze some oranges? I like orange juice with oatmeal."

A perfectly ordinary conversation. But seeing him naked had turned a switch in her brain. She wasn't going to be able to get back to their easy camaraderie of yesterday any time soon. Her hands put together the ingredients for the oatmeal dish without any participation from her brain. "Great, thanks. I think we may get home today."

Outside the storm had blown out, replaced by a picture perfect winter day. Calter Creek would spend the day after Christmas waiting for snowplows and digging out cars.

Jacob said, "I'll check on the power status in a little while. I'm sure Pat would be happy to see us out the door before too much longer."

"Morning, all." Pat came into the kitchen.

Amanda shoved her casserole into the oven and took the opportunity to escape, leaving the other two to set the table and finish squeezing oranges.

* * *

They were hovering over the table with cutlery and glasses when Jacob registered Pat's eyes on him, without a trace of humor. She said quietly, "Serious?"

Jacob sensed her meaning immediately. "Yes."

"You toy with her, I'll kill you."

"Not in the plan. She's got me."

"Does she know it? I somehow doubt it."

"I spooked her, Christmas Eve. Did she tell you?"

Pat nodded.

"It's as if we've known each other for years. But if I try to get closer …" His hand fiddled with the cutlery, repositioning knives and forks on the table. "I can't get past it. I want to, but there's this wall."

"Give it time, Jacob."

"I'm doing my best." He paused. "Pat, what was she like? You two go back forever. Was she always so all-business?"

Pat grinned at him and returned to distributing juice glasses. "She wouldn't mind my telling you she was really sort of geeky in college. Hitting the books, getting the grades. She started at SI in her mid-teens."

"Didn't date a lot?"

"Sorry, Jacob. Can't say any more. Ask Amanda."

Norah charged into the kitchen. He wheeled. "Hi, Pumpkin. Ready for breakfast? It'll be—how long?" he asked Pat.

"Amanda's oatmeal thing cooks in half an hour. Less time already served, let's say twenty minutes. Want a glass of juice, Norah?"

Jacob watched his daughter drink her juice, her legs swinging furiously under the table, and considered what Pat had said. He could give it time, especially when there wasn't any option. The mystery that was Amanda Sinclair just kept getting deeper.

* * *

Jacob bundled Norah up, Pat dug an old sled out of her garage, and they set off along Pat's quiet street. The plows hadn't reached them yet, and it seemed as if everyone who wasn't digging out a car or shoveling a walk was playing in the snow.

Norah set off at a run, fell into a snowdrift, laughed, and did it all over again. Jacob breathed deeply, reflected on perfect winter days, and asked, "Ever make snow angels?"

"Years ago," Amanda said. "Isn't this wonderful?" She turning to Pat. "Like winters when I was a kid. Snow forts and snowball fights."

"Want to shovel my driveway?"

"Give me a break, it's great." They followed the trail Norah forged, Amanda in the lead. Which gave him an excellent chance to watch her from behind.

"Snow forts?" he asked.

"Crude ones. James thought he could best me, but my brother's never been as good a pitcher as I am."

"The pleasure of watching a snowball splat on someone else's snowsuit?"

She looked back at him and grinned. "I was ruthless."

"So," Pat said, "let's deal with those snow angels. Norah, you want to play?"

Norah was several doors down the street by then, but she waded back to them through the snow. "Watch me." The little girl fought her way into the middle of Pat's lawn and dropped backwards, flailing her arms and legs.

Jacob leaned over to pull her up. "Not a bad angel, Angel."

Norah wiggled. "I've got snow down my back."

"Part of the fun." He brushed her off.

Pat dragged Amanda onto the lawn. "I might be too old for this," Amanda said.

"You don't go down on your own, you get pushed," he said.

The two women finally held hands and dropped down together, giggling, Norah shrieking with laughter. Jacob offered first Pat, then Amanda, a hand getting back up again.

Amanda stumbled as she regained her footing, leaving her close to him. Close enough that he wrapped an arm around her, just for a moment. She leaned into him, just for a moment.

"You know what's next?" Pat said to Norah. "We don't have any guy angels yet."

Norah and Pat exchanged a look, then headed his way.

"Hey, wait a minute. I'm the one who hauls you ladies up. I can't—"

"Want to bet?" Amanda asked him. Sweetly.

The three of them tried to topple him into the snow, but overbalanced, and all four of them ended up in a drift. Amanda lay next to him with one of his arms caught under her, laughing helplessly, while Norah, on top of him, decided to bury him instead. "Help," he whimpered to Pat.

"You're a guy, help yourself," she said, then scrambled to her feet. "I'm going to go start some soup for lunch."

Jacob watched Pat leave and wrestled with his daughter with his free arm. The other arm did very nicely where it was, because when Amanda started to get up he was able to hook the collar of her coat and pull her down again.

Their eyes met. He raised his brows at her.

"I'll get even before we go in," she said.

"Let's put this one on the sled and walk up the street." He toppled Norah off of him and pushed up, again offering a hand to Amanda. She took it, and once again ended up right next to him, their coats touching. His hand brushed over her hat, then down her shoulders and back to knock off some of the snow. Then he took her gloved hand. "Come on, Pumpkin," he called to Norah. "Your chariot awaits."

"He's silly," Norah said to Amanda.

"He can be."

Norah tried out the flat-bottomed sled, but wouldn't stay put. She ran ahead, came back, enthralled by a road closed by snow.

They'd walked most of a city block before Amanda pulled her hand free of his. He didn't comment.

But as he was squatting down to help Norah knock the snow off her boots before they went inside to indulge in Pat's soup, he felt something cold and wet go down his back. He twisted to look up. Amanda smirked at him.

Chapter 14

Amanda and Pat blitzed Pat's house after Jacob and Norah left, once the snowplows had been by and the power had been restored to western Calter Creek. As they cleaned up the remaining traces of their Christmas, Amanda found one plastic brick and tucked it into her pants pocket, absentmindedly planning to return it to Jacob next week.

They didn't really talk, beyond the superficial events of the holiday, until Amanda was packing her overnight bag to head home.

Pat perched on the bed. "Worn out?"

"It shows?"

"Yeah. So am I, to be honest. Best Christmas in ages though."

"It was."

"Norah's blooming now. You're good with her, Mandy. I wasn't sure, after that first meeting, but you really are. You've got a fan club in the McKinnon family, I'd say."

"Don't push it, Pat."

"I won't. But I'm glad. They're solid."

She knew. Working in the kitchen, the four of them sharing Christmas dinner, had felt normal, and right.

Almost.

He'd been careful not to push it too far, even as he and Norah were leaving, offering her only a restrained hug, his head touching hers for a moment before he backed off. Not the bear hug he'd given Pat. She supposed she should be grateful that he respected her boundaries.

Still, there were times she wished she could let her barriers down and be like other people. Like Pat, or Mel, who wouldn't think twice before wrapping Jacob in a hug.

She needed the distance, because he made the Jolt tap dance, and the Jolt scared the wits out of her.

He made her long for the peace and solitude of her usual days.

And to leave the peace and solitude behind.

She was uncomfortably aware that he had been the one to break off their kiss—both kisses—on Christmas Eve, not her. That required consideration. Or maybe not. Some things in life are surely better not examined.

After Brandon, she'd made a conscious choice not to trust, ever again, but if she had to, she suspected she could trust Jacob McKinnon.

Finally back home, she unpacked, soaked in a bubble bath—a rare waste of time—and, wrapped in her new pajamas and bathrobe, heated some leftovers she'd brought from Pat's for her dinner. The silence of her house after the excitement of Christmas left her vaguely unnerved.

Then, kitchen tidy, she took a pad of paper and pen into the living room, switched on her gas fireplace, and began to sketch out some of her ideas, new directions for Sinclair Imports. Lists always soothed her. They showed her how in control of her world she really was.

* * *

The short work week between Christmas and New Year's brought an expected surge in workload, which suited Jacob well since there was a lot he'd be better off not dwelling on. The controlled activity around him diverted those thoughts from his active mind, even if they didn't dispel them completely.

Amanda in a glittery sweater.

Amanda playing with Norah.

Amanda's face when she caught a glimpse of your naked torso.

There's a theme here. Figured out what it is yet?

He'd drop a gourmet basket and a thank-you card off at Pat's within the next day or two. What should he do to thank Amanda? Too many unknowns, from her rejection of him on

Christmas Eve to her laughing in the snow with him the day after Christmas.

Mid-afternoon Monday he appeared as usual at her office door. Without preliminary he said, "I want to thank you again for being willing to make the holiday so positive for Norah. That matters more than I can tell you."

Amanda had been pecking at her computer keyboard. She looked up and reached for her pen. "I had very little to do with it. Thank Pat." She fished a plastic brick out of her pocket and put it on her desk.

"It could have been a lot more awkward. I felt horrible when Pat told me you'd be there, but by then Pat wasn't letting me say no. And I'm not sure I had a choice anyway, given Norah. But you made it easy."

"It wasn't easy."

The coolness in her voice stopped him. She'd flipped again, returning to cool and rejecting. He studied her face a moment. "You kept it well hidden. I'm not here to pursue that today, I just wanted to thank you." He gave her a little nod, picked up the brick, and headed toward the door.

"Jacob?"

He hesitated, then turned back to her.

"You're right. It was a wonderful holiday. I've never spent Christmas with a child before, and I enjoyed it. Your daughter's ... well, I like her."

He smiled. "So do I. Thanks."

* * *

Jacob met Dave the Friday night after New Year's for a beer at a pub a few blocks from his house. He'd left Norah with a babysitter for the first time at night, and he was sticking close to home. He viewed the evening with both trepidation and a sense of freedom that surprised him. The pub was quiet and they could actually hear each other's normally pitched voices. Jacob figured everyone was either exhausted or broke, after the holidays.

Dave got right to business. "Might as well tell me straight out how the courtship's going."

He expected it, but wasn't sure what to say. "We could talk football. Microbreweries. The economy."

"All of which are on the top of your mind?"

Mugs of ale and bowls of nuts appeared in front of them. The waitress disappeared, limiting his options for stalling, and Dave would wait him out anyway, so he might as well get it over with. "We spent Christmas with Amanda."

"No kidding? How'd that happen?"

"The only way possible—accidentally. With the power out, Norah was in a state. Poor kid, with no lights, no prospect of dinner, no nothing, I had to do something, so I phoned her psychologist to get some suggestions. Pat invited us to her place."

"Don't tell me. Your psychologist and your uptight dream woman are friends."

"The closest of. It was a fabulous two days. Christmas, we fell asleep watching *Shrek*. Norah hasn't been this happy in years. Amanda built a castle with her. Who would have dreamed she'd be able to relate to a six-year-old?" Jacob shook his head in wonder at the memory. "Then we played in the snow the next morning. Norah was in seventh heaven."

"Careful, Jake. You're nesting."

Jacob decided talking about Amanda wasn't so bad. "Yeah. I can see the three of us by the fire, reading a story to Norah, or Norah reading to us. I can see family vacations. I can see her at night, getting ready for bed—"

"And in the sack, too."

"Oh, vividly. But—"

"She's got her hooks in you, doesn't she? Be careful, pal. This is your first time around since Deb. You might be ready to fall for the first pair of pretty eyes that look your way."

"In point of fact, there've been a few other eyes looking my way. I chose not to look back. But I don't think that's it. For one thing, those pretty eyes are doing everything they can *not* to look. She'd rather pretend nothing's happening."

"That doesn't surprise me. She's never sent out the signals. I've heard speculation she's frigid. Ugly talk, the kind of drunken clowning you get sometimes after a boring meeting, but no one's arguing she's one chilly woman. Do you really want the challenge?"

He wondered how much to say. But he and Dave were as close as he imagined brothers would be, and it might help if he spilled it to someone. "Between you and me — and I swear if this goes any further I'll murder you — she's not cold."

Dave sat up. "What have you been up to with Ms. Sinclair? Say more."

"None of your business." Jacob shrugged, paid some attention to his ale. "So I thought we'd be good to go, but the walls are higher than ever. I don't get it. I'm not the kind of guy women are scared of."

"Wouldn't surprise me if there was something not quite savory in her relationship with Caine."

Jacob raised his eyebrows. "I saw his name in the business section recently, a new mall north of town."

"Can't stand him, myself, but it's been years since I last ran into him. I'll be keeping an eye on that mall development, in case anyone cries foul before it's over. Probably not, as far as I know he's just good at what he does, but a man can hope. Now that we've got this connection, I'll be cheering for the other guy."

Jacob laughed. "You goof. That was years ago. What's it to us now?"

"Oh, pure spite. How the holier-than-thou can fall, and all that. Revenge for Ms. Sinclair. Wouldn't you like him to take a dive?"

"I'm not a complete idiot. We're not spring chickens. No one's counting what went before. Besides, I've mostly given her my life story, chatting over afternoon coffee. Sometimes I can't seem to shut up," he added. "That wasn't enough to make her run away, but any mention of this thing between us … she's blowing hot and cold."

Dave, for once, was quiet, so he ate a peanut, then finished what he had to say. "She'd rather I were an automaton designed to do her bidding, by which I mean the company's bidding. Pardon the hint of bitterness. Women are a mystery."

"You understood Deb, I suppose, or thought you did."

Jacob nodded. "Sometimes a guessing game, but most of the time, yes."

"Trust me, that isn't going to help you in the least this time around. Sooner or later you'll have to try to understand Norah, too. Now that, I want to watch."

"Yeah, I bet. You understand your daughter?"

"Easy. Right now, it's horses. Once she hits puberty, I don't kid myself."

Jacob chuckled. "Norah already gives me this look, and these big sighs, and this way of saying 'Daddy' that tells me I'm a clueless male. Where'd she get that? Is it bred into them?"

"But she likes Ms. Sinclair."

"Yep."

"She might prove to be your secret weapon."

"Or a millstone. Whatever happens, I can't let it hurt Norah. If it doesn't work out — man, this is complicated."

"I've got a news bulletin." Dave broke off to signal the server for refills. "It was ever thus. And it ain't gonna get any clearer. You and I, pal, we're along for the ride. The women rule the world."

* * *

"I'm not sure I get it. Am I getting it?" Amanda studied the charcoal lines running randomly, it seemed, around the big sheet of newsprint. The drawing class was Pat's idea. Amanda wasn't convinced.

Having fun. Right?

"Negative space. Holes. No clue." Pat frowned at her own sheet. They faced a pile of chairs, randomly tossed on top of each other at all angles. The lines represented their attempts to draw the chairs, outlining the spaces where the chairs weren't.

"I'm feeling mutinous," Amanda muttered. "You may have met your Waterloo with this one."

"I'm feeling martini deprived. This would be *so* much easier not quite sober."

Their instructor picked that moment to come around. "It's not, actually. Your straight lines don't stay straight under the influence." She chuckled. "Now this," she continued, pointing to a portion of Amanda's sketch, "this is exactly what I'm looking for. You see this right here?" Her finger indicated a little patch near the center of Amanda's attempt. "You've caught the angle between the legs of those two chairs perfectly. See how much easier it is to draw the negative space than to try to draw the chair legs themselves?"

"I did?" Amanda said, amazed. "Hey, I did!"

"Brother. Now I really need that martini," Pat grumbled. "I've got beautiful chair legs. How come yours are better?"

"Must be my natural affinity for negative spaces."

Later, over wine, not martinis, at Amanda's, Pat said, "I haven't seen you since Christmas, so talk to me. Christmas Eve. Jacob."

"How did I know you were going to say that?"

"Because you know I can't resist. Where's your head, Mandy?"

She expected it and had her answer ready. "Focused on staying safe, after what Brandon tried. I can't let this go on, I can't risk …" She broke off and made a fist, pounded it gently on the table. "Okay, I'm scared. I'm terrified."

"First, Brandon was five years ago, and you're a stronger woman now. Second, Brandon came with an agenda, and one that had nothing to do with building something with you and everything to do with using you, including trying to get control of SI. Third, Brandon was a jerk and not worth considering. Fourth, Brandon was the special kind of jerk that believes he's God. Any more questions?"

"My family—they trust me with SI. How can I be sure it won't happen again?"

"Brandon Caine was a manipulative louse, and he didn't succeed, did he? You kept his unsavory ass out of your company. He never got the power he wanted, and then you walked out on him, so he retaliated. According to him, you were a lousy manager, lousy socially, and basically lousy, period. All of that's demonstrably not true. It was mental abuse, based on lies. You know this."

Amanda shrugged. "I can't risk it again."

Pat's hand covered hers. "You got out of a disastrous relationship, and you rebuilt your life. You're not giving yourself enough credit. Sure you're scared, but look at it this way. Jacob's one of the greatest guys we've met in years, and you want to give him the boot because of what happened five years ago. That means Brandon wins." She squeezed Amanda's hand. "Jacob isn't Brandon Caine. With Jacob, it's still at the beginning, but it's special. And with Norah, and that isn't a small thing. It's okay to try again."

Amanda stared off into space. "To tell the truth, Pat, I'm not sure I can avoid it. When he's around, I lose my ability to think clearly. Christmas Eve, I'm pretty sure he knew I couldn't control it. And it was only a kiss, for heaven's sake," she stated, suddenly angry. "I'm building it up into this great big thing. I just wish it hadn't happened at the office—in my office."

"Yes, I get that. But Jacob wouldn't be able to. He doesn't know your authority at SI was ever at risk. I say, forget it."

Amanda was still off in her own reverie. "He can read me so well. It's only when he's not around that I can be rational."

"That isn't power over you. That's one soul talking to the other or something." Amanda rolled her eyes and Pat laughed. "Okay, not soul dialogue. Body dialogue? But he isn't going to fathom your fears on his own. Don't let him rush you, but don't hold him back too long, either. Level with him, is my advice. So talk. You two chattered over Christmas like you were an old married couple. My guess is he hasn't the faintest desire to wrench your company out of your grasp."

"Everything's so confused, with Stan, and now Jacob already has power, he manages the accounting."

"Remember last year? Boredom?"

"Back when life was simple? To change the subject, what did you think of the class tonight? Feel inspired?"

Now it was Pat's turn to roll her eyes. "Negative spaces? Sounds like science fiction."

"But if we got good at it, we'd become famous. I could spend my days with colored pencils instead of spreadsheets."

"Better, but not a way of life. Suppose you embed a martini glass in every picture?"

Amanda laughed. "And life would be a bowl of cherries, right?"

Pat shook her head. "It's still a pile of chairs, sorry."

"The idea of living without cares has more appeal than I like to admit."

"Having someone to share them is almost as good. Easier to obtain, too. I love it when you get silly." Pat clicked Amanda's glass and drank.

Chapter 15

Plan ahead. Avoid surprises.

Amanda didn't bother with New Year's resolutions, but she did make plans. She arrived at work on a Monday in mid-January with her three-pronged strategy to re-launch her life firmly in place.

One. She'd continue gathering ideas for changes at SI. She envisioned new product development, new software for their online presence, possibly even a move to a larger warehouse. The binder holding her ideas filled her with renewed enthusiasm, each time she caught sight of it on the corner of her desk.

Two. She'd get out and enjoy herself more. The art course didn't thrill her, but she might learn something. Pat was determined that they check out a yoga class. She'd research the courses at the local community college. Places where she'd learn something new, meet new people.

Three. She'd lead a simple, uncomplicated life. That meant dealing with complications, and that meant Jacob. Whatever his expectations, this thing between them wasn't going anywhere. He deserved better. Somehow, couching it in those terms made it more acceptable, less like a rejection. Less like throwing away a chance at —

No. Don't go there. You've made your plan.

But the memory of that glimpse of him, the wild hair, the stubble on his chin and a scattering of dark blond hair on his bare chest — did he have to look so *male*? Would she be able to see him in his suit and not remember the way his chest hair arrowed down toward —

It's your imagination. You didn't see that much.

I saw enough.

But she simply didn't have the courage to begin a new relationship.

Executing the third prong involved some discomfort. She accepted that. They couldn't avoid each other, but they were rational adults. They'd deal with it. She was skilled at handling difficult conversations, professionally and unemotionally. Once she was sure he understood, it would be over.

So when Jacob came into her office that afternoon with coffee and his notes on the January/February projections, she said, with a calmness she had to fake, "Would you close the door, please?"

He gave Mel a shrug, then pulled the door closed and turned back to her. "What's up?"

She studied him objectively before she spoke. Gray suit, pale pink shirt with a burgundy and navy striped tie. Direct gaze from those hazel eyes. He looked conservative, businesslike, competent. Perfect, in fact.

For SI.

"Please sit down."

He sat, a question in his eyes.

From behind her desk, and with her facts lined up, she was ready for this interview. Which didn't explain why her stomach felt like she'd swallowed a lead weight. To bolster her confidence, she reflected briefly on the number of uncomfortable interviews she'd conducted, over the years.

Never with a man you've tussled in the snow with. Or kissed.

Irrelevant. This was business. She could do it.

"I've deliberated on this. I don't think you believed me, and I want you to understand, for your sake mainly, but also to save us from any awkwardness. Despite what happened over Christmas, this goes no further. You and I have no future."

He didn't say anything. She couldn't bring herself to meet his eyes.

"Have I made myself clear?"

"You have." The usual casual ease was gone. His voice was as uninflected as hers.

"Good. Thank you for these." She gathered up the sheets he'd given her and squared them on the desk. "I don't have time for coffee today, so you can leave the door open when you go." When he didn't move, she added, "Jacob? I have work to do. I'd like you to go."

At last he spoke. "Hardly a suitable conversation for the office. Were you afraid to meet me somewhere else?"

Then he moved. Onto his feet, closer to her desk. She was used to amusement dancing behind his eyes, a lightness in his bearing. There was no sign of that now. "Did you think I might make a scene? Did you need your desk between us?"

She'd expected him to acquiesce. With bruised feelings, perhaps, but without anger.

"I can't be in a relationship with you." She stated the fact precisely.

She'd never seen him angry, never suspected this side of him. His face was granite. She tensed, but held on to her resolve.

"Let me get this straight." His voice was so low he virtually growled at her. "We talk, we share who we are, and we both look forward to it. We had a great time together over Christmas. Are you afraid of wanting me? We both know your desk isn't an effective barrier. If I came over to your side, do you think you'd be able to make yourself stop me?"

Her face heated. In tense business meetings, she'd always maintained eye contact, but this time she couldn't help herself. She looked down.

He paused. His hard glare lasered in on her. "But the minute you're away from me, you convince yourself you never want to see me again. You've dedicated your life to this other master, this—this *company* is more important to you than ordinary human relationships."

Amanda was on edge from his reminder of how readily she'd responded to him. Now her fury fought to boil over. How *dare* he? She stood. Her hands clenched. He'd thrown Christmas Eve in her face, then he'd topped it off by insulting her dedication to her company. But she kept her voice level and her words pointed. "Just go."

He straightened, making her aware of his height advantage. "It's more important to you than even giving us a chance. You aren't willing to risk anything personal because you've already chosen the goddamned *presidential*."

She gasped at his language, his bitterness, and started to retaliate, but he plowed right over her. "What gets me is we do both want it. I'm at my wit's end trying to figure out why you're denying it every chance you get." He turned toward the door, but stopped after one step and spun back around to face her.

"Here's a question for you. Something magical happens when we're together. Is magic that common in your life that you're willing to throw it away? Because frankly, I don't see it. I see good work done. I see plenty to be proud of. But I sure as *hell* don't see how that keeps you warm at night."

With those words Jacob left, leaving her door ajar, as she'd requested.

She felt as if he'd slammed it in her face.

When you were the one doing the slamming.

She regretted not asking him to close the door, because, inevitably, not a minute later Mel appeared. "Whew. Someone left in high dudgeon. Just as glad I don't work in Accounting right now. Want a break?"

Amanda sank back into her chair. In the aftermath, she felt as shaky as a child after a scolding, but she pulled her face and voice together for Mel's benefit. "Not this afternoon. I'm running behind."

"Might do you good. Something more than the import business going on in here, I think. The air's bristling."

Amanda ignored Mel's comment. "We need to go over these projections with the latest warehouse report later, if we can find an uninterrupted chunk of time."

"Yes, ma'am." Whenever Mel called her ma'am, insurrection was afoot. Her executive assistant was nobody's fool.

She moved on to the next task on her list, her senses alert to Mel's leaving.

Chapter 16

Amanda's doorbell rang. That never happened. She'd been drying the few dishes from her sad attempt at supper and wishing she weren't so unsettled. Frowning, she tossed aside the tea towel and went to peer through her security peephole.

Jacob.

For three days she hadn't seen or heard from him. She'd hoped that meant he'd cooled down and accepted her decision.

She sometimes wondered if she'd fully accepted it herself. Night times, say, like now. Or afternoons at three o'clock, when he no longer brought her a coffee and came in for a ten-minute chat.

Was there any chance this was about SI?

No. No chance at all.

When she opened the door, he said, "We're going to talk." He didn't ask permission, but stepped into her space like a man entitled. She could no more stop his entry into her private domain than she could stop her heart thundering in her ears or call back the sudden clamminess of her palms.

After he'd taken off his coat, he said, his voice tight, "Kitchen? I'm sure you'd be happier with a table between us."

She followed him almost meekly.

He faced her with his hands on her small kitchen table, barely avoiding the pot of winter mums she'd bought to brighten her mood. She stopped in the doorway.

"This is a one-time thing, you don't need to worry I'll keep barging in on you." His voice was flat, emotionless. "Let's put it in terms you can comprehend, shall we? You expect me to do valuable work for your beloved company. Since Monday, that hasn't been happening. I'm afraid it won't unless we get this sorted out. I'm damn good at my job, and I don't appreciate the effect you're having on me at the moment. It's going to stop, one way or the other."

Amanda stood across the table from him. This potent man, laying down the law. To her.

When she didn't reply he went on in a voice that worked toward conversational. "Funny, isn't it? I really believed kissing you would open up doors for us both. Instead I get this."

She cleared her throat. "I thought I was clear—"

"For heaven's sake, sit down. You're so tight you might fracture something. I'm not going to jump you."

"I don't want you here." But she sat, warily watching him settle across the table from her.

"Better if we keep this short, then."

"You have no right, and this isn't appropriate."

"Of course it's not. Right now, I don't care. Your telling me to get lost doesn't change how I feel." His elbows rested on the table, his hands clenched together in front of his chin. Under his blue shirt, his chest rose and fell with the force of his temper. "Right now, what I feel isn't pretty."

She took a breath. "I meant what I said, Jacob."

"I'm sure you did."

"You're better off without me."

"Why?"

Why? She paused. "There are things I prefer not to talk about."

"And that's the problem. You won't talk to me. You're scared, and I don't understand why."

"I am who I am." Her own anger surfaced. She gave it wings and let it loose. "You never considered that your impression of me might be incorrect, as if I don't have a brain in my head. I won't be managed or manipulated. Don't you *dare* think that."

"What?" He reared back, his eyes as bewildered as if she'd slapped him. "Did I ever suggest that? Imply that? I don't want to control you, Amanda. Part of what I love about you is that fire, what you've accomplished. You're an amazing woman. In fact, you awe me."

She heard the word — *love* — but it was rhetoric, wasn't it? It didn't mean anything. This was merely unfinished business. She was highly capable when it came to business. "So many people depend on me. This thing that happened between us." She stumbled when his eyes returned to her, but it was crucial she finish what she wanted to say. "It's in the way. I keep my priorities straight."

"Responsibility doesn't preclude caring. Relationships."

"Don't lecture me on how to live my life."

"It doesn't even preclude good old desire."

"Don't." In self-defense, she put enough venom in the word to make it a threat. The electricity between them tonight made the Jolt seem no more than the spark of a flint against stone.

He shrugged. "Now, why would I want to touch you? Why would I dream of how good it feels when we're together? Why would I dare to imagine what might be, where you're concerned? You're wrapped up so tight a nuclear bomb wouldn't break you open."

"And you're insulting and offensive." Amanda's hands, in her lap, were balled into fists. She consciously relaxed the grip, flexed her fingers. "You don't know anything about me, not really. I make my own decisions. If I choose not to include you — I've tried to be sorry. At the moment, I want you out."

Without warning his palm came down viciously on her little table. Every muscle in her body clenched, and her pot of winter mums skittered and almost toppled. "I swear, you are the most exasperating …." He tapered off, stared hard at her, then, curiously, at his hand. The tension vanished from his voice. "That hasn't happened since my last year in college. I was mad at myself then, not raging at someone else. I'm sorry."

"I'm being honest, Jacob." The attack on her table had rattled her, but she wasn't about to show it.

"You think you are." Jacob leaned forward, resting his arms on the table. His eyes never left her. "Is it because of

Norah? Or because I was married? Is it that I come with baggage?"

Shocked, she risked looking at him. "Of course not."

"Thank God for that."

They glowered at each other.

Jacob finally moved, rolling his shoulders as if to shake off tightness. "Before we kissed, I could have walked away and we'd have gone back to a normal business relationship. There was something there, but if you didn't want it, I could have accepted it wasn't going to happen. But now, if this is how you're determined to play it, I'll be leaving SI. It's uncomfortable for everyone. Am I clear enough?"

She didn't answer. This was a new factor in the equation, and not a welcome one, on a couple of levels. SI needed him. She'd grapple in private with her reaction to the idea that he might not be around.

He stood and prowled her kitchen. When he passed behind her and put a hand on her shoulder, she jumped, and her heart slammed into her throat. Not fear, no. The Jolt responding to him, but something else as well.

A need. Almost as if he were there to take care of her.

"Would you rather yell at each other?" he said. "Sometimes it's easier to yell. So they say, anyway. Personally, I don't like fighting."

She swallowed her heart back down where it belonged. "I'm not mad."

"No? I am, and I don't want to be."

He still stood behind her, his hand on her shoulder. His thumb massaged her back, as if it were somehow up to him to relieve the tension that threatened to blow her to bits. Suddenly aware she was holding her breath, she gulped in oxygen. "When you hit the table. You scared me."

"I scared myself. I really am sorry. Does this scare you?" He put both his hands on her shoulders, lightly working on her tense muscles.

It's as if he conveys comfort through his hands.

"I—" She broke off. His thumbs dug into the knots at the base of her neck. It felt so good.

Impossibly good.

"You're not supposed to be doing that."

He made a sound like a strangled laugh. "Why, because we're having a fight? I guess it's a fight. I'm not skilled at this confrontation thing." He released her and circled the table, sitting down across from her again.

Freed from his touch, she said, "It's better, Jacob. For both of us."

"Speak for yourself. Problem is, I'm not convinced it's that great for you, either. Whether that's true or not, we've come down to one option. We maintain a distant business relationship at work while you advertise for a new accountant, and I drop out of your life."

She didn't answer. Instead, she fastened her eyes on his hands, in light fists on her table. Competent hands. The memory of them on her shoulders settled over her, and she sagged a little as her muscles relaxed. The silence stretched like black elastic, ready to snap back at them.

"Right." He swung to his feet. "I'll talk to Marcia in the morning, but I'll stay around until you get a replacement. I take enough pride in my work for that."

"We'll be sorry to lose you."

Something way too close to bitterness coated his words. "Be honest. You don't want me around, so don't pretend you'll regret my going. As long as you can replace me, you'll be fine. You could drag Stan back early, he'd probably like that. What matters to you most will be taken care of, and that's what's important, isn't it." It was a statement, not a question.

He was at the door, putting on his coat, when she finally joined him. The hardness had left his face, replaced with resignation. "Like it or not," he said, "you matter to me. If you ever need a friend, call me. In the meantime I'll make a point of avoiding you as much as possible. Good night. Or—what the hell. Might as well end this with fireworks. Friendly fireworks."

He put his hands on her shoulders and stepped closer to her. She froze. His mouth brushed hers, then traced a line along her cheekbone to her neck, where he nuzzled under her ear. She gasped. Then her arms went around his chest, without her willing it or being able to stop it. She clung, pressed against him. His body went rigid, then relaxed against her.

He wrapped a hand around the back of her head and cradled her to him. He held her for a long moment, gently, then he moved his mouth to hers with a kiss that was unhurried, intimate without being in any way invasive, as if she were his, and he hers, and tenderness spoke as deeply as passion.

He broke it off and released her. They stared at each other. "Goodbye, Amanda," he said.

Then he was gone.

* * *

The next morning she found a note in her personal email. *"I'm sorry. This isn't what I wanted to happen."*

Of course it wasn't. Not even one day had passed, and she was beginning to get an inkling of what she'd thrown away. But if he was willing to be friends, she might be able to handle it.

His kiss had haunted her sleep. The need in it had scared her, but it hadn't hurt at all. Even if it hurt like splinters in her heart now.

Chapter 17

"Daddy?"

Norah stood by Jacob's chair, with that scrunched-up look on her face that told him she was worried. He'd been organizing his files for income tax season, work that was crying out to be interrupted, so he put down his pen and pushed back from the desk. "What's up?"

Norah wasted no time. "Daddy, I was thinking." She gestured at him. "I mean, none of the dads in my class have a ponytail. Well, except Frederick's dad, but everyone says they're hippies. Are we hippies?" Concerned, her brow furrowed.

"Not a bit. Are you asking if I'd cut it off?"

She nodded, mute, but gave him a look conveying the rightness of her world if only the ponytail disappeared.

At last. He'd waited months for this. She probably didn't even remember the tantrum she'd pitched when he'd suggested that very thing a few months earlier. "How does this sound? I'll pick you up after school tomorrow and we'll go to the barber's together, and you can supervise." He figured this was safe enough, and if her ideas were disastrous, well, the stuff grew back.

But Norah looked crestfallen. "Becky says her mom and dad go to the same place. To a *stylist*, so it'll be perfect. Can't we go to a stylist? You and me? Please, Daddy." She switched to abject pleading. "It would be *so* fun."

Oh, would it? Perhaps if you were a six-year-old girl. "Can we do a compromise? Usually, I think, with a stylist you need to make an appointment way in advance. Why don't we start with the barber?" He pulled the elastic out and shook his head so his hair fell around his face, down past his shoulders. "When we get used to me without all this, we'll do the stylist thing together. We'll both be beautiful."

"Daddy." Again that tone implying he was silly. "Men aren't beautiful."

"Then I reckon you'll end up more beautiful than I will. That's okay with me. Deal?"

Norah danced away.

Jacob was more than pleased, but for reasons that didn't concern Norah. In his mind, more than once—in fact, sometimes it felt like constantly—he'd imagined holding himself over Amanda, using his mouth and his body to bring them both to fulfillment. A picture that didn't include a foot of hair falling around his shoulders. Oh, yes, he liked the idea of a haircut.

Even if at the moment there was no Amanda to share the fantasy.

On top of everything else, she'd started invading his dreams. He was in good, tight control during the day, but more than once he'd woken breathless and aching. He didn't get back to sleep in a hurry after those dreams. He'd lie wide awake, lost in a toxic mix of emotional longing and physical need, wondering what he was going to do with the mess he was in.

Something in his mind didn't accept she was out of his life for good.

Time heals.

He knew it was true, he'd lived it over the last two and a half years. It didn't follow he had any faith in it now.

* * *

Mel was at reception when Jacob arrived for work two days later. She started to step aside, then stopped and stared. "Oh, my God."

"Don't tempt me with corny come-back lines," he said.

"My heart just did a swan dive. Jacob McKinnon, you are flat out gorgeous. Isn't he, Anne?"

Anne, their receptionist, nodded. "Not half bad, and I'm old enough to be your mother."

"And what brought this on? Ooh, I can't resist." Mel went up to him and ran an appraising hand through his short hair.

"Norah clued in that I wasn't winning any fashion points among first-grade fathers. It's a relief. Gotta go." Jacob rounded the reception desk and headed left down the west corridor.

In the Accounting suite, pushed for details, he elaborated. "Norah dealt with the barber like a pro. Told him how she wanted me to look, then sat with her arms folded and watched every move."

"You're going to have such an interesting life as she grows up," Bev said.

"You don't need to tell me. Would you believe, the guy wanted to keep the hair? Seems he can donate it to someone who makes wigs for women in chemo. I liked the idea, it sort of gives legitimacy to the years it took to grow it, but this is heaven. I only kept it for Norah, and she doesn't need it anymore." He remembered his amazement. "She picked up one lock. She found a ribbon to tie around it for a keepsake box—I didn't even know she had one."

"She probably doesn't," Bev said. "But trust me, she will."

He headed to his office, distracted. His mind was on the way Mel's hand had felt in his hair, wishing for another hand.

Forget it. So he commanded himself, and succeeded, to a certain extent, in not thinking about Amanda Sinclair's hands.

* * *

That afternoon Amanda went to the Accounting suite for a meeting with Jacob and Jim. The year-end figures were coming out, so reviews and developing budget projections for the coming year were a fact of life.

So far, she and Jacob had managed to co-exist in the SI building without more than the occasional frosty nod in the corridor. Marcia had begun advertising his position. Amanda didn't know what SI thought about this, but she did know Jacob wasn't saying anything. The grapevine, via Mel, told her he wasn't talking much at all these days, outside of business. What Mel suspected—well, she couldn't control everything.

When she returned to her office, she glared at Mel. "Keeping secrets?"

Mel feigned innocence. "Let's see. You had a meeting in Accounting this afternoon, right? Noticed the new haircut? Pretty great, huh?"

"Definite improvement. You might have told me."

"Didn't want to spoil the surprise. That man is so hot, and his hair feels *so* good." She shook her head and mimed a fan with her hand.

Typical Mel.

"I've seen hotter," Amanda said as she headed into her office.

Alone, she wondered in what possible set of circumstances Mel had become familiar with the feel of his hair.

* * *

"Tell me if we're having fun yet?" The end of their first yoga class that evening was the high point of her day, Amanda thought. "You honestly think I want to sign up for three months of torture?"

Pat, on the other hand, glowed. "I like it. This one might be a keeper."

"For you. For me, don't hold your breath."

"Oh, I think you'll be happy to limber up some. Before things get, shall we say, a bit athletic?" Pat glanced at Amanda and raised an eyebrow as they settled into her car.

"What do you mean? I don't—oh."

"Yoga's meant to be fantastic for getting ready for sex. I'm assuming you're still in the preparation phase, not the consummation phase."

"And suppose I said there isn't going to be a consummation phase?"

Pat sighed. Loudly. "I guess I'd harangue you until you came to your senses. I've known you too long not to be able to read the signs. You're falling for him, Mandy."

"I'm not."

"I'll give you a hundred to one there'll be a repeat of Christmas Eve."

Amanda didn't volunteer that the repeat had already happened, much less that it had affected her every bit as much as the first one had.

"This trajectory is leading in one direction only. So sign up for yoga." Pat parked in Amanda's driveway. "What do you have to eat?"

"Some leftover chicken. Nothing sweet."

"Amanda Sinclair—"

"Sorry, busy day. I didn't have time to go to the grocery."

In her kitchen, Amanda collapsed into a chair and let Pat rummage in her fridge. "I see lettuce. Chicken salads? I don't see Caesar salad dressing."

"Be grateful I've got wine."

"After I finish dropping dead from hunger I'll be grateful."

"I'll pour if you make the salads."

A few minutes later, wine and cold chicken salad served, Amanda said, "Before you say anything, I'm done with it. It's over."

"Mandy ..."

"We talked about it."

"And you sent him on his way. I bet that was your idea, not his."

Amanda shrugged.

"You'll never convince me he agreed."

"He did. Sort of." The wine interested Amanda more than the salad. She stared into her glass.

"Explain."

"I had a decision to make. I made it."

"Because you're scared."

"After Brandon—"

Pat's fork hit her plate, and her voice radiated frustration. "I am *sick* of hearing about that man. It's been five years. It's time you got over it."

Amanda's fork matched Pat's for reflected anger. They glared at each other. "Easy enough for you to say. I don't notice you exactly racking up the relationships."

"My love life's irrelevant. You need to let this go."

"Thanks for your psychological insight."

Hovering on the edge of one of their rare fights, both women looked away and focused their attention on their salads. Until Amanda abruptly put her elbows on the table and buried her face in her hands.

Pat brushed her hand. "I'm sorry."

"I'm so messed up. I can't handle it."

"Would you consider going back to the counselor you talked to?"

"My post-Brandon confessional? It didn't solve anything then, so I don't see why it would now."

"Is Jacob still dropping in every afternoon?"

"No."

"I didn't think he'd give up so easily." Pat pulled Amanda's hands from her face. She held on and squeezed. "I don't need to tell you you're in your head too much. You're overthinking this."

Amanda sighed. "Please, talk about something else. Tell me about the kids' group you're setting up. Your family. Anything."

Pat backed off and launched into a description of the discussion circle she was starting for kids in foster homes around Calter Creek. Later, as she was leaving, she said, "Yoga's good for serenity, too. I'll be here next Tuesday, six o'clock, to pick you up, so register for the class."

"I'm not sure I'll be able to move my muscles tomorrow, but if I must—"

"You must."

Chapter 18

Jacob surfaced from the pages of data filling his screen and shook his head to clear it.

For three weeks he'd pointedly avoided Amanda whenever possible, even to the extent of twice leaving the break room when she came in. He'd declined meetings and sent Jim or Bev when something had to be delivered to her. SI had noticed, but so far no one had said anything. Except Mel, who'd cornered him in his office one morning when he was alone in the Accounting suite. "Jacob, I just wondered ..." she'd begun.

Their eyes locked.

"Don't go there."

After another moment while they held that eye lock, she'd nodded and left.

It hadn't been fun.

He glanced around. He'd been dimly aware of the silence and realized quitting time was a good half an hour ago. He was long overdue at home. He made a quick call to let Norah and her sitter know he was on his way. Then he groaned, stood, and stretched with his hands on his lower back. At the printer in the corner of the suite, he scooped up a few pages and stowed them with his laptop in his computer bag. As he headed down the corridor to the front door, he glanced through the windows overlooking the Floor. He wasn't the only one still at SI. Someone was running around with the forklift, packaging up one last shipment before going home.

They're loyal, they go the extra distance. They like it here.

Someone didn't like it here enough. What he'd found in the financial records astonished him. Because someone had stolen from Sinclair Imports.

The papers in his bag dragged on him like wet cement. He'd put in the extra time today, making sure he'd interpreted the entry in the accounts correctly.

Jacob appreciated the team spirit that permeated SI. He'd been there long enough to be sorry to be leaving, although the unacknowledged tension between him and the president of SI made it impossible to stay. He was impatient for Marcia to find his replacement.

The new revelation made him sick, because this was going to devastate Amanda.

For three weeks he'd kept thoughts of her at bay. He'd managed not to mention her around Norah, to gently change the subject the one time she'd asked about Amanda. He tried to ignore the pain that had settled over his heart, a stone pulling him down.

God, how he wanted not to hurt.

The walk home didn't improve his mood. The weather had turned nasty as January inched into February and sleet stung his face. It made him wish for something warming and wonderful for dinner, like a chicken potpie — but his skills didn't run to anything that complicated. He supposed it was complicated. He and Norah ate adequately, but simply. Chicken potpie wasn't in the equation, but it was certainly that kind of day.

He found Norah happily building a structure out of cardboard and construction paper. Her sitter, a matronly woman who doted on her, hovered over his little girl, listening intently to her plans. She'd packed up her things, he noted, and he apologized again for being so late.

"It isn't a problem this once. Your daughter's a jewel, and it's a tough world, earning a living and all. Still, next time, yes, some advance warning would be good. So she won't worry."

Norah looked anything but worried, but Jacob took the point. He'd inconvenienced the woman he relied on for Norah's well-being. "It won't happen again." He pinched the bridge of his nose. "Stressful day. I got absorbed."

She gave his hand a little pat on her way out. "Don't worry. Bye, Norah," she called as she left.

"Bye, Mrs. Franklin! See you tomorrow!" Norah barreled into the entry and hugged the older woman.

The sitter dropped a kiss on Norah's head. "You bet. We'll do some baking if this weather holds. Not much point in going out." Her parting smile encompassed them both.

Jacob scooped up his happy daughter. "Now, why don't you show me what you're making? I think we've got an architect in the family."

"Daddy," she said in her silly-Daddy tone. She squirmed, and he set her down. He'd prayed for her to love her life again, but it came with a certain sadness, because it meant Deb was floating further away from her memory. It was bound to happen, but still. Jacob sighed and squatted down in the living room to admire the structure, whatever it was, engrossing his little girl.

Between architectural marvels, supper, and their shared bedtime rituals, it was well into the evening before Jacob was free to phone Amanda. This was a call he wanted to be over with, so it was a relief to punch in the numbers.

"Jacob?" Call display, but at least she'd answered. Her voice was brusque.

"I need to see you."

A pause. "Is something the matter?"

"As soon as we can arrange it, and not at work. I'll tell you when I see you. I'm not willing to talk about it on the phone."

"If you think I'm going out on some wild goose chase—"

"For once, trust me. This isn't minor, Amanda. It threatens SI."

While he waited out her silence he flashed to an image of a small animal, trapped and cowering in a corner. *Ridiculous. Not this powerful woman.* But the visual teased his mind.

Her voice was cold and businesslike. "All right. Expect me at eight thirty tomorrow."

They hung up with, he thought, a sense of mutual dissatisfaction.

Chapter 19

The next evening Jacob shuffled through the papers he'd brought home while he waited for the doorbell to ring. He'd devoted most of the previous evening and part of this one to cleaning. What he'd told Dave last autumn was true, the house was a little tired after over two years of his half-hearted attempts to keep it clean and tidy. Now the bathrooms gleamed, he'd swept and vacuumed, and, in the case of the kitchen, mopped. He'd had the exhaust fan going for an hour to banish all traces of their supper of frozen fish fingers, frozen French fries, and frozen peas. Norah had given the place her stamp of approval.

He watched his daughter arranging the books on the coffee table to meet her requirements. He'd started to clue in that she was house proud. His days of bachelor-style housekeeping were over, if Norah had her way. Amanda's visit pleased Norah, even if it would be after her bedtime.

"You're always alone, Daddy," she said when they'd stood together surveying their handiwork. "You need friends to come see you."

"Dave comes."

"He doesn't count." Well, perhaps Dave *didn't* count, in some calculus that her female mind grasped and his slower male one didn't, or he pretended it didn't. He'd never cleaned the place like this for Dave.

Amanda coming to his home. Belatedly, it occurred to him that he should have conducted this meeting on neutral ground, somewhere that would keep Norah out of the picture completely.

Always so much to remember. You can't think of everything.

He hoped the house didn't smell too badly of fish fingers.

Amanda was punctual. As Jacob steered her toward the living room, she said, "Let's get this over with as quickly as possible. I have a few other things to deal with tonight."

"Understood." He gestured to the sofa and sat beside her, leaving plenty of space.

Where to hold this meeting had occupied a fair amount of his mind over the last twenty-four hours. Logic dictated his office, but he'd given in to instinct and decided on the living room, in front of the fire. He'd scooted Norah's decorative touches to the side and put his own papers on the coffee table.

He noted the prim way she sat, with her knees locked together and her rigidly straight back, which he knew by now meant she was seriously displeased. *Efficient, businesslike.* He didn't waste any time on preliminaries. "There's something in the books that doesn't make sense. I don't have the full picture yet, but I have evidence to suggest that someone has stolen from SI."

A blank pause. "You've got to be kidding."

"I've got some papers to show you, some printouts."

She stared at him as if he'd spoken in Greek. Her mouth pinched into a thin line, and then she was on her feet, as if she might well storm out rather than face his facts. "I don't believe you. If something illicit were going on, Stan would have caught it. Stan—wait a minute. You're telling me it's Stan? Stealing? Because he isn't. You've made a mistake." Her voice rose as she spoke, anger overwhelming her cool shell.

He was on his feet, too, and clutched her left arm in an attempt to get through to her. "Just listen, will you? I'm not trying to get your back up or accuse anyone of anything. Something isn't right, and you need to know about it."

She shook his hand off and drew herself to her usual icy calm, but the inflexible set of her body signaled hostility. "You're wrong."

"I would love to be wrong. I don't want to be the one facing you right now, okay? But I'm not likely to put myself on the line unless I'm sure. Sit down, Amanda."

They both sat. Jacob gulped a breath, determined above all else to keep the whole encounter factual, not emotional. He picked up the first page. "Let's start here. By rights no one should have have found this, it's well buried. To give you the high level, we made a payment, ostensibly to this company, Shirai Distributors, back in September.

"It looks like I'm going to be stuck at SI for a while," he continued, and noted that her head gave a little tic when he used the word 'stuck'. "So I've spent some time reviewing the inventory system. I wanted to get a better feel for when it's crazy, when it's quiet. There's no record in inventory of receiving anything from Shirai. They're not even in the system."

He handed the profile for Shirai Distributors to her. She studied it, her face expressionless. "We haven't dealt with them in years," he said. "The account should be closed, but it isn't. That's why I caught the payment, Shirai's turned up in a couple of internal reports. I checked with them. No payment received, and they don't have an open account with us. I did find a stub in the purchasing files, but it doesn't connect to anything else. What I don't know yet is why the numbers balance. There's no discrepancy in the books. Stumbling on the payment entry was dumb luck."

He walked her through the information he'd gathered. Reviewing his limited facts took longer than it should have, given her facility with the company's accounting. But she argued with him, with the numbers, trying to force them to show something they didn't. Her anger seemed to have disappeared, replaced by puzzlement.

Half an hour later, Amanda showed no sign she was itching to leave. He stood to put another log on the fire. "While I'm on my feet, could I get you coffee or tea or water or anything? A brandy?"

Amanda sank back against the sofa cushions. "No—yes. Tea would be nice. Earl Grey?"

"The one adult in this household is a man. Earl Grey's for women."

"And the commander of the Enterprise."

Every time he thought he was getting closer to understanding her, she astonished him. "I'd forgotten. You *knew* that?"

"I catch it in reruns sometimes. They played around with metaphors and allegories, it wasn't all shoot-em-up."

"No Earl Grey, sorry. And some of the shoot-em-up appealed to us guys."

"No doubt." He caught a tiny edge of humor in her voice. "Whatever you have, then. I'm not fussy."

Oh, you are. You are one fussy woman.

Jacob headed for the kitchen.

When he came back he found Amanda staring at the reports, as if she could make the numbers change by force of will. Her eyes widened when he set the tray with cups and saucers, milk, sugar, and cookies on the coffee table. "This is beautiful." Her fingers traced the pattern on the sugar bowl. "Is it old?"

"No, just old fashioned. Deb chose it. I haven't used it since I lost her—no reason to, but it seemed appropriate. There's a teapot, but I didn't have any idea how many tea bags to use. I figured this was safer." He flicked one of the paper tabs hanging from the cups. "Try a cookie. Norah and the woman who watches her made them this afternoon."

Amanda removed the tea bag from the water and took a cookie. "I've never said—I'm sorry about your wife."

"Thanks, but no need. It's been almost two and a half years. It's hard when it turns up in the news or something, like last summer when they finally put the barrier down the middle of the highway through town—"

"I don't understand. She didn't ... I mean she wasn't ill?"

How have you made it this far without her knowing? Maybe she's right. Maybe you really are strangers.

"No, she was stuck in traffic going through town. This old guy heading the other way lost control and plowed into the side of her car. There was no way she could have avoided it. She didn't stand a chance." He paused. No matter how much time passed, discussing what happened to Deb would never be straightforward.

"I remember that. It was news for days." She focused her gaze on her tea, not on him. Another distancing mechanism.

"Norah was in the back seat, on the other side of the car. She came out of it without a scrape, physically, but it's taken this long for her mind to heal. That's why I make her such a priority, as well as being crazy about her. That's why the ponytail." He scrubbed his hand through his short hair. "After, I couldn't be bothered with anything except Norah for a long time. I lived in a haze, on automatic pilot, nothing mattered. When I finally sorted myself out enough that I was ready to get a haircut, she pitched a fit. Deb usually wore her hair that way, and I think it reminded her of her mom. You don't know how glad I am that it's gone."

Amanda nodded. "What happened to the person who did it? I can't remember."

He barked out a laugh, although without any humor behind it. "His car was a write-off, and he was too old to run. Late eighties. Why he still had a driver's license is beyond me. He lost his focus and hit the wrong pedal. I think he's in some seniors' facility now.

"We'd been thinking about another child … sorry, you don't want to hear all that." Jacob stared at his teacup for a moment. "Norah's healing, doing six-year-old things, making friends. I actually believe she prefers her after-school sitters to me. I'm sure she gets more attention. And I don't know where we'd be without Pat to get her back on track. She needed professional help."

Amanda nibbled at the cookie. "Good." She sipped, then put down the cup. "Yes, Pat's amazing."

"I'm sorry, I didn't mean to lay that on you. It's history now. And I remember you want to get home early."

"As for my time, this takes precedence. There has to be a mistake, but I can't see where."

"We don't have all the facts yet. I'll keep digging, but it's hard to do from work. This isn't exactly the quietest period in SI's life cycle. Plus too many interruptions."

"Could our check have been issued by mistake?"

"Unlikely, and Shirai didn't receive a payment. We know that much."

"Ask Stan. This happened before his heart attack. He might—"

"No." He softened his voice when she glared at him. "You must recognize that if something's going on here, there's a limited number of people who could be responsible."

"One person, you mean." She sighed. "I know, but I don't believe. I've known Stan since I was ten years old." She shook her head. "No. It's impossible."

"Still, you can't tell him."

She nodded.

"I'm swamped at the moment, but I'll do what I can."

"I'd like to take these." She picked up the papers.

"Of course."

Jacob escorted her to the door. While she donned her coat and boots he said, "Marcia hasn't found anyone yet to replace me. I keep hoping someone will turn up, but I guess that's the downside of living in Calter Creek. Not many of us in the market."

She looked nonplussed, as if she'd forgotten about his planned departure, then recovered. "We'll advertise in Columbus if nothing happens in the next week. I know you want to get on with your own opportunities."

"Yes."

"Only ..." She riffled the papers.

"I thought of that. If I'm not around, who's going to follow through on this mess? I don't know, Amanda."

She scurried through the sleet to her car. Jacob had seen the traces of shock that shadowed her face and didn't try to delay her. She'd need recovery time before she'd be up to speed again.

He realigned Norah's coffee table arrangement and carefully washed and shelved the tea set. The contradictions that made up Amanda Sinclair buzzed in his head. She'd handled his personal story with grace, yet the numbers that indicated theft had thrown her.

Well, her priorities didn't rank him anywhere near as highly as SI. He needed a strategy to deal with that. Because he wasn't blind or insensitive. He'd felt it again when he held her arm to keep her from bolting. Whether she admitted it or not, the electricity still zinged between them, as strong as ever.

* * *

Amanda had only the foggiest memory of how she got home that night. Her mind had stuck in overdrive, faced with the betrayal to her company. If it was true.

It couldn't be. It just couldn't be.

It was more than that though. Jacob had given her an insight into his own reality. The mystery woman she'd never know, the suffering in his life. Reality, too, for the delightful child she'd built a castle with, Christmas afternoon.

You've held him in your arms, and he's known so much pain.

Amanda came from a loving family, despite the ongoing tension between her and her father. A sudden death spelled catastrophe. Jacob's life seemed to be under control now, but the last years must have taken their toll, especially with the added burdens of work and caring for a traumatized little girl.

No matter what happened between them, Jacob insisted on being a full person. He refused to stay an abstract problem to be solved.

Still, she mused, his story wasn't personal to her. They'd proved tonight that they could work as colleagues and nothing more.

Entering her townhome gave her a jolt of another kind. Tonight, after experiencing Jacob's well-worn home, her preference for clean lines and minimalist décor seemed cold and lacking personality. Well, that just showed how different they were, didn't it? She'd never be happy in Jacob's lightly battered place.

Would she?

Amanda made herself a cup of tea, chamomile this time, and settled down at her desk to stare at the papers she'd brought home, even though she knew the explanation for what Jacob had uncovered wasn't in these reports.

Chapter 20

Amanda spent the next morning in the large viewing room with representatives from Honeysuckle & Thyme, a gift shop chain with stores throughout SI's catchment area. Most of SI's business came over the Internet now, with perhaps a third still originating with their sales team, but when the potential customer could contribute significantly to the bottom line, the display room helped to showcase their scope and solidity. It was a dog-and-pony show, and she was the ringmaster, on stage every minute.

H&T presented a homey, welcoming aura to the public, and a hard-nosed, challenging face to SI. There had been nothing comfortable in this morning's meeting.

Back in her office, she collapsed in her chair, drained.

Mel followed her. "Almost two and a half hours. Ate every pastry on the plate. Did we win them?"

"I don't know. If we don't hear from them in the next week we'll get Sales to follow up. Best we can do. I'm exhausted."

Her instinct said they'd done well, but she didn't run a business on instinct. They'd give H&T every encouragement to come on board with Sinclair Imports. If they went to some other supplier, she wouldn't shrug it off, but she'd seen it often enough that she no longer lost sleep over it. She'd like to win this one though.

Amanda snapped out of a light reverie. "Are you going out for lunch?"

"Want to come?"

"No, but could you pick me up a sandwich?"

"Chicken and pesto on multigrain?"

"You know me too well. Here." Amanda dug into the lunch money fund she kept in her drawer. "Take your time."

Jacob came in as Mel left. It was the first time he'd sought her out at work in weeks. He and Mel exchanged quiet words and big grins as they passed. Mel inspired people to share with her, feel close to her. Amanda almost sighed.

"You wanted the credit rundown on the company from this morning. I got Bev to pull up everything publicly available."

"Thanks."

"You're tired."

"I am."

Jacob went to her door and double-checked that Mel had left for lunch before turning back to her. "Seriously, how are you?"

"Shocked, if you must know, but it's filed away in another corner of my mind this morning."

"But it's weighing on you." He paused, as if choosing his words. "Amanda. I'm not pushing, but I'm here. I can be the shoulder to cry on, the sounding board. Whatever you need." His unemotional tone implied nothing more than a business transaction.

Which, given the state of things between them, made sense.

She narrowed her eyes. "You'll let me know if anything else turns up?"

"Of course I will. Take care." His voice remained matter-of-fact, and he didn't look at her.

"You, too."

He nodded and left.

She turned to her computer. The Jolt lay dormant. She refused to admit that she missed it. She wished she possessed the courage to ask him not to leave, to close the door, to …

Why couldn't she be more like Mel, those casual, almost intimate words he'd exchanged with her?

She pulled up a spreadsheet and ran her company.

Chapter 21

"You what?"

"I quit," Jacob replied calmly. As if quitting were an everyday occurrence. As if he didn't care. "They've started the search to replace me. I've got feelers out, we won't starve."

A Friday night for the books. Indiana lost, alcohol was minimal, and now Dave had to get on his case.

"Never thought you would. That's not the point." Dave had been nursing the same lager for an hour. The stuff had to be tepid by now. Apparently Nancy was on a weight and health kick. The little fridge in Dave's basement media room had yielded two beers each, no more. Maybe that's why he sounded irritable.

Back up. Who's irritable here?

He reached out to put his empty bottle on the coffee table, then stayed slouched forward, elbows on knees. "Your point? I can feel it coming."

"It's Amanda Sinclair, isn't it? You've been down in the dumps all evening."

"Yep."

Dave's groan conveyed dismay, and more than a little doubt that Jacob had any brain matter left to lose. "And here I thought you were the smart one."

"Amanda's call. She said get lost, I got mad, she got icy. End of story. No point staying at SI torturing myself."

"Bummer. So, two week notice and you're history."

"Not quite. I'll stick around until they replace me. Professional integrity and all that, but it's a mess. Things are tense."

With that on the table, the game over, and no beer, the two men turned their attention to the muted post-game show. Jacob waited the silence out, confident that Dave wasn't about to let this drop.

Sure enough. "When did this go down?"

"Three weeks plus."

"Hit you hard."

"Yup."

"Not like you to get mad."

"Nope."

"Apologize?"

"No. Well, sort of."

Dave whistled under his breath. "Don't think I ever told you, Nance and I've tried out that thing you had going with Deb about always saying you're sorry. It's smoothed things over once or twice, I can tell you."

Jacob slouched back, staring at the movement on the muted TV screen. "Point taken. But Amanda's not Deb. That isn't what's going on, not really."

"Then what is going on?"

Jacob shrugged. "No clue. Ask Amanda."

Jacob's fingers played with a pretzel while he waited out the silence. At the end of it, Dave came to life. He sat up straighter and aimed a finger at Jacob.

"Son, you've got work to do, and thanks to your impulsive nature, you've got a limited time to accomplish it."

"Forget it, Dave. I don't need to be kicked while I'm down. I'm done."

"No, you're not. You're morose. I bet your minions at SI know something's up."

He had to smile. "Mel—she's Amanda's executive assistant, she pretty much runs the place—she's been giving me these looks, like she's assessing what I'm made of. I'm not sure if she's planning to lecture me or yell at me or what. She's the company radar, and I'm in her sights."

"Get back in the ring, is what I say."

"No."

"Monosyllabic tonight, aren't you? You're rolling over and playing dead too soon, Jake. Your Ms. Sinclair has a long history of very, very cool. I figured your charm would wear her down before this since you know she's not indifferent. I assume she likes the kissy-kissy part."

Jacob's mouth twitched at that, fighting a grin. "Yeah, she does."

"So your job isn't to go all roll-over-and-play-dead on her. I expect she wants the walls down as much as you do. She just doesn't know it yet. Think of it as your sacred duty or something."

Jacob twisted around in his chair to face his friend. "When she freezes me out if I so much as deliver a report to her office?" He shook his head. "I need to get going."

"I'm putting the idea in your head, man. If a landslide isn't working, try the erosion technique. Chip away a sixty-fourth of an inch at a time. Make yourself irreplaceable, so she can't imagine life without you."

The two men stood and headed for Dave's front door. "Do not give up." Dave jabbed a finger in Jacob's back. "Do. Not. Give. Up. That's my sage advice. Consider it."

"If you insist."

He did consider it, driving home, tossing in bed. He considered it most of Saturday, playing with Norah in the snow. By Monday, he'd faced the reality he'd suspected the night they reviewed the accounts. He could no more walk away from Amanda Sinclair than he could stop breathing.

And that meant coming up with a plan.

Chapter 22

Jacob sat at Amanda's conference table and listened. Amanda had brought in Charlie from Warehouse, Marcia from Personnel, Ted from Technology, and Mel.

And Jacob himself, bemused at being included in her focus group. SI wasn't any of his business anymore, was it? Did Amanda think it still was?

Amanda put down the fountain pen she'd been feeding through her fingers and glanced around the table. "So that's where we stand now. Based on last year's figures and the trend over the last three years, and in spite of the global economic challenges, we're well positioned to expand. We can source new products, and the marketing team's positive about expanding our footprint. So, high level. Any preliminary thoughts? Problems?"

"The warehouse is too small," Charlie said. "A significant increase in stock would break us. We struggled over Christmas with the new stuff coming in."

"Agreed." Amanda made a note on the pad in front of her. "Expansion would mean larger premises, more staff, and increased pressure across the board."

She met each of their eyes in turn. Except his. She skipped over his.

A tell. She can't look at me.

Marcia reviewed personnel challenges, Ted discussed server capacity.

"Accounting?" She glanced toward Jacob, but still shied away from meeting his eyes.

Jacob kept himself loose and his information factual. "The accounting system doesn't integrate well with inventory or personnel—those bottlenecks would become urgent if you expand. Of course we're shorthanded at the moment."

"Last I heard, Stan could be back at work now, as far as the doctors are concerned, but Susan's been angling for what she calls a 'real' vacation, for years. Plus the daughters are on her side. My guess is another month, minimum, before his family releases him." She smiled. Whatever her current feelings about Stan, his plight amused her.

No one mentioned his own impending departure.

She sat back, passing her pen from hand to hand. "So, gut reaction. I want your thoughts and the probable impact on your departments, including cost implications. Should we expand at all, or would we compromise something fundamental to our company if we got too much bigger? I don't have the answers to those questions, so that's what I need from you."

Jacob scanned the table and saw mixed reviews on the faces around him. Charlie and Ted seemed excited by the possibilities, Mel doubtful, Marcia neutral.

"How long do we have?" Ted asked.

"Let's say two weeks. If we decide to do this, we should start the search for warehouse space as soon as possible."

"What about Colin?" Charlie asked. "Will you involve him?"

"He'd be ramrodding through the doors if I didn't, you know that. But the decision comes from us, not from him." Amanda stood, and the meeting broke up.

"You like it," Jacob said to Charlie as the two men walked together toward the west corridor.

"Sure. I don't expect any unsolvable problems. It's good to see Amanda take charge again, fielding the big plans. She's a real entrepreneur. She'd been a little flat for a while there. See ya."

"Later," Jacob replied. Charlie disappeared through the door to the warehouse floor.

Jacob continued the short distance to his office, mulling over the new information he'd just received. She couldn't look at him. She'd included him in the meeting, but she couldn't look him in the face.

* * *

"Daddy, can you show me how to play this?"

Jacob tossed the tax bulletin he'd been reading on the coffee table. These days work occupied far too much of his life as he struggled to keep up with Stan's workload and his own, with the added challenge of researching the mystery payment. In the quiet time between supper and bed, he'd rather be doing something with Norah.

She stood between him and the fire he'd lit in the living room fireplace. She'd dragged in a guitar case. "Where'd you get that, Sweetie?"

"From the junk closet. Where it's always been."

"Let's see." He knelt and opened the case.

Debbie's guitar. He'd put them both away, after. He hadn't thought about them in a year or more. They'd begun lessons together, he and Deb. Classical guitar, something they'd started after Norah's birth, a shared activity for the two of them.

"Let's check this out." The batteries in the tuner were dead, so he did his best manually. With the instrument more or less in tune, he strummed a few remembered chords, picked a few notes. Expectedly, his fingers acted like uncoordinated sausages on the strings.

"I want to do that. Can you show me?" Insistent, Norah stood close to him, her hand reverently brushing the surface of the guitar.

He shook his head and set Deb's guitar back into its case. "I'm not good enough to teach you. If you want to learn, we'll find you a teacher and get you a guitar that's the right size. This one's almost as big as you are."

"That's not true, Daddy. Let me try." She climbed on the sofa and held out her arms. He picked the guitar up again and placed it in her lap. She tried to stretch her arms out on the neck and around the body of the instrument.

"See what I mean?"

"I guess so." Norah treated him to a dramatic sigh. "I want to play this one."

"Your mother's guitar."

She nodded.

In his mind he'd been adding the newly resurrected guitar to the list of things he should deal with, aka things he should get rid of. That wasn't going to happen. Watching Norah struggle with the guitar, the far too familiar emptiness settled inside him.

Love doesn't mean you can keep them safe. Or that your own life's going to be any safer.

He refocused on the present.

"Why don't we put this one away and get you one that's the right size for you. Then when you're bigger and ready for a full sized guitar, this one will be waiting for you. Is that fair enough?"

She nodded again. She seemed so tiny behind the instrument. How was it possible that she was old enough to want lessons?

"I'll phone around. You know you'll have to promise to practice and not complain? It's work, and your fingers hurt until they get tough."

"I know, I remember. You and Mommy played at night. Mommy played for me when I took my nap, when I was little. When you had to go to work."

Ah. The pang wedged under his ribs. "I didn't know that, about your nap. Thanks for telling me."

"Can you take this now? I'm afraid I'll drop it." Norah squirmed, but never took her hands off the guitar.

"Do you want me to put it back in the closet?"

"No, 'cause you'll forget. We can leave it here, then when you trip over it you'll remember."

One of life's organizational maxims. He constantly heard his words, or the words of other adults, coming from his daughter. He laid the guitar in its case. "Not going to happen, Pumpkin, because I'll get mine out."

"Will you play it?"

"Maybe." Two and a half years. Memories.

"Okay then. We can go shopping on Saturday."

"Let's be sure we can find those lessons first. Off you go, now. I need to finish this work, and it isn't much fun. Then we'll try out those new bubbles if you want."

"Is that a bribe?"

"Yes, it is. Now scoot."

Norah vanished, and he set the guitar case in the corner of the room, propped against a wall. He'd take it to the junk closet later and swap it for his own. Dig out some of the old music, put fresh batteries in the tuner.

He'd expected the memory to be more painful. The ache lingered, but gently, a caress instead of a blow.

This is new, he thought. *I remember, but the pain's less. Softer.*

It was so easy for us, so simple.

He wondered if he wanted to play the guitar again, or if it had been enjoyable because he and Deb had shared it.

Only one way to find out.

He returned to his bulletin—then stopped, gazed at the fire without seeing, and let himself remember. Quiet evenings, free of hurt, playing duets with Debbie.

Chapter 23

Norah loved the swings best, so on a Saturday in early February, as Calter Creek experienced a mild spell, Jacob took Norah to the park.

There are worse ways to spend a Saturday afternoon. More stimulating ones, too.

The park wasn't busy, typical for the time of year, with snow covering the ground anywhere that the traffic of booted kids hadn't worn it off. Several other parents did their best to keep warm while their hyper-excited offspring ricocheted from one piece of playground equipment to another.

Every play day he spent with Norah meant dodging the urge to pack her in cotton wool and never let her out of the house. Celebrating her confidence and independence cost him, in a world so full of danger. Even something as innocuous as the swings. He didn't allow himself to imagine the catastrophes that could happen on a swing.

Instead, while he pushed her he thought about Amanda. Their afternoon coffees together—he'd started dropping in on her again. She seemed to lack the willpower to stop him. After the first couple of days, confident he was getting away with it, he'd upped the ante, covering her hand with his own or running his fingers up past her wrist before he left. He needed to find other ways to court her though. Touch her. Convince her.

Letting Amanda into his mind, even while pushing Norah, sent his system into a carnival ride of reaction, one moment exhilarated, the next plummeting down into some deep dark pit.

Melodramatic, McKinnon.

At least he had those brief afternoon conversations. Perhaps they'd find a way to be friends after all.

After ten minutes or so, Norah announced that she was freezing, so Jacob pulled her to a halt and watched her run to the geodesic dome structure the kids climbed on and swung from. Jacob followed, his cold hands bunched into fists inside his gloves. He figured the exercise promoted her strength and balance, as well as her self-confidence. By the time he caught up with her she was climbing enthusiastically, like a monkey. His daughter, able to laugh and play again.

He sent a silent thank-you to Pat, and to time, and to whatever god tended to the healing of little girls.

"Watch me, Daddy." She started working her way across the top of the dome, from one bar to the next.

"I'm watching," he called back.

So he watched as she missed her grip, then lost her footing. She tumbled to the ground from the highest point of the dome.

The blood drained from his head, fled his extremities, coagulated in his heart.

Norah screamed, tried to get up and cried out again, and collapsed sobbing on the cold mat beneath the structure.

Jacob fought his way through the openings in the bars and ran his hands over her.

"My arm. It *hurts*." He recognized fear, as well as pain, in her voice.

A man appeared beside him. A good thing, because he'd gone from competent to jelly in the split second it took his daughter to fall six feet. "Need a hand?" the man asked.

"She's—I'm afraid to move her."

"I'm a paramedic, lots of first responder training." He squatted down next to Norah. "Honey, what hurts?"

"My arm," she whimpered.

"Anything else?"

Norah shook her head.

"No headache? Bump on the head?"

"My arm. Make it stop hurting, Daddy." Norah sobbed, and his heart shattered.

"We will, baby. Lie still for another minute."

Jacob kept his hands on her, kneeling beside her, stroking her cheek and holding her shaking body still.

"So," the man said. "Tell me your name."

"Norah," she choked out.

"Well now, Miss Norah, let's see if you can move your other arm."

Norah raised her free right arm and wiggled her fingers. The other arm, the injured one, was trapped underneath her.

"Can you move your feet? Not too hard, now."

She obediently kicked both her feet out. The panicky sobs let up a little as she grew intrigued by the things the man asked her to do.

"We can move her," he said, after checking Norah some more. "It's going to be tricky, getting her out of the middle of the dome."

Jacob read the unspoken message—it's going to hurt— and nodded grimly. He was getting his bearings again, but he was far from coping. He'd never in his life been so frightened. "I guess we've got to immobilize the arm."

The man nodded. "Name's Neil."

"Jacob."

"Anyone with you to hold her if you drive?"

Jacob shook his head. "Just the two of us."

"So here's what we'll do."

They lifted Norah, supporting the painful arm against her. Between them and a couple of other parents who came over to help, they eased his little girl out through the bars of the dome. A little blood soaked through the sleeve of her coat. Every time Norah cried out, Jacob felt something rip apart inside him. Neil spoke to his wife, then carried Norah to his own car while Jacob stabilized her arm, holding it as still as possible and murmuring to his daughter.

The wrong man's carrying her. But his muscles weren't reliable. He wasn't even sure he could make it to the parking lot, much less handle driving.

At the hospital the system claimed Norah while Jacob checked her in, answering endless questions and receiving a sheaf of forms to fill out, before he could follow her to a treatment room. He sat next to her, alternately comforting her and working his way through the forms. The monotony of the paperwork calmed him somewhat.

Doctors and nurses came and went. Norah was wheeled away for an x-ray, with a promise of painkillers. After an interminable hour, a doctor sat down to talk to him. "It's an open fracture, so we'll put her on antibiotics as a precaution. We'll use a general anesthetic when we realign the bone, but it's straightforward surgery. We'll do a scan to be sure her bones are growing properly, but I'm reasonably sure it's bad luck."

His daughter, pain, surgery, scans, all whirled in his head.

He let them direct him back to the emergency waiting room, where Neil came over. "There you are. I'm off. Rotten thing to happen, but I'm sure she'll be okay. She's a game kid."

"You're still here? Thank you. I can't tell you how much I mean that. I hate that I've taken up so much of your afternoon." The two men shook hands. "How do I get in touch with you? Phone, email?"

Neil fished a business card out of his pocket. "Don't worry about it. Gave me a chance to schmooze with some pals. Most likely we'll run into each other on the playground. Can your wife come pick you up?"

He shook his head. "Not married."

"Well, if you need anything, money for a cab?"

"I don't. Seriously, thanks. I don't know what I would have done if you hadn't stepped in."

"You're underestimating yourself. Don't forget to take care of yourself, as well as your little Norah. You're still white as a sheet. And no alcohol."

"I figured that. Doesn't even sound good, to tell the truth."

Neil clapped Jacob on the arm and waved as he left the hospital.

A while later the young doctor appeared to say that Norah would be staying in the hospital. "She's going to be fine, but with an open fracture we prefer to keep an eye on her overnight. It'll be easier on you, too, you'll have enough to deal with once she's home. We're taking her upstairs to Pediatric. Go up to the waiting room, and they'll come get you when you can see her."

In the pediatric waiting room Jacob paced, and sat, and paced some more, sure that no other events in his life had ever left him so alone or so helpless. Not even the aftermath of Deb's death had been like this. Then, he'd had numbness on his side. This time it was all too vivid. They'd taken his daughter from him, she could be asleep or afraid or hurting or *anything*. He'd pound a fist through a wall if one more person told him she would be fine. His careful life lay in tatters at his feet, and he wasn't coping. He'd failed to protect Norah.

He needed to pull himself together, but for once he couldn't find the reserves to do it. Not alone.

He didn't give himself time to second-guess himself. He dug his phone from a pocket and called Amanda.

* * *

Amanda had half of a load of laundry piled in the washing machine when the phone rang. She listened on speakerphone, stuffing one last sheet into the machine while Jacob told her, not too coherently, what had happened to Norah.

Why would he call you, of all people? What can you do?

Why would you race off to be with Jacob at a hospital? Something in his voice? Something beyond desire or friendship?

Why should you care?

She stepped into the pediatric waiting room half an hour after she received Jacob's call, wondering at her own alacrity. But as Pat kept reminding her, sometimes it's possible to seriously over-think things.

And some lessons take longer to learn than others.

Although people passed through continually, the room itself was empty except for the man sitting hunched forward on an uncomfortable-looking molded plastic chair. His coat lay abandoned on the seat next to him, his forearms were on his knees, his head down. She put her own coat on top of his, then sat and draped an arm around his shoulders.

She, Amanda, who never instigated a touch or a hug.

Don't think.

Her hand slid down to rest between his shoulder blades. "Jacob?"

He turned a haggard look on her. "You're here." Then he looked away.

She waited.

"I hate this," he managed after a minute. He took a deep, gasping breath, still leaning forward with his hands clasped between his knees. His voice was tight and quiet. "It's so impossibly lonely sometimes. I've had to be everything for her. Deb's gone, and sometimes it's so damn hard, facing it alone."

Amanda was skilled at handling crises, but she'd never dealt with a crisis like this one. Rather than risk saying the wrong thing, she chose silence and waited.

He straightened, fixing his gaze on something beyond the room. His voice sounded hollow, his face looked haunted. "I was standing right there, and she wasn't safe. I'm just so tired. I don't have any right to ask, but—stay close for a little while, would you?"

Definitely safest not to think.

Her hand moved from his back to grip his shoulder. "Kids take tumbles. Parents cope somehow. Trust yourself."

His gaze remained fastened somewhere off in space. "I couldn't have prevented it, my rational mind accepts that. The rest of me's in shreds."

Amanda's hand left his shoulder to rub circles on his back. A friend, she thought. Friends comforted each other, fair enough, but being here was deeper, more intimate. Even more than when he'd kissed her. She didn't have a nurturing bone in her body, so what explained her need to wrap this man in her arms, hold him safe?

Is this you? Where have you put the real Amanda?

The real Amanda wouldn't touch this situation with a ten-foot pole. The real Amanda stayed aloof, avoided entanglements. Instead, she found herself in a quiet hospital waiting room on a Saturday afternoon, with Jacob McKinnon, hoping that somehow she was making the right guesses about what to say and do. Who was this woman, anyway?

And wasn't that a monumental joke since you've done her best to kick him out of your life?

But he'd phoned. She'd rejected him, and he hadn't stayed rejected.

Abruptly, his words registered. Deb's gone, he'd said.

And that brought her musing to a sudden, shuddering halt. The joke was on her.

After all, Deb had to be the one he wanted. Deb, who'd given birth to his daughter, who'd shared the first four years of Norah's life. She, Amanda, was a stand-in. She'd never be Deb.

The reality, not a daydream. How perverse is that? Just when you might even be able to —

Jacob got up and prowled around the deserted room. He didn't say anything until he'd sat back down. "I wonder why they think bunnies and nursery rhymes make good decorations in a waiting room," he mumbled. "It's not as if the kids are in here." He locked his hand into hers but kept his gaze on the floor.

The nurse sought them out a few minutes later. "She wants you. I told her you weren't alone," she said to Jacob, "so she demanded a description, then announced she wanted both of you. She's one for speaking her mind, isn't she? She'll be groggy and strange for a while yet. Don't be surprised if she's as cross as a bear tomorrow, but she's going to be fine."

* * *

Jacob found a washroom and splashed cold water on his face, determined to show Norah his usual composure. She was half-awake, confused, woozy, and unhappy. Her arm in the temporary splint, until the swelling went down, looked beyond fragile. He bent over his daughter and kissed her forehead. "Better?"

"I feel funny, Daddy."

"That's the medicine. It'll go away." He kept his hand on Norah, brushing back her hair, touching her cheek. She claimed his other hand and held on. Her grip was weak though, and the sight of her, so frail, stabbed his heart again.

Norah didn't need to know that. He'd had years of practice keeping his deepest pain hidden from her. "Do you want anything from home for tonight? One of your animals?"

Norah revived briefly. "Will you bring Bobo? I want to show him this whole place. And they said I get applesauce *and* pudding for supper."

If you're awake to eat supper. Her voice was slurring.

"Applesauce and pudding? I think you'd like to break your arm every day." Jacob grinned at his daughter.

He got an answering giggle and felt relief down to his toes.

"It was pretty horrible," she said in a small voice. Her smile vanished, and her hand clutched his. "I was scared. I'm glad you were there."

"So am I, Pumpkin." Jacob perched on the side of the bed, cupping his daughter's cheek with his free hand. He longed to pick her up and cradle her, but couldn't bear the risk of hurting her, so he contented himself with leaning over to kiss her again.

Norah's eyes closed. "I'm sleepy. You should go home with Amanda. You can get Bobo."

Amanda had waited near the door. Norah had noticed though.

"Bobo'll be here when you wake up. I love you, little one," Jacob told her. "Sleep and get all better again."

"G'night, Daddy." Her voice trailed off, and she was asleep before she got the last word spoken. Jacob kissed the tiny, perfect hand, now limp in his, and he and Amanda tiptoed out.

* * *

Night had fallen when they left the hospital. Jacob was uncharacteristically quiet in her passenger seat during the drive to pick up his car. He stared out the window without moving or speaking. Amanda concentrated on her driving, but the silence nagged at her. The flash of insight she'd had in the waiting room wouldn't go away and leave her alone.

At the hospital, she'd assumed the right to touch him, to comfort him. She'd behaved as if she had a role in their lives, as if they were building something together. As if they were a family. She and Jacob and Norah.

Which meant she'd capitulated. Somewhere during this strange afternoon she'd admitted Jacob into her life. In the waiting room — even before, when she'd answered the phone, if she was honest — she'd realized that with him was exactly where she wanted to be.

Except this puzzle had a missing piece, and that piece was Deb McKinnon. To make the picture whole, Deb had to be in it. Right now, she was no more than a stopgap. He needed his late wife, the mother of his child. He wasn't over her loss. He might never be.

Jacob must have grasped it, too.

This electricity thing, this Jolt, that was sex, wasn't it? It had nothing to do with the depth, the emotional connection between a man and a woman. His wife had claimed that part of him years ago.

Logically, that meant whatever had been fighting for life between them had to end.

Only this morning, she would have welcomed the ending, with a little regret. As she drove and the silence in the car grew denser, Amanda steeled herself against the words he would use to tell her she would never be a part of this tight unit he and Norah made up.

At the playground, Amanda pulled in next to his SUV. He stared out the side window, turned a little away from her.

"Jacob?" She touched his arm.

"Would you come over for a while?" He didn't move.

"Jacob, what's — I mean, where are you? Are you all right? Of course you're not," she said, suddenly brisk. "You must be exhausted. And hungry." This wasn't the time to discuss their misaligned relationship. He needed her friendship tonight. "Go home. I'm picking up pizza."

"You'll come?"

"Are you okay to drive? You need to get Bobo back to the hospital, but I suspect you're in shock. Pizza's a great shock remedy, I hear." The corners of his mouth twitched, but the flash of amusement didn't last. In the parking lot lights his face was all hard planes and angles.

He gave his head a shake, as if clearing away cobwebs. "I can drive. So you know, Bobo's a purple monkey. But here's another idea. I'll get Bobo and drop him off. You get pizza. Could we meet at your place? It's a lot closer to the hospital, and it'll save your driving to the other side of town. We can hang out for a while. If you want to."

"Good plan, so go. Deliver Bobo before Norah wakes up. I'll see you later."

He nodded in reply. She watched him change cars and drive away, a little muscle of hope twitching inside her. Out of habit she fought it off. Before heading home she pulled out her phone and speed-dialed the pizza place.

Chapter 24

Waiting on her doorstep, Jacob was aware that Amanda's home left him with mixed feelings. He'd only been there once before, the crazy night he'd confronted her and ended up holding her as if neither of them would ever let go. He'd left with an impression of precision, of orderliness and polish, so perfect it was hard to imagine anyone actually living there. To him it felt cold. Yet it suited Amanda.

Ne'er the twain shall meet, eh?

He was starting to get a grip on normality. Having things to do cut through the shock.

Or maybe it's the thought of an evening with Amanda?

Well, no. It didn't get much more surreal than that. Jacob managed an inner chuckle at his own expense.

Still, she'd come to the hospital. And surreal or not, you're here now.

At home he'd smelled the stress on himself, so he'd taken a few minutes for a quick, hot shower. He'd dressed in an old pair of jeans and the blue and gray sweater. Above all, this fraught evening, he wanted relaxation and comfort. He'd gone to the hospital, fought tears as he tucked Bobo next to his sleeping daughter, made arrangements to spend the night with her, then driven to Amanda's.

She opened the door and hurried him in. The air had turned cold under a clear sky; the mild spell was over. "Pizza's in the oven. I got one with pepperoni."

He shrugged out of his coat, mildly astonished. "You did? I never pegged you for a pepperoni gal. Vegetarian, or Hawaiian."

"Not Hawaiian, too sweet. Pat says the way to a man's heart is through pepperoni pizza. I figure she's the psychologist, she should know."

"Isn't it odd we've never yet had pizza together? All these firsts we still have ahead." He was sniffing his way to the kitchen. "And you've figured out the way to my heart, I think, but at the moment I agree with Pat. I'm starving."

"You should be." Amanda slid the pizza out of the oven and served up wedges dripping with cheese on pre-heated plates. She'd also set out an array of baby vegetables, little carrots and broccoli florets, cherry tomatoes and celery sticks with some kind of dip. She caught his look. "I'll eat the pepperoni if you eat the veggies. It's a fair trade."

He shook his head at her, in wonderment rather than denial. It was some minutes before either said anything. Hunger overtook them and they attacked the food.

Jacob absentmindedly reached over to where she sat catty-corner from him and swiped a finger across her chin. "String of cheese."

"Thanks."

"No problem."

A strange expression flickered on her face for an instant. He smiled at her, then returned his attention to the food.

With the first hunger pangs extinguished, Jacob surveyed his surroundings, noting the quiet order, her kitchen's peaceful, pale yellow color scheme. He felt less raw, less hurting, as if he'd shed a truckload of tension. "So, talk to me. All afternoon I've been trying to convince myself that everything's going to be all right. I'm having a hard time with being in your kitchen and wondering if it might be better than all right."

"Yes." A line appeared between her eyebrows. She put down the half piece of pizza she held and fixed her eyes on it. "I've been thinking." She took a breath. "I want to set your mind at ease about this. Today in the hospital, I recognized I can't take the place of what you lost. When you said, 'Deb's gone'."

"Hold on. I said that?"

She nodded. "With Norah hurt, you'd want her with you, not me. I understand. Today I overstepped. I thought I could help by feeding you, but I feel as if I've intruded—"

"Stop." He wasn't sure how to react, this was so far from what he'd expected, so running on pure instinct he reached across the table and covered her hand with one of his own. "Look at me." He studied her; it wasn't possible not to. She clenched her lower lip between her teeth and turned her gaze from the pizza to him. Amanda had lost her protective, all-business cloak for once. She didn't speak.

"I called you, and you came. That's two unbelievable statements right there. It makes me wonder if the door's opened again, a little." His fingers wrapped around her hand, his thumb absentmindedly tracing lines on her palm. She looked down again, following his thumb. "I sometimes think it's me, and some part of you, pitted against that ultra-logical mind of yours. Trying to compartmentalize what's happening between us."

Jacob paused, but didn't release her hand. He let it flow through him—Amanda, Deb, need, responsibility, loneliness. Love. He saw the way their joined hands seemed to mesmerize her.

"Where Deb's concerned, you're wrong. I mean, no, of course you can't take her place. The thing is, I don't want you to. What's happening between us doesn't have anything to do with Deb. She's gone. That's the reality."

He paused again, to regroup. He'd wounded himself with the brutal honesty of his words, even though they were completely true. "I don't remember what I said in the hospital, other than wanting you to understand how lonely it can be. I try not to talk about her too much, to you or anyone, because she's my past. It's been two and a half years, Amanda. I loved her, but it's over."

He let go of her hand, leaned back in his chair, and closed his eyes, his thumbs hooked in his jeans pockets. He spoke slowly, with pauses to help him get beyond the residual pain of his words. "I think about her less as time goes by. I won't lie to you, she's never going to be out of my life completely. We were happy together, but I've had to let go of it. Now, there's you.

Only you, so we're clear," he repeated. The words hung in the air.

He sat forward and reached for her again, tapping their joined hands on the table. "It's you I phoned. When I needed you, you came. Not Deb."

He'd never tell her how much it hurt, denying Debbie so adamantly. But that was between him and his past. His heart sent out a silent apology.

When she was quiet he spoke again. "I want to show you something." He let go of her hand to pull his wallet out of a back pocket, and took out a photo. "I want you to know what she looked like."

He watched Amanda absorbing the picture he handed her. Deb. He knew that picture by heart. Far from glamorous, she'd been slightly overweight, with blond, untidy hair tied back in a ponytail, and bright, laughing eyes. "It was taken at a park, not long before she was killed. It's good of her. She loved playing with Norah, they were always concocting some scheme or other."

There was another picture in his bedroom, a studio shot. He thought about putting it away, trading Deb for the possibility of the woman sitting across from him. One day.

Amanda handed the photo back to him. "She looks like she loved life. Did she go out to work?"

"She taught third grade, but she wanted to be at home once we had Norah. She'd even considered home schooling. That would have been a mistake, Norah's like a bird who's discovered her wings at school, but we didn't know it then."

He put the photo back in his wallet, shoved the wallet into his pocket. "Whatever happens between you and me, Deb was — is — a part of my life. Not actively now, I guess, but she's always going to be in the mix. Every time I look at Norah, at least when she's not with you, I see Debbie. That may change over time, but I can't turn it off on demand."

He took a breath before he went on. "But none of that has any bearing on you and me. I'm not making comparisons, and I'm not pining for the past."

"You must be, a little."

"Sometimes. Not usually. And not now."

He held on to his own composure by the thinnest of threads. Norah's accident had already pitched him into some peculiar mindset, and this evening threatened to slip the bounds of ordinary reality.

Still, surreal or not, he also had something he had to say.

She picked up the congealing piece of pizza and took another bite.

Jacob left the silence for a minute. He shoved his fingers through his hair and fixed his gaze on the table. "You need to know something. About me. I fell apart this afternoon." His voice barely managed a whisper. "I couldn't handle it. I failed when I couldn't afford to. One of the other fathers stepped in to help, but I was one step from useless."

He wondered if she heard the disgust he felt. He had to get it out though. All of it. "I called you because—I don't know why I called you. I wish you'd never seen me like that."

Her chair scraped on the floor. He looked up. She'd repositioned the chair to face him directly. "Jacob, don't. After the shock of the accident? Norah's everything to you. How would anybody react? The truth is, I'm more ... I guess, more at ease with you."

"I can't believe that. You can't possibly respect someone who fell apart the way I did. Hell, I can't respect myself."

The puzzle that was Amanda. Will you ever be able to predict her?

She swallowed. "I wonder if you've considered how much you've determined the whole course of things up to now. I mean, between us. You present this perfect image of father and professional, someone who's confident in what he's doing, who expects to be in control. Today at the hospital, I saw a little past the exterior, and it may sound funny, but I'm grateful. You're more real to me now."

"I've needed all the control I can muster, to get Norah and me both safely through it all."

"Yes, I see that."

"Today's going to haunt me. I can feel it."

"It shouldn't, Jacob. You love your daughter. And I'm glad you're human."

"We both are. Just two people, Amanda. Two ordinary people."

"I see myself in what you said. It's less scary when you're in control."

He picked up on the uncertainty in her voice. "But it can be less rewarding, too. We both have ghosts. We're adults, we can't help that. But we don't have to let those ghosts run our lives now.

"I think we're sort of stuck with each other," he went on, with the first hint of his usual good humor in his voice. "Whatever we have to do, whatever the demons and memories. I see you as my future. I want to be yours. You do know I'm in love with you, don't you?"

He watched her face, taking it in. "Not good news?"

She straightened her chair. "I'm sorry, Jacob. It's confusing." She appeared to be seriously uncomfortable, her hands moving aimlessly before settling in her lap. Her words, when she spoke, came out fragmented, as if she struggled for each one. But she wasn't running. "I can't separate what might be … love, and what's … desire."

Her hesitation over those words. Love, desire. The intricacies of intimacy. She's admitted she wants you, in a roundabout way.

So he chuckled. "Isn't it the truth. The desire part's overwhelming sometimes, it's a force field with a mind of its own." He grew serious. "It's kind of a relief to admit I'm not infallible. I've had to put myself in this image, to keep it together for Norah, but there's other stuff underneath. I want to trust again, and love again. You, by preference."

Amanda frowned, and followed this with what to him was a complete non sequitur. "There must be dozens of women better suited to you. I've never been particularly nurturing, or intuitive about what people are feeling."

He smiled at her and dragged up some of the old mischief. "What an image, women lining up, wanting to get their hands on me." She raised her eyebrows. "Every guy's dream?"

"Oh. I guess. But what I meant—"

He sobered in a hurry. "You're afraid of this, so I can guess something's spooked you. Let's not go there tonight, okay? All I ask, if I have any right to ask, is that we try. Baby steps, whatever it takes."

"I'm not sure, Jacob. It isn't fair to you to let you think something that isn't true. It's as if I'm two people. Logically it's so clear—"

"And I come along and mess it up. You and me—I don't see a lot that's logical. That doesn't make it less right. Here, give me that." Abruptly he stood and snatched the remains of her pizza slice from her plate. "We're inching closer, and I'd say we deserve more than cold pizza. We deserve *hot* pizza." He put their two partially eaten slices back in the oven and brought over the box with hot ones.

"I think I'd like to be friends." She looked up at him as he maneuvered a pizza slice onto her plate.

"I said that, didn't I? Friends for now, we can do that. If that's the most it can be."

She smiled at him. A genuine smile. Jacob felt warm inside for the first time in hours.

Then she dropped a handful of carrots on his plate. "A deal's a deal."

Their eyes held for an instant before he laughed, relief bubbling up in him. She'd seen through his shell to the real, the vulnerable man inside, and she hadn't bolted. He might not have penetrated the mystery of Amanda Sinclair yet, but he had hope that he would one day. Now, Amanda was joking with him about pizza and carrots.

"For you, anything." A yawn followed the laugh. He sat back down and popped a carrot into his mouth.

When he left an hour later, he brushed her cheek with his lips. It wasn't much, as kisses go, but it was all he could manage, and all she was ready for.

Chapter 25

Of course it wasn't over that easily.

After leaving Amanda's, he spent Saturday night at the hospital, on a cot in Norah's room. Sunday he did his best with an irritable and uncomfortable six-year-old. She drove him nuts, alternately demanding and whining. She'd captivated the nursing staff though, so she got some spoiling and extra desserts with her meals.

When he was able to get away while she napped, he threw himself into preparations. He changed her sheets and set up her stuffed animals to be a welcoming committee. He found movies for her to watch, pulled out a new coloring book he'd been saving for emergencies, and made a quick stop at the grocery. At the hospital pharmacy he filled prescriptions for antibiotics and painkillers. He accepted the information they pressed on him about Norah's care, wondering when and how he'd find the mental focus to absorb it all.

Late afternoon Sunday they released her to go home.

Once Norah had settled for the night, he sent emails scattershot to SI, letting them know he wouldn't be there Monday, then started phoning around to arrange for sitters for the next few days, until she returned to school.

At nine o'clock, he stopped. He'd barely eaten, and his body rebelled. He found a leftover in the fridge, and ate it cold, standing at the kitchen counter.

At nine thirty he phoned Dave. After outlining what had happened, and Norah's impossible mood, he said, "I'm glad she's asleep now and looking so angelic. It might be the only thing standing between me and murdering her."

"Ain't love grand? Brings out these higher instincts."

"I feel rotten, Dave."

"You're thinking yourself into it. With your brain power, I expect you can think yourself out of it."

"Fat lot of help you're being."

"My kids are older than Norah, so I've had experience. We parents were born to suffer every calamity they get themselves into, then the little monsters pull through and go merrily on their way and never have a clue what they've put us through. It's ever thus, pal."

"It sucks."

"Yup."

At ten o'clock he went to his home gym and pushed the weights around for half an hour. He felt marginally better.

At eleven o'clock, exhausted and plagued by chaotic thoughts, he reached the ragged end of the day. He dropped into his bed and completely failed to sleep. His mind spun, thinking about his little girl, the extra challenges while her arm healed, and where he'd find the energy to deal with it.

Grow up, McKinnon. He got up and made tea.

And that brought Amanda into his mind, front and center.

She'd asked for Earl Grey, so he'd bought some. In his expert opinion, it was horrible. Maybe women liked tea that tasted like flowers, but as far as he was concerned, they could have it. Tonight, he'd go for no-name grocery tea. Caffeinated. Since he wasn't going to sleep anyway, who cared?

Amanda. He'd kept the thought of her at bay all day. Now she was so real she might have been in the room with him.

She thought other women out there would suit him better and were no doubt dying to get him in their clutches. Well, he knew from experience over the last couple of years there probably were one or two. Sexy women. Norah-loving women. Uncomplicated women. None of them the right woman.

Perhaps it's the challenge.

Perhaps it's pheromones or something.

He and Deb had never questioned where their love had come from. It simply was what it was. Debbie hadn't had Amanda's extra layer of complexity. Or possibly he saw things differently now that he was forty-two, not twenty-nine. If Deb hadn't been killed, they'd have continued on their straightforward way through life, raising Norah, growing old together. For most of the last two and a half years he'd railed against the fate that had snatched that possibility away.

He glanced at the clock in the kitchen. One thirty. Jacob heaved himself from his chair, yawned — a promising sign — and once again wandered off to bed.

Chapter 26

Jacob was driving, his SUV being more suited to the roads following a light February snowfall the night before. He'd returned to work, leaving Norah to be spoiled by Mrs. Franklin, her favorite of the roster of sitters. He and Amanda had an appointment to view a warehouse recently on the market. They'd be rendezvousing with Charlie, Marcia, and the real estate agent.

Calling themselves friends had relieved something in Amanda, he mused. Given her some breathing room.

He had the feeling SI had breathed a collective sigh of relief as well.

Speaking for himself, his life felt a runaway train. Never in his wildest dreams had he seriously expected to find himself driving out the highway with this alluring woman beside him, as if it were the most natural thing in the world. At the moment she relaxed beside him, even if focused on business.

"Would you fill me in on the specs of this place? I didn't have time to review before we left."

Amanda read off statistics from the real estate listing. Because their warehouse was also their head office, they had to assess it for business, as well as warehousing, functionality.

They were chatting comfortably about what they might want and expect from this viewing when Amanda went quiet. He glanced at her, sensing a change in the atmosphere. She'd drawn in on herself. A couple hundred yards along, he got the clue he needed. They'd been passing a new development, advertised in prominent signage at each entrance.

A Brandon Caine development.

He checked the clock on the dashboard, then pulled to the side of the road, safely out of the line of traffic. He was breaking their unwritten rule about how they'd behave around each other at the office, but in his mind some crises outweighed the rules. He shoved the car into Park and turned to her. "Amanda," he said quietly, "I think you'd better tell me."

"Oh." She came back to the present. "I'm sorry. It's nothing. Why did you stop?"

"No, it's not nothing. Something's upset you, and I think it's the sign back there. The one with Brandon Caine's picture."

"Oh, that. I knew him once—it was a long time ago. Let's go on."

Fair enough, this wouldn't be the best time or place to encourage her to talk about Caine. She had a business meeting to attend, and she needed to be on top of her game. Still, perhaps it was time he told her.

"Since it's right in front of us, you may as well know that I've heard he was a part of your life once." He put the car in gear, checked the traffic, and pulled onto the highway. "Come over this evening. Talk to me."

"I don't have anything to say."

"In that case, come over for supper and visit with Norah. She's been asking about you, how she saw you at the hospital on Saturday and hasn't seen you since. I'll make spaghetti."

"Honest? From scratch?"

"You know me better than that. You can buy bottles full of sauce. Just add pasta."

"Even I can do better than that. Italian sausage, mushrooms, green peppers."

"And watch the child of your heart pick out every vegetable and stack them neatly on the side of her plate. Come eat with us. I'll add the mushrooms and you can be a good influence."

"As long as we're clear that I don't want to talk about Brandon."

"We're clear."

As they drove the rest of the way, they might have continued to discuss what they hoped to find at the warehouse, or joked about spaghetti, but instead they were silent. His thoughts had no place in their work relationship. He suspected it was the same for her.

* * *

Amanda enjoyed their casual supper. The spaghetti was a qualified success. Norah had indeed eaten a single bite involving a mushroom, then had watched Amanda take the ones she'd picked out and add them to her own plate. Once cut up and armed with a spoon, the meal was easy for a child to eat with one hand. Jacob had been right, Norah was delighted to see her.

Norah had some latitude around bedtimes since she wouldn't be back in school until next week. Amanda rinsed and stacked the plates while Jacob settled her in the living room with a DVD. "Wash or dry?" he asked when he returned.

"Dry, please. I need gloves to wash. I sometimes get a rash."

"Dry it is." He pulled a fresh dishtowel out of a drawer and handed it to her, then ran hot water into the sink. "And while we clean up, we can somehow not talk about Brandon Caine."

Her temper flared. "You're bullying me. I told you I don't have anything to say."

"I've known for a while that you were involved with him, but what happened—"

"It doesn't concern you, Jacob." It was no use; curiosity got the better of her. "How did you hear about Brandon? And me?" She kept her hands busy, drying the plates and glasses he passed to her. Something new to grapple with, the idea that Jacob had heard about Brandon.

"Turns out you know, not well I don't think, a good friend of mine, Dave Carter. He owns the U-Brew downtown."

She stopped drying. "And they say women are gossips."

"Men don't deny it, when we're cornered. Were you together long?" At her glare, he added, "I've told you a fair amount about my history. I know next to nothing about you. He was in your past, and my impression is that it didn't end well. I'm not asking for a play-by-play."

Amanda felt her temper settling. He'd been up front with her, true. She sifted what she might say, to meet his openness with something of her own.

"The sign, it reminded me. Of why I won't risk involvement."

Jacob's eyes stayed focused on the dishes in the soapy water. "After the hospital, you can't claim we're not involved. What we are is frozen at this point where we can't move forward or back."

She studied him for a moment. A man, talking to her while he washed dishes, untainted by the memory of Brandon.

No alarm bells. No fear.

She started speaking, watching her hands rub the towel over the plates.

"It lasted almost two years and didn't end well. I packed up the things I'd taken to his house and changed the locks on my own. He was furious. Image mattered to Brandon, and I met his requirements there. Young entrepreneurs, attractive people. We made a great couple, on the surface. But he had expectations I didn't live up to. He made sure I knew it." The bitterness crept in beneath her calm recital; she felt it but couldn't suppress it. "He didn't want me to be a person. He wanted an appendage. I had to fight, constantly, to hold onto myself."

"How long ago?"

"Five years."

"He's the reason you keep me at arm's length." Jacob's voice gave nothing away.

"The worst was, he tried to get his hands on SI. He'd never have been able to actually own it since it's locked up in my family, but he did his best to control how I managed it. We hit a rough patch about then. He used that. He wanted me to make him managing director." She gave a humorless laugh. "The daughter of the owner to add eye candy or something. I'd be the figurehead while he made the decisions. He tried to convince me I wasn't competent, Jacob." Her voice dropped to a whisper. "He almost succeeded."

"Bastard." Oddly, the venom in his voice comforted her. When Brandon had used that tone, she'd been terrified.

"He said horrible things. It's so obvious, once you're out of it. When you're in the middle it's not so straightforward."

"You saw through him and got out. It seems logical to me. And incredibly brave."

It hadn't been logical. It had been a morass of confusion, fear, and determination, but she wasn't willing to talk about it. Not yet. "I guess so, yes."

He stared into the darkness out the window over the sink, unsmiling. "So you wonder, if we become lovers, if I trust this man enough to open my heart to him, will he do the same thing? Will he try to influence me or take over my company? And nothing I can say or do can convince you otherwise, especially since I already play a major role with the finances."

He went back to washing. "I understand now. I thought SI was my competition, but it's not. It's the fear that I might use you to get control of SI. I don't guess there'd be any way to hurt you more."

"Probably not."

"And I don't know how to fight it. How to convince you that I have no interest whatsoever in running your company. Or controlling you, for that matter. I love your independence, your competence. I guess it's something you need to see for yourself, but I'd hoped you'd know me well enough by now to know that."

"I'm sorry." She stacked the last plate and made a self-deprecating sound. "Trusting—it's not that simple."

Jacob washed the pasta pot. His voice was matter-of-fact. "I'm stronger than I look. I'll kick his ass into Missouri if you want me to."

She turned from him and hung the wet towel on the stove handle. Turning back, she said, "Remember what you said about ghosts? He's a ghost, so you can't kick him anywhere."

"It'd be worth a try, if it meant he'd stop haunting you."

"I'm sick of it," she burst out, surprising herself. "He's still in there and I want him out. I've tried, Jacob. I've honestly tried."

Jacob wrung out the dishrag and draped it over the faucet, keeping his eyes on his hands. "I'd sell significant body parts to hold you right now."

She touched his arm, then vanished into the living room with Norah and the video.

Later, when she prepared to leave, he said, "On the bright side, we've gone a day without talking about the stolen money." He bent down and gave her a gentle kiss. The kind it was easy to walk away from, if she chose to, except for the look that went with it. "Sleep well," he said, and kissed her again, on the corner of her mouth. "Your company's safe from me."

Chapter 27

A fresh layer of snow on the lawns shone in the sun. Despite facing another meeting about Shirai Distributors, the scene delighted Amanda as she drove to Jacob's house the next Saturday morning. Her mood was buoyant, and not only because of the crisp winter day. The figures were in, and they'd had an excellent Christmas season, even better than she'd thought.

And Jacob knows about Brandon. He'd given her his support, in his own way. She'd developed this weird image in her mind of Brandon, butt naked, flying over the Mississippi with a boot print on his ass. Yes, she liked that. She caught herself grinning.

Jacob's house had a comfortable, lived-in feeling, and its owner had a comfortable, lived-in feeling, too. Being with Jacob was like wearing her favorite old clothes and curling up by a fire with hot chocolate. At least until he got mad. Then he turned into some kind of alpha male and made his presence felt. But even that one time, he hadn't scared her. Shocked her, yes, but she hadn't been afraid of him.

Not like you were afraid of Brandon.

And the Jolt was alive and kicking. She hadn't been able to get her little collection of his kisses out of her mind. She could, and did, replay them one by one. Tasted their different intensities, explored their intents. Correlated them with the Jolt, its strength, where it had affected her. The Jolt always lay in wait to ambush her, and when it did, the only stability was to cling to Jacob. It had taken her a while to figure that one out.

He was right. Obviously it isn't over at all.

Jacob opened the door before she had a chance to ring the bell. He smiled when he saw her. "You look cheerful. Hurry in, it's cold out here." He stepped out of the way. His hand brushed her shoulder, then her back, as he hustled her indoors. "What's going on? Why are you so happy?"

"Nothing really. I like this. It's fresh and clean outside. It reminds me of candy apples and cocoa. Snowmen."

"Ice skating, snowball fights. I know what you mean. Here, I'll take that." He hung her coat in the entry closet while she took off her boots. "I've got facts and figures for you. One more piece of the puzzle, and confirmation of what we already knew. This guy's good. Without dumb luck I don't see how anyone would have found it, other than a forensic accountant."

On his desk was a bunch of carnations in mixed colors in a vase. "How lovely." She brushed a hand over them, then stuck her nose in them. "I love the scent."

"Good. They're for you."

She frowned, puzzled. "Why?"

In reply he claimed her hand and kissed it. "Valentine's Day?"

"Is it?"

Jacob shook his head. "We have to get you a life, love."

They worked at his desk. She followed as he walked her through the financial and inventory archives of Sinclair Imports. But she also found herself achingly aware of the tidy appearance he made in jeans and that blue and gray sweater, the way the skin around his eyes crinkled when he focused on the screen, the way his brows drew together as he led her down the tracks of his investigation.

Her eyes wandered to the flowers occasionally. Once she caught him smiling a little, and he nodded to her, a *let go, be happy* nod.

Once, their eyes met. Up close, his were brown with flecks of green and gold. Breaking that eye lock had been hard.

Awareness of him threatened to mess up her concentration.

Jacob had been watching her, too. She was sure he knew the toll the missing money took on her. More than the numbers, it was the 'why' and the 'who' behind them. The betrayal to herself and her father.

"So that's it," Jacob said, drawing her wandering thoughts back to the hard facts. "Simple on the surface, but masterful, the way it's been buried. And the kicker's this." He tapped a transaction with the end of his pen. "New news. He paid it back. More intricacies, to make sure the two transactions match, but won't be obvious to casual scrutiny. He's not leaving himself or you hung out to dry. Speaking of which ..." He paused.

"What is it?"

"I've been mulling this over. If you want me to, I'll stay at SI until this is sorted out. That's one disruption you don't need."

Since they hadn't been able to find a replacement, it hadn't been on top of her mind, but the thought of his resignation had niggled at her, until finally she'd had to admit to herself how little she wanted it to happen. Knowing he'd be around, she puffed a breath of relief. "Thank you."

By then it was lunchtime, and Jacob didn't ask, he simply set her a place at the table and fixed her a grilled cheese sandwich with a pickle. She enjoyed chatting with Norah over lunch, even if Norah's father was uncharacteristically quiet, lost in his own thoughts.

The meal finished and the plates in the sink, Jacob said, "Let's go to Creekside Park. We still need to figure some things out, but we don't have to sit in a dark office to do it. And Norah's got enough pent-up energy to climb the curtains."

Amanda looked out the window at the storybook winter day and surprised herself by agreeing. Half an hour later they were in the parking lot at the end of the Creekside Walk. After Jacob squatted to explain the ground rules to Norah, they set off along the mile-long walkway.

Amanda breathed deeply and lifted her face to the sun. "Oh, I needed this. Thanks for the idea. I feel better, getting out in the fresh air."

"Me, too." He took her hand, and the Jolt snaked its way up her arm, dampened somewhat by their gloves.

She glanced at him. "Do you have any ideas about how to handle this, down the road?"

She meant the Shirai Distributors mess, but belatedly realized she might have been speaking about their joined hands. Fortunately, he picked up on her intent.

"That's your decision, but I'm happy to talk it out with you if you want me to. The refund check confuses me. Whoever did this wasn't in it for the money. Less than three months? I don't get it."

"Or that Stan could be involved. I know what it looks like, but it doesn't make sense in my mind. He taught me so much. He and my dad are old friends. I don't see how it's possible."

The sun on the snow was blinding; she heard the ice on the creek crackling in the warmth.

His eyes tracked Norah as she ran along the path then back to them, ignoring the cast on her arm. "I don't have the answers for you. We have some facts. And there's something I'd like you to think about."

"What's that?"

"How much of your financial exposure is concentrated in the hands of one person."

"Always back to Stan."

"I didn't mean personally. But whoever controls the reins in the Accounting department."

"I hate this." Hated talking about a nasty issue that transcended business to become personal, when this moment offered sun, snow, a perfect winter day.

A day with a man you want.

The thought she'd avoided for months. From the first Jolt to Christmas Eve. Telling him about Brandon. Until now she'd never told a soul, other than Pat and the counselor Pat had sent her to once it was finally over.

He squeezed her hand. "What I want you to think about—" He broke off and called, "Norah! Slow down!"

The little girl ran back toward them while Amanda thought.

Friends. Surely we can hold onto being friends?

When Norah had once again taken off along the path, he spoke. "I was hired to be a part-time supplement to Stan, and on contract, not regular staff. You need a more permanent presence. SI's like a family, but that's risky for you, and it's like an open door for anyone thinking of taking from your company, because who's going to be suspicious of a family member?"

"Oh. You still plan to leave? But I thought you said …"

"Not until this is over. Don't worry about it."

"But …"

"Look at it this way. If I have years of walks with you ahead, I might prefer not to be your employee. If I don't have those years, well, we already know how awkward that is."

"I see." She saw, but the thought took her one step past her comfort level, personally or professionally. So she returned to the immediate. "I want this over, Jacob. This whole mess with Stan. I hate what's happened."

"There's steel in your voice. I'd like to ask you a question, but don't answer if it's too personal. Were you so driven before that realtor got his hooks into you?"

Amanda sighed. "Yes. Maybe less rigid. There's so much riding on my not messing up. That's why this whole business about Stan has to be resolved. Soon."

"All this talk about control—that's what we're talking about, isn't it? Control, so failure won't happen, so nothing can go wrong. Except it doesn't work that way. We all mess up from time to time."

He pulled them to a stop, moving to the side of the path. His eyes constantly tracked Norah, even while he spoke only to her. "I'll tell you a story. From when I'd just turned twenty-one. I was making the grades, setting myself up for a glorious career. Parents so proud of me, the whole bit. Until one lovely autumn day in my senior year I was busted for marijuana possession."

"You?" She stared at him, shocked.

His face was grim for a moment before he recovered and threw her a self-deprecating grin. "Yeah, me. Mister clean-cut nice guy. I was guilty as hell, Amanda. It's a miracle I wasn't charged with trafficking. Bottom line was, my folks found a top-notch lawyer, and I got off, no record. It took years to pay back my parents for the lawyer's fees, and I lost a year of school. More than that, it cost me enough shame and humiliation to last a lifetime. So don't think I've never thoroughly fucked up. I have. I know what it's like to fail, big time."

She looked down. "I don't know what to say." His story didn't mesh with the man she knew, nor did his words. He hardly ever used coarse language. She took it as a mark of how deeply his story had affected him.

"Well, you might be shocked and horrified that you're consorting with a covert law-breaker." He sobered. "Just because I got off doesn't mean I didn't do it. I keep that little fact in mind when I'm tempted to get cocky. Or when I fall flat on my face. Failure's the pits, but it happens. I learned from it. In a way, I'm not sorry it happened. Easy to say after more than twenty years," he added. "Nothing was easy back then."

He started them walking again. "Have to keep moving when you've got my daughter with you, or you'll be left in her dust." His eyes constantly scanned the trail ahead, keeping Norah in sight.

They walked a few minutes in silence. Their joined hands did something warm and tingly to her nerve endings. Had she ever, in her life, held hands like this?

He squeezed her fingers again. "I think," he began tentatively, "when two people find themselves where we are, what needs to happen is, where their lives intersect they both give up some control. Because they trust each other. Because they're building something between them."

When she didn't answer, he tightened his grip on her hand. "This isn't easy for me, either, you know. I wasn't kidding when I told you I'm in love with you. Had you forgotten?"

No, she hadn't forgotten. She probably never would.

They walked silently. Amanda was aware of the strength of his hand in hers, anchoring her in the perfect winter day.

After a minute he pulled them to a stop and turned to her. "I'm a simple guy. For me, it doesn't get any better than this. This day, Norah and you."

Her thoughts flashed to her parents, her uncomplicated, secure childhood. She glanced at him, then down the trail, but felt his hazel gaze on her. "I'm talking about a lifetime, Amanda. A lifetime of walking along Calter Creek together." He grinned. "Plus, my thoughts about you are liable to cause an early and very steamy summer, any moment now."

Ahead of them, Norah had stopped and seemed to be building a baby snowman with her good arm. "If anyone can do it, she can," Jacob commented.

He went to work on their gloves, shoving his own into pockets, then peeling hers off, thoughtfully, one finger at a time. He brushed her knuckles with his mouth. "Stop me any time."

He turned her hand over, kissed her palm. She shivered. He did it again, then grinned. "We're shelving the whole discussion of what we are to each other for a minute. Look around. See anyone you know?"

"I ... no, but Jacob—"

"Good." He methodically unbuttoned her coat.

"What are you doing?" Her voice held an edge of confusion.

"Expediency. I like to be efficient." He unzipped his own coat, then pulled her in to him. His mouth was on hers, his arms inside her coat, before she got another word out, before she even had time to think, to absorb the effect he'd already had on her, shooting from her palm into deep, deep places. His kiss was quiet, not demanding, a public kiss.

Not enough, her traitor mind said, and afterwards she didn't remember how it started. She fused to his mouth, which parted hers, giving her no options. His tongue experimented with her lower lip, then deeper, while his hands drew her more tightly against him, his body hard against her. Her own hands shoved his coat out of the way, desperate to feel the leanness of him in the blue sweater.

He ended the kiss and held her a little apart from him, puffing out a giant breath. "For the record, it's not only the attraction thing, but right now that's playing a very large part." He let her go and turned away, facing the creek. "Oh, boy."

She struggled to find her voice, but it was a lost cause.

"I need to concentrate on glaciers." He glanced down the trail, toward Norah. "Quickly. Baseball statistics. Should've worn a longer coat." He scooped up a handful of snow and rubbed his face in it. "The things we men do to avoid public embarrassment," he said from behind his hands. His shoulders shook; she realized he was laughing while she stood watching him, stunned.

He turned to her, discarding the snow but still caught in the laughter. "Sorry about that. It's been a long drought. But that's partly why I'm not giving up. And the friendship, and the magic."

She couldn't come up with a single sensible thing to say, so she shrugged and made a helpless gesture with her hands. Standing on the Calter Creek trail next to him, the sun warm on her head, she was a stranger to herself, delighting in the aftermath of the near total obliteration of her senses.

Norah ran up to them. "Daddy, you kissed Amanda."

"I sure did. I liked it." Jacob smiled at his daughter, and Amanda felt her face burn hot enough to melt the snow for several feet around.

"Neat," Norah said, then she raced away again.

I liked it, too, Amanda thought. But right out in public?

She couldn't have stopped it. Part of her was grateful. Most of her, actually, because she suddenly felt giddily, overwhelmingly happy.

"Reaction?" he said. He buttoned her coat back up and took her hand. They moved along the trail.

She took a breath. "I've never done anything like that."

"Lusty guy, beautiful woman, romantic setting? Ringing any bells?"

"Don't grin like that."

He pulled her closer, tucking her arm under his. "Walk with me, Amanda. We'll sort it out."

They'd ambled to the end of the gravel path and turned around before either of them spoke again. He looked at her occasionally, and once she gave him a shaky smile. Control was back within her grasp, so out of habit she seized it. She was coming down from the sheer giddiness his kiss had spawned in her, and the implications were starting to pile up.

"A lot to work through?" he asked.

"I guess so."

"We're in this together, so we both really have to deal with the trust issue." At her frown he shrugged. "You must know you've hurt me. I need to learn to trust as much as you do."

Of course you've hurt him.

She'd reframed it, making it for his own good. Making it something minor, something easy to walk away from. "I never meant to."

"Here's what I don't think you've seen yet. We have a long way to go, but you're not alone. We'll get through it together."

That stopped her, literally. She stood anchored on the trail while his words sank in. The one thing she'd never considered was that she might not have to face her demons alone.

But how was she supposed to think straight with Jacob right next to her, his eyes on her, and the memory of being in his arms—in public—still floating through her mind and body?

A kiss. It was just a kiss. She'd never known kisses could hold so many messages.

He turned his grin on her. "Until you catch up with me, we'll be friends and have fun together, and I'll kiss you and touch you, and I'll back off, God help me. I want you to believe in me. In this."

He paused. When she didn't answer he said, "Speaking of friends, Norah's got this thing going on at school, like the little girls are forming cliques. Her best friend's blowing hot and cold on her. Any female insights on that one?"

Normality.

"I remember those days. I was the skinny, geeky one."

"So was I, actually. She's the born leader, but she feels threatened. Should I talk to her teacher?"

And sooner than seemed possible, they'd arrived at the parking lot. They drove back to his place, where she gathered her work papers and the carnations in a plastic bag, and left them.

She'd spent five hours with this man. He pecked her cheek when she left. She felt gypped.

* * *

Jacob ran a bath while Norah chose her pajamas and selected the stuffed animals to cuddle with her that night. "Come on, Honey Bun," he called.

"You have so many silly names for me," she said. "Bubbles?"

"Lots. Give them a chance."

Norah kicked out of her jeans and sweatshirt, let Jacob wrap a plastic covering around the cast, and climbed into the tub.

Soon she won't want you in here with her for bath time. She's growing up so fast.

"Is it hair washing night?"

"Not tonight. Did you have fun today?" He skated around the kiss she'd witnessed. He wanted to know what she thought, but he had to treat it like it wasn't a big deal.

Norah gave a massive yawn; their walk had done its work. "I like doing stuff with Amanda."

Whew.

"So you like Amanda?" he asked cautiously.

"Um hmm. Pat's fun, too. Amanda's quiet. You don't kiss Pat."

"No, I don't." When Norah didn't add anything, he went on, putting up the safety shield around his daughter. "But you know, Sweetie, Amanda's busy. She may not be able to spend much time doing stuff with us."

Norah yawned again before she spoke. "Daddy, I think she needs us."

What? Did little girls really see so much more clearly than adult men?

Best not to respond to that insight. Jacob switched them back to normal. "Let's get you all sweet and clean and cozy for bed, shall we? It's been a long day, and you are one sleepy kid."

* * *

Not alone.

Through far too much of the night, Amanda thought about the carnations on her kitchen table, and the fact she'd forgotten about Valentine's Day. She thought about how they'd been able to switch so easily from the hard realities of SI's accounting, to that kiss, to a relaxed afternoon walk full of so much to say to each other. Even if not all of it was said.

Why did the whole thing have to be so impossible? Was it impossible?

Why did being with Jacob have to feel so good?

Could she risk letting someone, anyone, get close enough that he could threaten her control over her company? She'd tried once, and what a disaster that had been. But Jacob wasn't a threat. Could she truly, deeply believe that?

Not alone.

She sighed, pummeled her pillow, and resumed her battle with sleep.

Chapter 28

Amanda sank into a chair at one of the large tables that filled the art room, already suffering from a serious lack of enthusiasm. The end-of-class exhibit of their drawings was a minor interlude, given everything else going on in her life. Changes at SI, theft from her company, Jacob …

Jacob.

She was rudderless, with no North Star to steer by, whatever the outward appearance.

It had been just over two weeks since Norah broke her arm and she broke every life rule she had by rushing to Jacob. Two weeks, and her life was topsy-turvy. He knew about Brandon, she knew about his marijuana bust. He'd shown her the picture of Deb, and virtually denied Deb's place in his life—and thought she hadn't seen the cost to him to do it. He'd kissed her on the Calter Creek Trail, in front of Norah and a handful of strangers, and she'd loved it.

Amanda hadn't managed to get a firm grip on the new direction her life had taken, though she was aware of the lens that brought it all into focus.

Jacob.

Was it any wonder she was reeling?

She snapped herself back to attention. The art room bustled around her. She had to admit most of the pictures the art class had produced were interesting, even good. Their teacher kept a stack of frames for this purpose, so they'd all been buzzing around, slotting their pictures into the frames, dithering over where to hang them.

She was pleased with her own picture. She'd found the original in a magazine and followed the mechanical steps the teacher had outlined, which involved a black-and-white photocopy and a grid. Their teacher had given them each a sheet of high quality drawing paper and told them to go for it. Hers was a mountain scene with a river. Its creation had occupied several empty evenings when otherwise she might have been dwelling on the money, or Jacob.

Jacob. Always back to Jacob.

Pat had chosen an old photo of a dog she'd had as a kid. Side by side, you'd never guess they'd attended the same class. Despite the technique, it was evident the pictures were by different aspiring artists.

Mostly, she was glad March had come, and with it the end of the art class. But maybe she would be grateful for the minimal skills she'd picked up, sometime in the future.

She hadn't had a great day.

Jacob hadn't uncovered anything new about the theft, but that wasn't necessarily good news. She longed to talk to her father, but it was like a childhood wish that he'd make it all go away. Rather than practical help, she was more likely to get rage at any suggestion Stan could be involved. Besides, she ran things now. Her father had a hard enough time dealing with that. If she started taking problems to him, their already uneasy relationship would become even more confused.

Customs had held up yet another shipment. Legal Robert was all over it, but it wasn't resolved yet.

Two men had resigned, both from the Floor. She'd be meeting with Marcia tomorrow to review the exit interviews. She prayed it was coincidence, and not a systemic problem.

Another day at Sinclair Imports.

Pat was across the room, laughing with the others. Amanda knew she should make more of an effort. This was supposed to be a celebration, after all. The whole point of hanging the pictures was so that first the class, then family and friends, could come in to see what masterpieces they'd created. But tonight she didn't have it in her.

Pat flopped in the chair next to hers. "Let me guess. You didn't invite your parents. Or Mel or anyone else from SI. Or Jacob and Norah. Right?"

"Call it a crisis of confidence."

"You could show off your picture anywhere. I hope you're going to get it framed properly."

Amanda nodded. "I might. I like it. That doesn't mean I want to show off."

"You look tired. Things not going well?"

Amanda gave her friend a smile. "Assorted crises at SI, all at once. And nothing I can do about any of it right now. This thing tonight should be fun. A positive triumph, to have survived the class. I can't seem to work up the energy."

Pat leaned in closer, frowning. "Rages? Headaches?"

"No, thank God. I hope I've left that person behind."

"The money thing? Do you want to talk it through? We could go someplace quieter after this shindig."

Amanda shook her head. "I'm drained."

Pat's eyes probed. "Jacob?"

"He's got my back. And he's given me all the facts and figures I need, for when it finally hits the fan."

"When you're ready, we'll talk. You know I'm here."

"I do. Thanks."

"Hey, I've got a present for you." Pat rooted around in her oversized bag and pulled out a flat, giftwrapped parcel. "Open it. Might cheer you up."

Amanda perked up a bit. "Thanks for whatever." Her fingers slit the tape and peeled back the paper. She laughed out loud.

Pat had created an eight by ten pencil drawing of the pile of chairs they'd tackled on their first lesson. Not quite balanced on top she'd collaged a martini glass, with olive, in full color. She'd had the picture framed in an olive green frame. "If at first you don't succeed."

"Pat, this is fantastic. How'd you do it?"

"Easy. I took a picture of the pile with my phone before it got deconstructed. Then I cheated and traced and photocopied.

There's no question I've got too much time on my hands. I wanted you to have it as a souvenir of the wonderful time we've had."

"The whole class deserves to see this. You've taken our innate artistry to a whole new level." Amanda rose and hung Pat's picture from one of the hooks.

Things loosened; she had her bearings again. The world seemed more familiar, more stable. Funny how a pile of chairs and a martini glass could lighten up her world.

Chapter 29

Amanda stood in the door to Jacob's kitchen. He'd set the table with a light blue tablecloth, dark blue napkins, shining cutlery and wine glasses. In the middle he'd put a crystal vase full of white and yellow Peruvian lilies, flanked by brown candles in polished silver holders. With his brown plates, the overall effect was stunning.

"Impressive," she said. "What's the occasion?"

What they had now wasn't quite friendship. It wasn't quite more than that, either. She accepted that he was perfectly capable of kissing her into a quivering mess, ripe and swollen and desperate for more. And that she was perfectly incapable of stopping him. She was uncomfortably aware that whatever the nature of his kisses, every time—*every single time*—he'd been the one to pull away, not her.

This is keeping control?

She had a good idea of why he pulled away first, and it had a lot to do with control, at least physically. She was well aware of what she was putting him through. The thought gave her a tight, sort of tickly sensation starting around her stomach and working south—like right now. She ignored it.

But in the meantime, they spent time together, and she felt safe. He still turned up for afternoon coffee, and he still touched her hand. In the two weeks since the walk along Calter Creek, they'd gone to a movie and cuddled, a first for her. One Saturday she'd run into him with Norah at Monroe's Bookstore in downtown Calter Creek, and they'd gone for burgers at Joe's Café. Otherwise, she'd seen him only at work, and she worked hard to convince herself that was enough.

He'd never once suggested they take it further, even if he did make it clear, constantly, in the subtle signals in his face, his posture, that he wanted a whole lot more.

They were relaxed around each other. Their conversation was sometimes bantering, sometimes thoughtful, sometimes intense, but their mutual interest never waned. He wanted her around, and more and more, she wanted to *be* around.

So when she received Jacob's unexpected call inviting her to dinner this Friday night, she'd accepted. She'd put on a teal blue velour top with orange maple leaves appliqued on the front, with black slacks. Her tapestry slippers to keep her feet warm, and no headband to keep her hair under control. She'd shed a lot of tension, and recognized his role in making it happen. Taken all in all, she was happy.

He'd rolled up his long sleeves and his hair was tousled, as if preparing their supper so far had been nerve-wracking. But he seemed cheerful, even a little bit manic. His voice cut through her musings. "Let's say I have a few finer instincts left. You like?" he said, gesturing at the table, then pulling out a chair for her. "Might I pour milady a glass of wine? There's a clever little Chardonnay keeping cool in the fridge."

Amanda giggled. "A *what*?"

"Very clever indeed. With the barest whiff of oak, and finished with hints of cherry and—oh, jeez. I can't keep this up. The man said it was good. Want to try?"

"That's a relief. I was afraid I'd have to believe your nonsense. Yes, please."

Jacob took the wine out of the fridge, uncorked it, and poured. He returned the bottle to the fridge on his way back to the stove. "Dinner in about ten minutes."

"Smells good. Why's the table set for two? Where's Norah?"

"Columbus, visiting her grandparents for the weekend. They've promised to sign her cast. We're having my personal gourmet specialty tonight—chicken cordon bleu, made fresh by the nice people at the deli in the grocery. With mashed potatoes and broccoli, both of which even a helpless male like me can handle."

"She won't be back until Sunday?"

"That's right. It means you and I can have a quiet dinner together and talk about things that don't involve a six-year-old. Like adults." Jacob glanced over. "It's not a planned seduction, so stop worrying. Would you mind lighting the candles? Matches are in the drawer at the end of the counter." He carried the pan of potatoes to the sink and drained them, then went back to the stove to add butter and milk.

Amanda lit the candles. "It doesn't seem to me you plan your seductions. It seems to me they just happen."

Had she said that?

She sat.

He grinned. "You're right. Blame it on you being irresistible. But tonight it's hands off and adult conversation. Cross my heart and hope to die—and I've just injected the first hint of child into our wonderful adult conversation. Sometimes I wonder if I can still talk like an adult. Not surprising, really."

He focused his attention on the potatoes he was mashing, not her. Which didn't stop her from watching him. With his rolled-up sleeves, she was intensely aware of his forearms as he worked. "Norah for day-to-day and milk, and occasionally my friend Dave for male conversation and beer, and we could debate how often that qualifies as adult. That summed up my life until you turned up in it. I amaze myself that I seem to be able to use multi-syllable words, given my usual companions."

"That's not fair. I can't speak for Dave, but Norah's vocabulary is pretty extensive."

"I hope you like the tablecloth. I got it with the napkins yesterday at the home furnishings store in the outlet mall. I thought blue would suit you."

He's buying tablecloths because they'll suit me? "I love this shade of blue."

The timer rang. "Ah, ze broccoli," he said, sketching a little bow in her direction. "Finished with ze hint, shall we say a soupçon, of garlic and parmesan—"

"Soupçon? Stop! You're cracking me up." Amanda laughed and sipped the wine.

"You don't appreciate my sophisticated French? Wait till you taste the cooking. This cookbook I found said the broccoli thing would be good. We'll see. With Norah it's tons of cheddar or she won't touch it. I sometimes wonder if I've lost my taste for finer things. No, I'm sure I haven't, it's just underground. Hang on, we're heading for the plates."

Amanda found herself touched by the image of Jacob, poring over cookbooks. Buying a tablecloth. For her. Had any man done anything like that for her before? Ever?

A couple of minutes later, Jacob had their meal on the table, the kitchen light dimmed but not too much, and the two of them were eating. It *was* good. And Jacob was cheerful, so she was, too.

Then, out of the blue, in the middle of a joke he was telling involving a frog prince, she remembered their pizza together on the day Norah broke her arm, the way he'd absentmindedly brushed a string of cheese from her chin.

Everything fell into place.

She ignored the swarm of butterflies fluttering in her stomach and made a resolution.

Later, with nothing outwardly changed, Jacob cleared their plates, and put an ice cream bombe and the bottle of Chardonnay on the table. "This thing is supposed to be pistachio on the outside and chocolate cake inside. Hope you like pistachio."

"I haven't had pistachio in ages."

"My favorite flavor." He topped up their wine glasses and sat. "To you, Amanda." Jacob reached over and clinked her glass with his.

"To you. Maybe to us both." She didn't give the words any particular inflection, but she heard his intake of breath.

He started to sip his wine, then stopped and put his glass down. "Maybe to us both. May I hold your hand for a minute?" He rested his hand open on the table near her, waiting for her to decide. He kept his gaze soft, without any intensity and with that funny half smile he sometimes assumed when he wasn't sure what would happen. "Tonight it's your call. I'd suggest you go with your gut," he added, "assuming it isn't roiling around from the meal I fed you."

"It was good. You don't need to knock it."

He waited, not moving. She put her hand in his—*like a magnetic force,* she thought. Magnetism shot through her, drawing every cell in her body toward him.

He raised her hand to his mouth. This time he kissed the tip of each finger, one at a time, then rolled her fingers into a fist, wrapped both his hands around it, and gave a squeeze. "Now, in the totally unnatural order of things, I let you go, so I can cut this ice cream thing before it melts." He did so, leaving her feeling vaguely abandoned. "Quarters? This is the smallest they had, but halves would be mighty big, or maybe I'm getting old. Quarters okay?"

"Sure. Fine." She accepted her plate from him and took a bite while he put the leftover in the freezer. "You're right. Pistachio's good." As he came back toward the table their eyes met. And this time, they both knew; she could see it in his face as clearly as she felt it burning through her body.

"I'm sorry, Amanda. I honestly didn't plan this." Instead of returning to his chair he was next to her, reaching for her hands, pulling her up and against him, holding her so she felt the whole length of him. Her hands found his back. "I said it's up to you, but this feels so good," he whispered into her hair. "Can we just stay like this for a minute?"

Not alone.

Every decision from now on was hers to make, triggered by the mood, the meal, her memory of his touch on her chin, the evening with the pizza. Her body was reorganizing itself, as if he were melting her structure into its molten, bubbling essence. She pulled away to look at him. "Have I told you about the Jolt?"

His eyes danced. "No. But I think I've experienced it. The first time our hands touched, at SI's front door."

"The answer is no," she said. "No, you can't just hold me." Her body was behaving oddly, the nerves misfiring, but she got one hand behind his neck. She pulled him down to claim his mouth for her own.

The bombe might never have existed. "I can't fight this," he said, his voice choked, when they came up for air. Then she was drowning, and he was right there with her, in a need that overwhelmed them and drove their mouths, their hands, the movement of their bodies against each other.

He led them staggering into the living room where they collapsed on the sofa, side by side, stunned, turned toward each other and touching, ramping up senses already threatened with overload. His hand was inside her pullover top, smoothing up her side, over her midriff, his fingers exploring over her bra. Breathing became more and more of a challenge

He closed his eyes. "Are you going to go home?" he asked quietly.

Through the haze swallowing her senses she heard the implication, *Are you going to run from this?* She didn't hear any judgment.

"If you're going to leave me, please go now. I'm going out of my mind. This is *way* better than pistachio," he whispered, making her giggle against him, but his voice was shaky. "What you do to me." He freed his hand and showed her; he was trembling. Then his hands were on her again, pulling her tighter against him, resting his head on her curls. She snuggled against his shoulder.

After a minute he repeated, "Are you going home?"

"No."

He'd lost control of his breath; his words came out in short bursts. "Thank you. For staying."

They stayed there together, letting the quiet of the house fall around them. Despite the need crackling through her, she didn't want to move, to shatter the moment. He must have felt the same way because he was still, other than a tremor in his arms. Wrapped in rightness, Jacob's arms meant safety to her. All the fears she'd had, the ways he might dominate her, hurt her, simply weren't happening.

As for what would come next, she had to know. She couldn't not know any longer.

After an eternity in heaven, Jacob pulled back and tipped her face up to his. "You can say no. But — maybe we should get it over with?" he asked quietly. His eyes met hers. "Before my courage fails?"

"I didn't think you were the one short on courage." She couldn't have kept her voice steady if her life depended on it.

He chuckled and rested her head against him again. His breath whispered through her hair, his chest rose and fell under her cheek, his hand smoothed the curls back from her face. "Over a decade since I last made love to a woman for the first time. Talk about anxiety. It's a cross we guys bear. We try to keep it a secret."

She laughed, too. "How can you make me laugh when I'm terrified?" She turned her face into his neck, where she first kissed, then gave a gentle nip. She heard him gasp.

"As long as we both are. Tonight?"

Their eyes met, and his were naked, dark with longing and need. Amanda pulled away from him and touched his face, stroked her fingers over his cheekbone, down to his chin. His body convulsed under her touch. "It's like I've never seen you. Like you've been wearing a mask. It's like—"

Jacob gave her a shaky smile. "Don't we all have masks? The last thing I want tonight is a mask. This is me," he said. "All of it." His smile was gone. Their eyes met and held.

The magnetism was going to turn her inside out if she let it.

She'd let it.

You're caught. You never had a chance.

They fell together again. He pulled her closer, and this wasn't the sort of kiss she could run away from. Amanda felt desperately weak and powerfully strong at the same time, needing to cling to him, needing to feel his body spasm under her touch, the effect her hands and mouth had on him.

She pulled his shirt loose to dig her fingers into his skin, running one hand over his hip and down his thigh, brushing the swelling in his jeans. His hands were everywhere, on her breasts, struggling with the waistband of her slacks. This was the kind of kiss that promised more, that promised all she would let him give her. His mouth broke free from hers and she lost track of where he tasted her, nibbled her. She let him lead, let him take her. It had gone far beyond a conscious decision to trust. Breaking off, the two of them staring at each other, he said in a husky voice she barely recognized, "Tonight."

Somehow they stumbled up the stairs to his bedroom.

* * *

In the morning they threw away the melted ice cream, ate scrambled eggs and fresh tomatoes for breakfast, and made love again, slowly, gently. As if they had all the time in the world. As if the world would stop for them while they explored the wonder they had opened up between them. Much later, still caught in enchantment, they went grocery shopping, and cooked together Saturday night.

Amanda didn't return to her townhome until Sunday afternoon, when Jacob had to go pick up Norah. She thought she'd deal with the work she'd brought home with her. But she didn't. She drifted from room to room, unable to settle, unable to shift her mind to anything but Jacob.

So this is what starstruck means.

Her usual pep talks wouldn't do any good, so she didn't even try. She gave in to the sheer luxury of loving and being loved.

Chapter 30

The next morning Amanda strode into the office, seemingly her usual crisp, efficient self in a gray power suit with white shirt and sensible two-inch heels. To any other observer, she might have pulled it off, but an hour later, she paused at the door connecting their offices when she overheard Mel on the phone, talking in a half whisper.

"What's happening in Accounting?"

Amanda hovered out of sight.

There was a silence, then Mel giggled. "Yeah, I agree, based on Madame this morning. She's out of focus. Cloud nine's pretty much filled up our end of the building. She's trying for all business, but—"

Amanda cleared her throat and entered the outer office with more bustle than usual. Mel just grinned.

* * *

A little later, in the Accounting suite, Jacob stared at his desk and wondered what he was supposed to be doing. No urgent deadlines loomed, although there was no shortage of work waiting. Minor things like income tax filing. But how important was that?

Norah was cheerful after the visit with her grandparents. The sun was shining on the fresh snow; he and Amanda had watched it fall Saturday night, wrapped up in each other. He expected she was in her office now, doing whatever it was she had to do today, and no doubt doing it impeccably.

But for him, concentration wasn't in the cards. He wondered whether more caffeine would ground him or launch him into outer space. "I'm going to the break room," he said. "Anyone want anything?"

"Not for me," Jim replied, while Bev said, "Hang on, I'll walk with you."

Jacob found himself uncharacteristically tongue-tied, so he listened to Bev chat and responded with vague noises about Norah being away for the weekend. "Ah," she said, as if that explained something.

Well, perhaps it did. Two or three people they passed in the corridor sent smiles and knowing glances his way, as if they were in on some private joke. It wasn't possible they *knew*, was it?

He expected he looked spaced-out and goofy. Being head-over-heels did that to you, he'd heard.

And wasn't it inevitable he'd find Mel, with her antennae on the alert, in the break room? She took one look at him and launched a giant smile. Then she gave him a hug and whispered, "Congratulations," in his ear.

Congratulations?

"What is it about this company?" he whispered back. "Can't a guy keep a secret around here?"

Mel glanced at Bev. "With the vibes you're both putting out? Are you kidding?"

Busted. Here's hoping Amanda won't mind.

"So the way it works is, now we start plotting your future together. Wedding, babies … give up on keeping it to yourselves."

Jacob groaned. "Tell me the call Jim got fifteen minutes ago wasn't from you."

Mel smirked at him.

He looked at the two women and shook his head. "I surrender."

Mel did a happy dance. "Want to volunteer a play-by-play?"

"Not on your life." Coffee in hand, he headed for the door. "Work to do, so they say. Worth a stab, anyway."

As he left Mel and Bev put their heads together. He could swear they were giggling.

* * *

By Wednesday, Amanda thought it was time she told Pat. She fired off a text.

"Invite me over?"

Pat texted back. *"Are you okay? Suspicious silence."*

"No crisis. Come on, ask me over."

"Roast chicken?"

"Gravy. Cranberry sauce. See you later."

Amanda had always told Pat everything, and Pat had done the same. She relied on Pat to ground her in this strange new reality. Besides, telling someone would prove, in the best possible way, that she'd purged Brandon Caine from her life. And Pat would be thrilled.

Lots of people would be thrilled. Her parents, the staff at SI … oh, she'd seen the looks, especially from Mel.

Her enthusiasm and energy were at a new high. And the boredom, the frustration, were things of the past. If she was honest with herself, they'd disappeared the day Jacob McKinnon first turned up in the break room.

She got to Pat's on time and called from the door, "I'm here."

"Good, you can help me with supper." Pat came through the living room from the kitchen, drying her hands on a towel. And stopped short. "My God, when did you get so gorgeous?"

"Pat, I'm in love." Amanda threw herself into her friend's arms, and to her own surprise found herself in tears.

"At last." Pat tossed the wet towel onto the bench in the entry and rubbed Amanda's back, then eased them both toward the kitchen and produced a bottle of cabernet sauvignon. "Absolute best thing for newfound love. Helps keep the palpitations at bay."

"Maybe I don't want them at bay." Amanda grabbed at self-possession along with a tissue and blew her nose. "Am I crazy?" She settled at the kitchen table, leaning forward.

"In return for being your ministering angel, I want details. Here, drink up." Pat put a wine glass in front of her. "I still have kitchen tasks to do. You're welcome to take notes, assuming you're about to have more demands on your questionable cooking skills. Tell me what happened."

She'd regained her composure, although in a global sense she suspected she'd be off balance for the foreseeable future. "Let's say thank God for yoga," she joked, earning a snort from Pat.

Then she turned thoughtful. "It was when Norah broke her arm. We were having pizza at my place. He reached over and brushed a string of cheese off my chin. I doubt he even noticed doing it. And I knew. I just wasn't ready to admit it."

Pat nodded and peeled potatoes. "Go on."

"So he threw this dinner for me Friday, I mean he bought a tablecloth and napkins, and candles. Norah was at her grandparents."

At that, Pat turned, her eyebrows up. "Have I mentioned this man's got great moves?"

"And the first thing he said was he swore he wasn't out to seduce me. Like it was a joke between us. Then over dessert it fell apart. I sort of made it fall apart."

Potatoes roasting, Pat joined Amanda at the table. "Mm hmm?"

"He sort of asked permission to hug me for a minute. I heard 'a minute', and I said no, that wasn't enough. And from there … I felt so safe. He was trembling, Pat. It wasn't only me. I didn't feel alone."

Pat's eyes were dancing.

"It was like I was a goddess. I never knew. It's never been like this."

"Isn't it in the Bible somewhere? 'With my body I thee worship'?"

"I don't think it's the Bible. I don't know where it is." Memories swamped her. "All those years of being afraid. He was so gentle. But the things he did … Oh, God, the things he did. The way he touched me. I must have tried him to the limits of his endurance. And then, I've never experienced …" She giggled. "That was Friday night. We missed dessert. The ice cream was melted by the time we found it Saturday morning."

"A sin. No sex is worth ruining the ice cream."

"News bulletin, friend. You're wrong."

Pat laughed and twirled her wine glass. "Mandy, this is beyond wonderful."

"Mel caught on the moment I walked into the office Monday, she saw right through my power suit. Jacob says it was the same in Accounting. People keep giving me these looks wherever I go. I have to get my feet back underneath me. I focus on something, then wham, I'm hit with this, this feeling." She waved her glass a little wildly, punctuating the thought, and giggled again when wine sloshed over the side. "So you're the psychologist. Do I need help? Am I out of my mind?"

Pat had been watching her, elbow on the table, her head propped on her hand, a bemused expression on her face. "No, no help needed, and yes, you are out of your mind. You're into your body and your heart for once. I have a lot of affection, and even more admiration, for Jacob McKinnon. I knew he was worthy. If he's a god in bed, it's no less than I'd expect."

Amanda was calming down. "You're the best friend imaginable. You not only listen to me babble, you feed me, too."

"Aw, shucks." Pat got back to her feet. "It's obvious you're in no state to make gravy, but can you handle chopping cabbage?"

"These days, I can handle anything."

Over supper the conversation was quieter, but no less intense. No matter how hard she tried, her focus stayed fixed on Jacob. "He'll get sick of me. I've become a groupie."

"No, he won't, and no, you're not. You don't recognize what's happening, because it hits most of us at nineteen, not thirty-nine."

"He's stuck in my mind. I'm reviewing a contract or going over the sales projections, and suddenly he's there. My efficiency's shot. I can't even imagine how this will play out."

"And you don't much care. But you've always been good at compartmentalizing—"

"Until he turns up in my office with a report or something. Or comes in for afternoon coffee. Monday we sat there like dunces and grinned at each other."

"Enjoy it. When it's time to think Jacob and hot, crazy sex, think Jacob and hot, crazy sex. Then kick him out and do SI stuff."

"The overlap's a problem. I take your point though. It ought to be possible to separate business from pleasure. But his hands, his mouth, all of him." She groaned. "How do normal adults ever even *think* about anything else?"

"To the extent they do, I'd say practice. Lots of practice. Doesn't always work though. Eat your chicken."

* * *

There was a break in the action; Jacob muted the television and let the basketball analysis go on without them. Dave crunched a pretzel.

"Glad you came over. Norah's wearing me out. She's not sleeping well these nights. I expect the arm's bothering her, or she can't get comfortable with the cast. She's grumpy."

"Much longer?"

"A couple of weeks. It's healing well. I'll be beyond glad when she's okay again, what with exercising her fingers and keeping the cast dry, and doctor's appointments and special treatment at school. At least it's her left arm, so she can write. But no swinging, no getting jostled, no roughhousing."

"Sounds like single parenthood sucks."

Jacob laughed. "Big time. I try to concentrate on other things to help me stay the loving daddy." He took a swallow of his beer, grabbed a handful of the pretzels.

"You need sex, pal."

"Not desperately."

Dave sat up and spoke around a mouthful of pretzel. "Got a question for you. Have you *ever* had sex for the sake of sex? No strings, no long-term?"

"When I was eighteen? Somewhere along the line I grew up. You recommend it?"

"You? Nah. Not in your nature. But if you're going to stay sane, you need something in your life besides Norah and

196

columns of numbers." Dave stuffed another pretzel in his mouth, crunched and swallowed.

Jacob treated himself to a full-body stretch, arching off the chair. "It doesn't follow that I don't already have something in my life."

Dave stared at Jacob, hard. Then he grinned. "You devil."

"Took you long enough. At SI it averaged two seconds per person. Ten minutes for the news to be all over the building."

"You've chosen a rare specimen, but I expect you're in for a steep learning curve."

"I'm anticipating a lifetime's fascination. She's a mystery, so much to learn. Every little scar and freckle. First pizza together, first shower together ..."

Dave treated him to an eye roll. "We guys are better off keeping some things to ourselves. If I went rhapsodic about first pizza, Nancy'd never let me hear the end of it."

"I suppose. It's all good, anyway, with the bonus of balancing out Norah these days."

"You've got this romantic streak a mile wide. Next thing, you'll be booking halls for the reception and shopping for a house—"

"House? What's wrong with this one? Norah's happy here."

Dave shot him a pitying look. "It's Deb's, Jake. No way can you expect Amanda to live here."

"Oh." Jacob scooped up a handful of pretzels, then dropped them back in the bowl as if they'd caught fire. "Uh oh. I guess I'm still sort of zoned out. Nancy's still got you on that diet. I got a lecture on snacks when I phoned. She'd kill me."

"Pretzels are safe. Peanuts, she'd kill you. Go on."

"I never considered the house thing."

"You'll need a clean slate. Bigger, too, with little Sinclair-McKinnons running around, and two home offices instead of one—"

"Hold it!" Jacob waved a pretzel, then, for no particular reason, launched it at Dave, who snatched it out of the air and ate it. "Stop right there. First, I'm not so sure about Sinclair-

McKinnons. Deb was thirty-two when she had Norah. Amanda's thirty-nine. It gets riskier after a point."

"A conversation lurking in the wings. Maybe the lady wants. Maybe the lady comes from a long tradition of triplets."

Jacob slumped back in his chair and studied the movement on the TV screen. "Kill the romance, why don't you?" he grumbled.

Dave was relentless. "So you're looking at new digs, minimum four bedrooms plus offices. You'll have to take Norah house hunting with you. She'll have first refusal, being the reigning female of the family. Then there's location near the best schools, safe sidewalks, convenient to shopping. You've got your work cut out for you, man."

Jacob glanced at his friend, then returned his gaze to the silent television. "You're way ahead of the gun."

"For you? You're gift wrapped and waiting for her. And from what I've seen and heard of Amanda Sinclair, she's not the casual type either."

"How about letting me catch my breath, instead of terrifying me with houses and rug rats?"

Dave smirked, and Jacob got that smirk well enough. His friend had stood by him through the rough years after Deb. This was payback time. He sighed. He foresaw months of ribbing ahead before he closed the deal and won the woman for keeps.

Chapter 31

"We're going for ice cream. Want to come?"

Jacob's call had surprised Amanda since she'd assumed he was at his desk at the other end of the warehouse. "You and Norah?"

"The cast is off, and that's cause for celebration. So leave early and join us."

"You're bad for my work ethic, Jacob McKinnon. Is she excited?"

"Oh, Lordy. Her arm though, it's sort of pathetic, like it hasn't seen the light for a month, I guess. Tomorrow she'll be a teenager and fighting everything I say, but right now she needs ice cream. Possibly I need it more. Want to come?"

She glanced at her watch. It was four o'clock on a Friday, so leaving early wasn't out of the question. She pulled up her electronic calendar and considered.

"Amanda? You still there?"

"Sorry, yes. That sounds like a nice ending to the week. Should I meet you somewhere?"

"Creekside Mall, it's the closest to the hospital. In twenty minutes?"

"More like half an hour. I need to clear my desk and pack up."

Jacob groaned. "Tell me you're not working this weekend."

"Not much. Personnel reports for a meeting Monday morning. Which I'd planned to review this afternoon," she added pointedly.

"It makes me happy to lure you from your workaholic ways. I wish I could stand here and indulge in phone sex, but maybe best not?"

Her cheeks flamed. "I hope Norah didn't hear that. And don't you dare."

"Norah's so antsy she's half way across the lobby. See you in half an hour."

Before she organized her files for the weekend, Amanda leaned back in her chair and studied the quiet, restrained workspace she'd created for herself. She loved this room with its rosewood and gold leather, its clean lines, nothing extraneous. But then she loved all of SI. The Accounting suite was utilitarian, Stan's preference, but she was as happy there as here.

And isn't that a change. You're happy again in your business. You're optimistic. It's ... it's fun.

The words echoed in her mind. She was having fun.

She enjoyed the yoga now that her body had more or less adjusted, and while she hadn't taken out her drawing supplies since the class ended, elaborate doodles covered her note pages. Nowadays, she let herself do crazy things like leaving work early to go out for ice cream. She laughed when someone told a joke. She wondered if she and Jacob should take up square dancing, he looked so hot in jeans.

At that, she shook herself and drew her attention to packing up her work.

When she got to the mall she found that Jacob had claimed a white wrought iron table in the corridor outside the ice cream shop. Norah sprang up and ran to Amanda, waving her newly freed arm. "Look! I can move it again."

"Careful," Jacob called out.

"I *know*." Norah seized Amanda's hand and dragged her to the ice cream display. "He said we had to wait for you, but I'm hungry *now*." Norah clearly wasn't in the mood for the subtleties of manners.

"Big day, huh?" Amanda said. "It must feel wonderful to have that cast off."

"Yeah." Norah did a whole body wiggle, like a puppy. "Chocolate's my favorite. I bet it's yours, too."

"I like some others more. Mint, for instance."

Jacob joined them at the counter and draped an arm around her shoulders. "You're having a double scoop, minimum. We can all get one scoop of each of our favorite flavors."

"We'd be sick," Amanda said.

"You're right. Terrible idea. So, Cupcake," he said to Norah, "what's it to be?"

"That one. Chocolate with …" She stumbled over the second word on the label.

"Praline. It's a crunchy caramel with nuts," Jacob said.

Norah nodded. "And chocolate syrup."

He raised his brows.

She turned a begging face on him. "Please?"

They all had the chocolate praline ice cream, although Amanda declined syrup. "It's funny," she said as they settled at the table. "I've never sat in a mall for the fun of it. Pat and I sometimes grab something after shopping, but that's expediency. This is just because." She looked at Jacob, propping an elbow on the table. "You're teaching me so much about how to live. I'm amazed." She watched the activity in the mall while Norah hopped up and down and danced around them, too excited to stay still.

"And you're adorable with ice cream all over your mouth."

She snatched up a napkin, but he laughed and caught her hand.

"I'm teasing. A little spill right here." He took the napkin and patted her lower lip. "Malls aren't all they're cracked up to be. If we were at home, I could have nibbled that drip away. Indulged in chocolate kisses. We need to investigate the possibilities of chocolate syrup."

"Don't." She laughed, even though for the second time in an hour he had her cheeks flaming.

"You've heard the rumors? That it's all guys think about? Mostly they're true. But when nothing else is on offer, there's always chocolate."

"I love you," she whispered.

"I love you, too. But don't tell."

"Like the whole world doesn't know."

"I know, Daddy." Norah had danced up to the table to catch the tail end of their conversation. "You're in love with Amanda. Becky says when grownups get in love they go mushy and make goo-goo eyes at each other. Do you do that?"

"Goo-goo eyes?" he mouthed to Amanda. To Norah he said, "Nope. I'll save my goo-goo eyes for you."

"And get me a guitar and lessons, remember? I bet you forgot. We could go Saturday."

Jacob looked at Amanda and shrugged. "Puts a whole new spin on romance, doesn't it?"

"Sort of—domestic romance? It's a good spin."

"I'm beyond happy to hear you say so. You get to take her shopping for her summer wardrobe."

"Pushing your luck, McKinnon." But she thought it might be fun, clothes shopping with a six-year-old. She and Jacob exchanged smiles and ate their ice cream.

Chapter 32

Amanda had been planning a trip to the grocery when the phone rang. She checked the call display and considered not answering. Her parents had returned from their southern sojourn a few days earlier, despite the mud and melt that made up an Ohio spring. Call display didn't tell her which parent was on the other end of the line. She sighed and figured she might as well get it over with.

It was her mother. She slumped with relief. She really didn't want to talk to her father, not with the money issue unresolved. "Hi. Welcome home."

"We're glad to be back. Or at least, I could have stayed in Arizona for another month, but your dad was itching to be here. I need to catch up on laundry and gossip. It was wonderful, going west, the landscape's sensational. We've stored the van there for the summer, so next year we'll start in Arizona, then drive to Florida. Now, when can you come for supper?"

"Mom, there's someone I want you to meet." She'd been rehearsing this conversation in her head for days. "I'd like to bring him, too."

"Mandy! Of course, any night except Tuesday, that's my bridge night. Tell me about him. Is he gorgeous?"

"Calm down." Amanda chuckled. She'd said the right thing to thrill her mother. "Pat and Mel say he's gorgeous. Me, I'm not so sure. I'm not sure it matters."

"Oh, baby."

While her mother struggled to get words out, Amanda fed her some facts. "His name's Jacob, he's forty-two, a bit under six feet. Blondish. Thin. He's an accountant."

"You mean the young man who's been filling in for Stan. Your father's been curious, so I'm sure he'll want to meet him. We're old school, so it's hard to believe anyone could fill Stan's shoes, but—"

"He can. He has. Assuming Jacob's free, how does Wednesday sound? Food-wise, he's easy to please. Grateful for home cooking, same as me."

"Oh, my goodness." Amanda imagined her mother doing a soft shoe in the kitchen. "I'm so excited, I can't wait to see you both."

She took a breath, unsure what reaction to expect. "There's more. He has a daughter. Her name's Norah. I want you to meet her, too."

"A daughter." She caught the uncertainty in her mother's voice.

"Jacob's a widower. Norah's six. You'll like her. Remember the accident two years ago, on the highway through town? When the car crossed the center line and plowed into another car and killed the driver? That was his wife."

"This sounds complicated, Mandy. Are you sure?"

"Never been surer. You'll see. You'll love both of them."

"And you'd be a step-mother?"

Amanda chuckled. "If it ever goes that far. And I'll be totally evil, like in Cinderella. Don't fuss, Mom."

"Well, I'll keep it simple. Maybe roast chicken? A child might eat that."

"Cook a nice, mid-week meal. They're people, not exotic birds. I happen to know she picks out her vegetables though, so be prepared. See you at six?"

"I can't wait to tell your father. And don't worry, honey. It'll be fine."

Worried about what? Amanda gave an affectionate shrug as she hung up. She couldn't imagine any set of circumstances in which her family and Jacob wouldn't get along. And Norah was bound to charm the socks off them.

Any set of circumstances but one. At least her parents hadn't heard, yet, about Stan and the missing money.

* * *

Amanda relaxed in her seat at the dinner table. So far, so good. The meal drew to a close while her dad quizzed Jacob about his work at SI, his relationship with Stan, his ability to fill Stan's shoes—no surprise there. They touched on the history of the company, the various models they'd used for stocking, the first accounting software they'd tried and how Stan had thrown the discs across the room in frustration.

"Best accountant you could hope to find. I worried after the heart attack. In fact, I phoned Stan as soon as he could take calls to tell him to get his butt back to SI and help Amanda—"

"Not that she needed help," Amanda interjected.

"You might have, and you know it. It's a tough business. Rock of Gibraltar, Stan is. Solid as they come."

"I admired him during the short time we worked together," Jacob said.

"So you've been heading Accounting for about four months now?"

Jacob nodded. "You needn't worry. I'll be happy to step aside when he comes back. I have to say though, the team's made it easy for an interim department head. Jim especially knows his stuff. You have solid employees there."

Amanda noted the pride in her father's face at Jacob's use of the word 'you'. Many of the staff at SI, including Jim, started after she'd taken over from her father, but he still needed to be—*insisted* on being—a part of the company.

The men's conversation segued into an analysis of Ohio State's last football season, and from there to a critique of a new fantasy series on cable. This was a new side of Jacob, one she hadn't suspected, so she eavesdropped.

Norah had her mother wrapped around her little finger within a few minutes of their arrival. Her mother had taken her off to the kitchen to 'help', as she explained with a wink to Amanda, and Norah had eaten it up. She'd set the table, folding the napkins with care, and solemnly brought a bottle of wine to her father for his approval before they opened it. During supper the little girl chattered to her rapt audience of one about school, her broken arm, and her current dream of having a pet, a monkey being the preferred option. And, inevitably, her father's relationship with Amanda.

"He kisses her," she said in a mock whisper.

Her mother said, "Oh, does he now? And what does she do?"

Norah giggled. "Silly. She kisses him back, of course. They're in love." She faked a love-struck swoon. At her over-the-top delivery, the men broke off their conversation. Jacob met Amanda's eyes, while Amanda sent up a silent prayer Norah wouldn't mention sleepovers.

"Nothing wrong with love," Amanda's mother said. "And now I'd be grateful if you gentlemen would go away and leave the table clearing to us. We'll have dessert ready in a few minutes."

"Dessert—oh, I'm so stuffed." Norah slouched back in her seat and rolled her eyes. Except for some green pepper in the chicken stew, she'd cleaned her plate, a sure way to her mother's heart.

The voices flowed, everyone talking at once. She could barely distinguish who said what.

Jacob: "Karen, that was sensational. If you aren't careful, you'll find Norah and me camping on your doorstep begging handouts."

She got a sentence in edgeways. "Trust me, his cooking's fine, Mom."

Norah: "If I can't eat all my dessert, do I get to take it home?"

Her dad: "Back twelve, fourteen years ago, we hit this period, suppliers dried up. Plenty of customers, but we couldn't get the goods."

Her mother: "Mandy, would you whip the cream, please? Norah, can you load a dishwasher?"

Norah: "We don't use ours, so I don't know."

Amanda let the noise wash over her and found herself comparing this evening to the few times Brandon had come for supper. It had been nothing like this happy chaos. He'd lectured her father on real estate investments and never lifted a hand to help.

Brandon's gone, at last. This is family. This is home.

* * *

206

Jacob and Norah left her parents' house early, because of Norah's bedtime. The door closed on them, and she turned to face her parents.

"He's a good one, Mandy." Her mother's opening salvo.

"Knows his business, has his head on straight," her dad said. "I'm glad you warned your mother about his wife's accident. Not that we would've said anything."

Amanda picked up a few dessert plates and headed for the kitchen, talking over her shoulder. "He's okay to talk about it. I didn't want it to come up with Norah here. She's had a rough time."

"He's handsome," her mother said, following her with more plates. "And it's obvious he's a good father. Are you planning children?"

"We haven't made it to marriage. It's way too soon." She began loading the plates into the dishwasher.

"Well, you know how old you are. There's not much time if you want to start a family, not that Norah's not a delightful child, but you might want one of your own one day."

"Don't rush it." She straightened and began filling the sink with soapy water.

"And I suppose they like him at SI?" her father asked. "What does everyone think about all this? I bet Mel's thrilled."

"Mel's the ultimate romantic. I'll never figure out why we get along so well. Jacob and I both keep getting these looks, so I'd say everyone's happy for us."

"And no awkwardness? What if he does something you don't approve of?"

"I can't imagine that happening. But if it did, I'd speak to him in private and we'd work it out. He's never presumed on my position or tried to take advantage of our relationship."

Trust her dad to grill her. "It still could be awkward when Stan gets back."

"I doubt it will be. Jacob's not worried, but we'll see. He had a six month contract, so he might not even stay. He's got the integrity to handle it, whatever happens."

"Will you be moving in together?" her mother asked.

Amanda sputtered with laughter, then helped her mother finish up in the kitchen.

Chapter 33

Amanda faced Jacob across the round meeting table by the window in her office, her door closed behind them. They'd played all weekend, she and Jacob and Norah. Now it was back to business, the business she'd been dreading.

"Stan phoned," she said. "He says he wants to return sooner rather than later. I asked him to come in for a talk."

Stan had been off work for almost four months. Only a couple of those months could be justified by his health; the rest had more to do with his wife and daughters and their determination not to let him work himself into an early grave. Susan had dragged him off on vacations, one to Hawaii and the other to Europe. Otherwise he'd been at home, loafing and working his way through a list of home improvement projects Susan had created for him.

Jacob's pen hovered over the pad of paper in front of him. Amanda forcibly put aside any thought of his strong arms, lightly furred with dark blond hair, under the sleeves of his dress shirt. She was learning to compartmentalize. "First question," he said. "Do you want me there?"

She had the answer ready. "Yes. You're the acting senior accountant, and you found the entries. But I need to run the meeting."

He gave her a small nod. "I'll speak up if there's a question about the books, otherwise I'll be the witness."

She and Jacob had slipped into a comfortable working relationship with remarkable ease. They were completely professional; she thought they were both most comfortable that way. Even his teasing touches of her hand following afternoon coffee had ended. Despite the emotional overload of evenings and weekends, their work protocol was formal.

"Have you decided how to play this?"

She nodded. "First, the staff's going to want to see him. It's probably best that it happen before our meeting. We arranged that he'll come in about three thirty, day after tomorrow, and plan on a social time first in the break room. If this plays out like we expect, coffee afterward would be awkward, and if he chose not to socialize, it would raise questions we might not be ready to answer."

"That works. And it's thoughtful of you. Have you decided what you're going to do?"

"There are so many variables. Does he admit it or not. Is he prepared to explain, or not. Will he resign, or am I going to have to fire him."

"Do you have your answers?"

"I think so."

He didn't press. "Do you want a rehearsal? A dry run?"

She shook her head. "I've rehearsed in my mind so many times."

"What do you need from me?"

"I want to put the complete Shirai account in front of him. Purchases and payments, when the account was opened and closed. Everything we have. Then we'll see."

"You'll have it today."

She started to stand, but he put his hand on her arm to stop her. "There's one more thing to consider. Mel." He took his hand away.

"She's fiercely loyal. I trust her. I hope she'll think we're discussing the handover, but she's so intuitive she may suspect something else is going on. Depending on where things stand, we might have to tell her more."

"Something we we can't plan in advance, then."

"I'm afraid not."

"Anything else?"

"No." She saw concern on his face and smiled at him. "Don't worry, I can control this. I'm not about to let sentiment get in the way."

"I'll have your back, just in case."

She returned to her desk. "Thanks. It means a lot."

He gave her a smile, not the full-bore one that seldom made an appearance in public, but a polite, businesslike acknowledgement. She turned to her computer and the next task on her list. He punched the appointment into the calendar on his phone, then left her to her work.

* * *

Two days later, Jacob entered Amanda's office suite as Stan arrived with Mel. Stan looked good. He'd lost weight, his color was healthy, and he had the robust air of a man with a lot to live for.

Jacob saw immediately how well Amanda had positioned herself. She wore a tailored, dark gray business suit with a severe white blouse. She'd had her hair cut the day before, so it was controlled against her head, and her makeup was immaculate. Sitting behind her desk where she wouldn't be available for spontaneous hugs, she looked remote and untouchable, every inch the executive in charge. She offered a polite smile to them both.

This was business, and she'd keep it rigidly businesslike.

Jacob had heard the gathering in the break room, down the hall from the Accounting suite, but hadn't gone to join in. Possibly it would have been the right thing to do; after all, Stan had hired him, and he'd been keeping Stan's chair warm for the last four months. But he wasn't sure he could pull it off, knowing what lay ahead. So he let the others welcome Stan back from his forced recuperation and vacation time and didn't greet the older man until they were both in Amanda's office.

The grapevine extended to Stan from several directions, so he must have heard about Amanda and himself. How might that affect the dynamic of this meeting? He hoped it wouldn't. Jacob could be every bit as businesslike as Amanda, and he'd participate as little as possible, as he'd promised. This was Amanda's show, all the way.

"Let's talk over here." She slipped from her desk to the far side of the round conference table before there could be any opportunity for a hug.

She glanced at Jacob, who quietly closed the door before he joined the two of them.

"Amanda, you look great," Stan said. "The Floor's busy for this time of year. And Colin tells me you're toying with the idea of expansion."

Never one to indulge in small talk where business was concerned, Amanda said concisely, "Things are going well. We had an excellent holiday season, and spring sales are positive. But there's a problem that's getting in the way. That's what we need to talk about."

Amanda picked up the report Jacob had prepared for her and placed it in front of Stan.

She let the room go silent while Stan studied the pages, which included the entire record of their dealings with Shirai Distributors, right back to the beginning twenty years before. The red line she'd drawn between the legitimate entries and the much later ones told its own story. Stan looked puzzled only for a moment as he flipped through the pages. Then he went still.

"You did your homework," he said finally. His glance flicked to Jacob, then he returned his attention to Amanda.

"I believe there's only one person who could be responsible for those last entries. Who understood the system well enough and had access to the files. We no longer have an account with Shirai. I don't want to believe it, but I don't know what else *to* believe." Amanda kept her voice level and devoid of emotion. Jacob could only imagine how tightly she was holding herself.

Stan looked down and made a show of going through the pages again. Silence hung in the room. He kept an eye on Amanda, worried about the weight of that silence and how much she could bear. Other than that he held himself to what he'd promised, an observer and witness.

She finally spoke up. "Stan, why? I know you care about SI. We could have arranged a short term loan if you needed it. Can you tell me why?"

Again silence filled the room. Stan looked a little gray. After a few seconds he shook his head. "I'm sorry, Amanda. I can't tell you."

To Jacob, her tension revealed itself in the uncertain phrasing of her next words. "You must know that you're leaving me in an impossible position. If there were a good reason for the … the theft … then we could deal with it. If you've … well, if it's something like debts … But without that …" She trailed off and waited for Stan to draw his own conclusions.

"It was paid back."

"But it was taken in the first place. With no authorization."

"It's a situation. I can't say any more than that. I suppose you'll want my resignation. You'll have it. But I can't tell you why, Mandy. I'm sorry, but there it is."

Jacob turned his gaze to Amanda and recognized the exact moment when she finalized her decision. Her face tightened and she sat more upright, if that were possible. "You've been a friend and a friend of my family since I was a child. But I can't keep you on staff, and I won't give you a recommendation. I'm sorry, but you're not giving me anything to work with."

Stan sighed. "I love this place. I've even loved working for you, even if you were a kid when I first started teaching you. You've been a good employer and a good company president. You have my admiration. I can't tell you how sorry I am." He stared at the report. "And what I'll say to Susan …"

"She doesn't know about this?"

"No."

"I haven't figured out what to say to Dad, either." Amanda wasn't giving him space to put a guilt trip on her. Jacob gave her a short nod of approval.

The mention of Colin galvanized Stan. He sat up straighter and seemed to be on the verge of saying something. But he didn't; his gaze returned to the table. "I'll tell him," he muttered. "It's my dirty laundry."

"I don't think there's anything more to say. I'll arrange to advertise for a new accountant immediately. Do you have any personal possessions still here? And I'll need your key."

Stan was playing with the edges of the papers in front of him, nervous and looking twenty years older than the man who had entered the office fifteen minutes before. Amanda had that close-to-fracturing expression he'd seen a time or two when the pressure threatened to overwhelm her.

"How about this?" he said, addressing Amanda. "Could Stan bring in a resignation letter, and at the same time clear out his desk? Let it look like a voluntary retirement. That would stop any potential gossip."

"Good idea." Amanda nodded at Jacob, then turned to Stan. "That's the most I can give you. If you could get that letter to me … let's say three business days." She stood. "You're welcome to leave by the side door if you'd rather avoid going through the main entrance."

Amanda and Jacob watched Stan leave, then Jacob again closed the door. "Good," he said.

"I feel as if the heart and soul of SI has been ripped out." Amanda circled her desk and sank into her chair.

"You're wrong about that," he said gently. "You're the heart and soul."

She smiled, although it barely touched her eyes. "Thanks. You're good for me."

"You want me to leave you alone now?" At her nod, he gave her his tentative half smile. "Mel?"

"Tell her that Stan's thinking of resigning—retiring. And ask her not to mention it. This is still confidential." She sighed. "I'm hoping for a miracle, but I don't see where one's coming from. You're right." She gestured with her hand at her door. "The less this is known out there, the better."

"Take care," he said gently. In planning for this meeting, they had addressed every possible situation. Except broken hearts. He met her eyes briefly, and what he saw in hers led him to reach across her desk to grip her fingers with a light squeeze.

"Come over tonight?"

She nodded.

He left her alone and went to face Mel.

Chapter 34

The meeting with Stan had left Amanda raw, as if a shredder had attacked her, so she was less than thrilled the next morning when her father appeared unexpectedly at her office door. She stood and circled her desk. His face was red, as if he'd been out in the sun, but she knew better. She'd seen the simmering anger before.

"Dad. Hello."

"Amanda."

She gave him a light hug. He shrugged her off and pushed into her office.

She frowned. Her father was never demonstrative, sometimes making her doubt there was any affection there, but it was unlike him to push her aside. "It's early, but there may be a few people in the break room." She glanced around him at Mel, but her executive assistant twisted her mouth into an I-don't-know expression and turned back to her computer.

Amanda, sensing trouble, closed the door behind him.

He faced her. "Let's be clear. I'm not interested in the damn break room. I want to hear what you have to say for yourself."

Silence gathered while she considered. This had to be about Stan, and her father blamed her. She was certain she'd done the right thing. Regret weighed like lead on her shoulders, and she doubted he'd lost the sleep she'd lost last night, because of it.

Where her father was concerned, the only viable option was to face him head-on. Her hand still on the door handle, she said, "You're talking about Stan, aren't you? He doesn't deny taking the money. How could I have handled it differently?"

"There's such a thing as loyalty. Looking at the whole picture. Stan's kept this place together." The unspoken thought, *since I was forced out,* hovered in the background.

He questioned her competence, and that shook her. She'd trained with him for years, soaking up everything he could teach her. She knew she'd made mistakes since she took over from him, that was inevitable. She'd recovered from them, learned from them.

This time though, it wasn't a mistake.

"There's also such a thing as acting deceitfully, not to mention illegally."

"The money came back."

"It was taken in the first place." Finally she released the door and circled him to get to her desk. She still didn't sit, but stood with the rosewood barrier between them.

"You made the wrong decision."

"I had no other option." She paused to catch her breath and see if he would break the stony silence. They faced each other across her office. The office of the president of Sinclair Imports, a symbol of the power that first he, and now she, wielded.

Since he refused to speak, she did, as an explanation, not an apology. "I'm sorry, but I don't see that I had any choice. If you see something I don't, please tell me. He took the money, Dad. There's no question about that."

"And this new guy claims he found it. He had no business poking in the old accounts. You're so sure he didn't orchestrate this whole thing?"

"Yes, I'm sure. In fact, I'd have been more concerned if he hadn't made time to familiarize himself with the business. As soon as he noticed the suspect account, he came to me. This isn't about Jacob."

He leveled a hard gaze at her. "I founded this company. You wouldn't have your fancy position if it weren't for me. I expect you to give Stan his job back, Amanda."

"I can't do that."

"We'll see about that." He wheeled and stalked to the door. With his hand on the knob, he turned and pointed at her. "You never were good at admitting your mistakes. You can fix this one. I suggest you do. Don't forget that between your mother and me I still control enough of this company to usher you out of your fancy office and onto the street." He yanked the door open and left her standing, astounded and speechless.

She had made the right decision. She understood her father's loyalty to Stan, but his vehemence in the face of the evidence didn't make sense.

* * *

That night was rough, despite Jacob's solid presence next to her. They didn't made love and didn't talk much. Mostly he held her, and she clung to him. The confrontation with her father had more than rattled her. It had given her a hopeless, empty feeling in the pit of her stomach that wouldn't go away. Jacob provided the stable point in a world that had rocked off its axis. Amanda dreaded causing a rift in her family even more than she feared losing her company. Her father's threat had to be hollow, but he and her mother did have a controlling interest, barely. If he chose to, he could do it.

When the phone rang the next morning, Amanda eyed the call display before answering. Her parents' number. It could be her mother, although she rarely phoned her at work. Her father? Telephones weren't his style. He was more likely to confront her in her office.

Well, she'd find out soon enough.

"Honey?"

Her mother. Thankful, Amanda closed her eyes. "Hi, Mom."

Silence. Near silence. Her mother was crying. "Mom? Are you okay?"

Her mother drew a shuddering breath. "No," she managed. "No, I'm not. He did it, Mandy. It wasn't Stan at all."

"He? Did what? He who? Mom, what are you talking about?"

Her mother moved swiftly from incoherent to indignant, which at least made for clearer communication. "You all think I don't have any interest in SI and I don't pay attention. I know a lot more than you give me credit for. Your dad handles our accounts, but things weren't adding up, so I did some poking. It's there, the missing money. There's a deposit in our checking account for same amount. It wasn't Stan, Mandy."

"Mom," Amanda said through a forced calm, "are you saying Dad took the money?"

"That's exactly what I'm saying. And when he gets home—"

"Calm down. You're sure about this?"

"That money didn't create itself. What do you think?"

"I don't know. I'm not processing. Give me a second." She let the line go silent while she caught her breath and re-oriented her mind. "Dad's not home?"

"No, he's off getting the oil changed in the car."

"When he gets back, would you tell him to get himself over here? And I'd like to see that bank statement."

"I'll scan it and email it over."

Once again she longed to turn to a parent for comfort. "Mom, right now I wish I were ten years old and I'd just fallen off my bicycle."

"You haven't done anything wrong, honey."

"I don't know how to fix this."

"Remember, it's not yours to fix. I love you. Your dad does, too."

"I love you, too. Would you mind checking whether there was a withdrawal a few months later? Someone paid the money back."

"I'll let you know what I find."

"I hate this, and I don't see how to untangle it. Bye, Mom."

She collapsed in her chair. The part of her brain that still functioned wondered how things could get worse.

* * *

She found out how, early that afternoon. Her father bypassed Mel and stormed into her office, livid. "You involved your mother in this. How dare you upset her? How *dare* you?"

Amanda dodged around him and closed the door before sitting behind her desk and facing him. Her father quivered with rage.

"I didn't involve Mom in anything." The thread that kept her attached to her cool demeanor stretched almost to breaking. She fought to hold onto it. "Can you explain why your savings account shows a deposit, two days after the embezzlement, for the exact amount that was taken?"

She got her first hint that he had stormed over to SI to confront her without a plan. He said nothing, then stated with a little less heat, "My personal finances are none of your business."

"The missing money is my business."

"You got it back."

"We've been through this."

He leaned over her desk, in her face. "This is *my company. Mine.* You think you've sidelined me, you can do anything you damn well please, but it doesn't work that way. You have no right ..."

"Sit down, Dad."

He didn't hear her. "Oh, no, you're above it all, aren't you? You're so almighty powerful, sitting there in that fancy chair of yours, breaking your mother's heart."

"You did that." Amanda's voice was flat. This was her father — her *father* — and she barely recognized him. She was even a little intimidated. He'd always been a blusterer, and she'd seen his bitterness over his forced retirement, but she'd had no idea he resented her so much. She'd tried since she was fourteen years old to be the successor he'd be proud of. Instead ...

"You took the money," she stated. "I assume, with Stan's help. It's *our* company, not yours, and if you'd asked I'd have arranged a loan or an extraordinary dividend or something. But no. I can't believe the underhanded scheming against your own company."

"You could have kept it quiet and relied on Stan. Instead you forced it out into the open. Now look at the mess."

At least he didn't say, 'the mess you created'. But she sensed the thought floating around in the office. "Tell me why you needed the money."

The fight left him. Her father sat down, diminished somehow. "Your mother wanted Arizona. The motor home, the trip across the country. There were investments that didn't … the downturn caught up with us." He looked at her, his eyes cold. "It's my money. I earned it, and I had a right to it. I figured you'd make a stink."

Amanda shook her head. "You're wrong. I'd have been happy to figure out something."

"You have a funny way of showing it. I'm out of here." Her father was gone before she had a chance to say anything else.

After a minute she closed her door again. She then made two calls. The first was to her mother. "Mom, watch out for him. His color's not good. I'm worried about his heart."

The second call was to a much closer location. "Jacob?" she said when he answered, no trace of emotion in her voice. "I need you here. Could you come? Now?"

* * *

Jacob rushed through the outer office. Amanda's voice had sent his heart plummeting to his shoes. Mel was at her desk, and from her face he figured she'd heard enough to know they were in the middle of a crisis. She didn't say anything, but gave him a little shake of her head. He let himself into Amanda's office and closed the door behind him. One look at Amanda and all the unspoken rules about their relationship, how they would conduct themselves with each other at SI, vanished into thin air. He circled her desk and gathered her up in his arms.

With his embrace came the tears, and when they let up she told him what had happened, stumbling over the words. Nothing could ease the grief she suffered at this betrayal, so he held her, letting her borrow his strength. A part of him wanted to seriously kick ass, punish the man who'd done this to her. Another part, the saner part, said to do what he was doing. Wait, don't make matters worse.

Logic's a bitch, sometimes.

When she was calmer he stuck his head out the door and said, "Mel, could you bring a couple of coffees, please?"

"Will do." Mel was a rock, he figured, and he was right. She didn't ask a single question, or even send a questioning look his way. She rose from her desk and headed for the break room. He sent out a silent blessing for Mel.

Coffee delivered, he and Amanda sat at the conference table. He took a box of tissues out of the credenza, then sat beside her, her left hand in his right one, sensing she needed the ongoing contact.

"How could he do it?" she asked him, confusion and pain in her voice. "What were they thinking? Dad never said Stan was involved, but there's no other possibility. Those two men, they love this company, how could they *do* it?" She looked at him bleakly, her eyes reflecting her turmoil. "I thought he loved me. How could he threaten me? How could he trust me so little?"

If she'd been looking at him she would have seen the stab of pain that pinched his face. He quickly banished it. "Not now," he said. "You can't make sense of this yet, much less sort out what to do about it."

"It's going to tear up my family. He has to deal with my mother, and she's furious and hurt. Will they ever invite me for supper again? Will they even *speak* to me again? And what about the money coming back? Mom didn't find anything in their bank statements."

"Stan, probably. We'll find out, now that we know the basics."

She was growing more and more wound up, so he released her and stood behind her, his hands working the knotted muscles in her shoulders. "I'm here, love. It's a nightmare, but you're not alone."

"There's nothing I can do. I've never felt so helpless. Stan—I didn't have a choice." She was repeating herself, convincing herself.

Sensing she hovered on the edge of meltdown, he let his hands move up to brush her face. She turned her head, resting her cheek in his palm.

You thought you knew how much you love her. You haven't even begun to plumb the depths of it.

What Amanda needed now was light sympathy and a lot of logic. Helpless wasn't her style, and his best option was to support her while she regained her focus. "They'll figure that out. You acted in the only way that showed integrity and competence and respect for the company your father built. It *will* happen. I wish it could happen sooner, but I'm afraid it'll take time." He put a finger under her chin and turned her to look at him. "Please. Trust me. We'll get through it."

She reached a hand up to touch his. "I couldn't without you."

"You could. I'm glad you don't have to."

It was midafternoon before Jacob left Amanda's office. He paused at Mel's desk to ask that she clear Amanda's schedule for the rest of the afternoon. At least it was Friday, so she had the weekend to recover.

* * *

That evening Amanda answered her door to find Jacob on her doorstep. "Have you eaten?" he asked. "I've brought Chinese." He handed her the bag, then peeled out of his coat and boots. "It's a good take-out place," he said, as if it were a normal day and he'd dropped in for a social chat. "Over on my side of town. I'd bet you haven't had supper, right?" He led her to her kitchen.

She sat at her table and watched Jacob track down plates and cutlery. He put a plate of chow mein, fried rice, a beef and vegetable dish, and an egg roll in front of her and prepared another, smaller plate for himself.

He would have eaten earlier, with Norah. "You're such a family man," she said.

"I guess so. Why do you say that?" He pulled out the chair next to her and sat.

"Never mind. I can't possibly eat this much."

"We'll throw out what's left, so eat. Somebody slaved over a hot stove to make this meal for you."

"All right." She sighed and took a bite. It was good, and although she found it hard to believe, she realized she was hungry. She picked up the egg roll and crunched into it.

"It's a way for me to take care of you, like when you fed me the day Norah broke her arm. After we've eaten, I'll go, or I can stay with you for a while. Your call. I want to be your port in a storm, and I'd say this qualifies as a storm. Use me any way you need to. I'm here."

She put a hand on his forearm where he'd rested it against the edge of the table. "You're a good man, Jacob. Thank you."

Predictably, he picked up her hand and kissed it. "If you knew how often I have to censor my thoughts about you, you might change your mind. But I try."

They ate the meal in silence. She'd never have believed it possible, but she almost finished it.

"Come home with me? I can't stay here because of Norah."

She shook her head. "I need time."

He brushed her hair back from her face and cupped her head for a moment, meeting her eyes. In his she saw all she needed, or could ever want.

He squeezed her hands in his, gave her an almost-not-there kiss, and left.

Not alone. She'd held the thought for weeks. Now it was a part of who she was, the final brick in this unit they'd been building. She'd never needed help before, not like this. He gave her what her spirit thirsted for, more deeply than she had the words to tell him. Somehow, she suspected he knew anyway.

She didn't sleep well that night. The fact that she slept at all astonished her when the alarm went off.

Chapter 35

"I do not believe I'm doing this," Amanda groaned. "You've subjected me to some harebrained schemes in the last few months, but this one takes the cake."

"That's the hope," Pat shot back. "There are several cakes up for grabs. I happen to be extremely good at Bingo, it's a talent I have. We'll win ourselves a cake, then we'll gorge. And between us we'll raise a fortune for Norah's school. Perk up, you'll slay 'em."

Perky wasn't in Amanda's vocabulary, although Pat was in high spirits. Her mother's revelation a week ago had taken its toll, and being here was, for her, more duty than fun. But she'd promised, and Norah had wanted her to come, and she suspected Pat and Jacob had some kind of agreement to keep her mind off things, so here she was. Pat found a parking place in the school lot, and they made their way into the gym. She thought half of Calter Creek must be jammed inside to play Bingo for the school.

Jacob stood up and waved to draw their attention to the table where he was holding seats. Norah took off like a bullet to hug first Pat, then Amanda. "I'm way excited," she babbled. "I've got two cards of my own and Daddy's been teaching me how to play. You have to know numbers way high up."

"All the way up to seventy-five," Pat said "Can you count to seventy-five, Norah?"

"Sure. Daddy said he'd help. He's got two cards for you, too. Come on." She was pulling on Amanda's hand, hustling them toward their table. "They're here!" she shouted from several tables away, then broke free and ran to her father.

"Whew," Pat said, and sank into a chair, leaving the one next to Jacob for Amanda. "Nice to be welcomed."

He draped an arm around Amanda's shoulders and kissed her. The kind of kiss that's acceptable in an elementary school gymnasium, she thought, and hugged him.

"Hey," he said. "It's not a death sentence. Go check out the prizes."

"Good idea. I need to whip up some enthusiasm."

"I'll come, too." Norah took Amanda's hand and danced across the floor, where they studied the promised cakes, along with assorted children's toys, electronics, and kitchen appliances.

"I'm going to win that one, and that one ..."

"Wait a minute." Amanda squatted down. "You know, don't you, that you might not win anything? There are lots of people here, and not everyone can win. Maybe we will, and maybe we won't. Playing is the fun part, not winning."

"That's what Daddy said, too. He said it'd be okay to pretend, just not too hard." Norah paused, and her brow furrowed. Her voice quieted as she said, "Are you going to be my new mommy?"

Amanda felt like she'd had her feet kicked out from under her. Why would Norah ask her? Why not her father? But the little girl needed an answer.

"Why do you think that?"

"Because Daddy kisses you. He doesn't kiss anyone else."

"He kisses you."

"Oh, yeah, but that doesn't count."

"Counts a lot, I'd say." Still squatting, so they were more or less at eye level, she said, "How would you feel about that? If I were your mother?"

Norah squirmed. "I miss my mommy sometimes. She's not coming back."

"No. She can't come back."

"Because she died. But you're okay. Daddy's happy when you're here."

"Well, I'm happy, too. About being your mother, I don't know, Norah, but I'll make you a promise. If your daddy and I decide that I am, you'll be the absolute first person we'd tell. And it would probably be a secret for a while. Can you keep secrets?"

Norah's eyes widened. "I guess. I've never had a *big* secret."

Amanda smiled and stood. She held out her hand to the little girl. "Something's happening up there," she said, nodding at the stage. "I guess we'd better get to our seats."

"Okay." With their joined hands swinging, they returned to their table.

Norah didn't win anything, but Jacob did, a set of tools for decorating cakes. "Sort of a consolation prize," Pat quipped as they walked out to their cars, Jacob carrying his exhausted daughter.

"My eyes are crossing," he said. "My brain's fried." No surprise since he'd had to keep track of his own and his daughter's cards. "Who knew that Bingo would challenge the skills of a supremely qualified numbers man?"

"Cutthroat Bingo. We'll expect you to throw a party when you recover. Bake a cake. Seems to me a cake was promised, like a lure to get us here," Pat said.

"I'll buy one instead. As for this decorating thing, I'll put it away for Norah's hope chest, if that's okay with you ladies."

"Not yet," Amanda said. "It looks interesting."

Jacob groaned. "Out of curiosity, have you ever made a cake in your life?"

"Sure. Cake mix. Failsafe."

"Not quite the same," Pat said.

They arrived at Jacob's car first. He tucked Norah in, then stood. "Call me?" he said quietly to her.

"Later," she replied, and they went their separate ways.

* * *

"Hi," Jacob said into the phone. Another minute or two with Amanda, he thought, even if he was reeling with fatigue.

"Hi, yourself."

"Tell me what you look like."

"You aren't thinking phone sex, are you?"

"I wasn't until you put the idea in my head. It'd be more fun to catch you one day at SI."

"Did I mention my repertoire of revenge strategies?"

He chuckled. "I'm intrigued, but nothing tonight, I'm too tired to be creative. Tell me."

"Okay, bunny pj's and robe."

"I love those pajamas. Especially when they're not on you."

"Jacob ..."

"Sorry. I'm a zombie, anyway. How are you?"

"Holding up, more or less. I enjoyed it. It was an adrenaline rush when I only had one or two numbers to go. You know what I mean."

"I do. Will you be able to sleep?"

"Better with you."

"Come over."

"Not tonight, even though I'd love to. I have a client meeting tomorrow morning first thing, and you aren't always the most conducive to a solid eight hours."

"I bet you're blushing."

She ignored that. "There is something you should know though. I didn't want to wait until I see you. While we were looking at the prizes, Norah asked me if I was going to be her new mommy."

Jacob missed a beat. "Whew," he said. "Is this a can of worms?"

"Is it?"

"Well, not where I'm concerned, but perhaps for Norah. Does it worry you? I haven't said a thing to her, Amanda. I promise."

"I didn't think so. She says you don't kiss anyone else, and you're happy when I'm around."

"Both true. My thoughts are taking a long trajectory these days, but I don't intend to ask you to marry me over the phone.

I don't have a clear plan yet, but I guarantee it won't include telephones."

"I sure hope not." She laughed, as she hadn't in the last week. Something loosened in him, knowing the happiness was still in there.

"You're good with her. That's so important to me. Not as important as you, the fact of you ... you know what I mean, I'm not coherent. But it does matter."

"Thank you," Amanda said. "The fact of you, too. Thank you, Jacob."

"God, I love you."

"I love you."

His heart always gave a funny hiccup, hearing those words from her. It was like putting an official seal on what they had, giving it a name.

"Sleep well, my love."

"You, too."

But Jacob went to bed with his mind troubled.

Her new mommy.

After failing to fall asleep he got up and took out the picture of Deb, the one that had been in his bedroom since before her death, the one he'd banished to a drawer before Amanda first spent the night, that incredible night. He studied Deb's face and, whether he wanted them to or not, the memories washed over him.

I'm doing the best I can, Debbie. She'll be good for our little girl. Sometimes I still miss you. I do.

Memories haunted the night, and once he woke with tears on his face. Yes, he thought, there were things about Deb and his first marriage he'd never tell Amanda. Even though Amanda was now his hope and his future.

* * *

A few nights later, after her bath and story, Jacob tucked his daughter into bed and kissed her. He hadn't solved, to his satisfaction, the problem of how to approach the subject of mommies with her, but he had to speak soon, because he couldn't bear to think that Norah was worried.

He stroked her cheek with the back of a finger and said, "I want to ask you something. All right?"

"Okay." Norah snuggled down into her pillow.

He took a breath. "Do you miss Mommy?"

Her face sobered. "Sometimes. Not all the time. Not like before." Her forehead wrinkled. "Is that bad?"

He smiled. "No, sweetheart. It's natural. She left us a long time ago. We can always love her, even if we don't miss her every minute."

"Good," Norah said. "But she'll always be my mommy, won't she?"

"Always."

"Even if I get a new mommy?"

Jacob pulled back the covers and scooped his daughter up into his arms, then settled himself down on her bed before he answered. "How would you feel about having a new mommy?"

"I don't know. Jessie has a new mommy and she was really nice at first but now she lives with them and she keeps sending Jessie to her room and off to camp and stuff. She doesn't get to have supper with her dad anymore."

"So Jessie's not happy."

Norah shook her head, making her curls fly. "Sally and Becky have their mommies, and they have so much fun and go shopping and try makeup and cook and stuff."

"You want to do all those things, too."

"Sure. I guess. If I had a new mommy …" Norah paused.

Jacob sensed he was about to hear her real worry.

Norah took a breath. "Do I have to call her Mommy?"

A valid concern. She wouldn't want to call Amanda 'Mommy', any more than he'd ever use any of his pet names for Debbie with Amanda. "No. We'd figure out what you want to call her. Whatever it is, your mommy's always going to watch over you."

"And I can keep her picture?" Norah had a print of the same picture Jacob had shown Amanda, on the dresser in her room.

"I'd want you to. You won't lose her, Pumpkin. I promise."

"That's okay, then." Norah snuggled against his chest. "Are you going to marry Amanda?"

He grinned at her. "Not so fast. Maybe one day."

"I like Amanda. I think you can marry her. I can be a bridesmaid."

He looked down at her and raised his brows.

"You kiss her and take showers with her. That's what you do when you're married."

She knew about the showers?

"Well, tell me if you ever don't feel good about it. Because I want you to be happy."

She nodded against him. "I'm glad we got that settled," she said. "You can go now. Becky says we girls need our beauty sleep a lot."

Jacob buried his face in her blonde curls for a moment, wondering how a six-year-old became a sixteen-year-old overnight. "Get your beauty sleep, then. And I'll keep you safe all night."

He settled her back in her bed, kissed her forehead, and tiptoed out, relieved and also a little discomfited by his daughter's insight.

Chapter 36

Jacob stood on the Sinclairs' doorstep and hesitated before knocking.

It's not as if you haven't been over what to say a hundred times.

The situation between the Sinclairs and their daughter was a festering wound. He couldn't avoid being a part of it, because Amanda was a part of him. Nor could he avoid resenting Colin for putting Amanda through so much grief. She hadn't heard from her family in two weeks, and he knew the silence weighed on her like a dark cloud fully loaded with rain.

But this wasn't about the stolen money.

There was no logical reason for his visit to turn into a confrontation, but it was a step into Colin's territory, and given the current messed-up situation, he couldn't predict how it would go. What Colin was dealing with now, in front of his wife and daughter, was as tough as it gets.

Perhaps because he hadn't changed out of his suit from work, he felt like a traveling salesman—but he hoped he had something Colin and Karen would buy. His presence on the Sinclairs' doorstep had nothing to do with the embezzlement, or with SI. It was practical and as old as the hills.

He rang the doorbell.

Karen answered, and froze in the doorway when she saw him.

He kept his face neutral, even though it was unnatural not to greet Amanda's mother with a smile. "Hi, Karen. It's good to see you. But it's actually Colin I'm looking for. Is he in?"

She didn't smile, either. He'd hoped she would, to make things less awkward. "He is," she said. "But I'm not sure you're welcome at the moment. Can you tell me why you're here?"

Amanda's mother looked older, and careworn. The last two weeks had taken their toll. There was no positive spin to put on the affair, and when it involved the man you'd married over forty years ago …

"It's a man-to-man thing, but I expect I'll be talking to you, too, later." He wanted to speak to Colin first because it was a man-to-man thing, but also because that's where the deepest wounds lay. "It's nothing to do with SI. May I come in?"

Karen was speechless for a moment, studying him, then said, "Do you mind waiting in the entry? I'll go find him." She held the door open for him, then hurried off.

Colin emerged from the kitchen after a minute or two, anything but pleased. "I suppose Amanda knows you're here?"

"No, this is just me."

"And you thought you'd be welcome to barge in on us like this? What are you doing here? I'd rather kick you out on your backside, to tell the truth. You have a nerve turning up this way." Belligerent and defensive, Colin wasn't going to make it easy. Jacob had hoped that wouldn't be the case, but accepted the possibility.

"Could we sit down and talk? This is important to me. I hope it will be to you, too."

"Come on." Amanda's father turned on his heel and stormed into the living room.

Jacob chose one end of the sofa and waited while the other man settled in the chair across from him. He'd been calm enough at the door, but that was changing. He took a breath. When he had the older man's attention he said, "Colin, I intend to ask Amanda to marry me. Before I do, I'd like your blessing."

There was a moment of stunned silence. "You *what?* What are you talking about? This isn't the eighteenth century. Amanda will do whatever she wants. Nothing whatsoever to do with me."

"In my mind, it's a lot to do with you. I'm asking to become a member of your family. I want you to be my father-in-law and Norah's grandfather. It's up to Amanda in the final analysis, but I hope she'll have me. I'd like a positive word from you first."

Colin was watching him, his eyes narrowed. "I wish I knew what your real agenda is. You've wormed your way into my company. You've damn near destroyed this family you're talking about."

Jacob didn't mention that Colin himself had started the events that had brought grief to the family. "Other than marrying Amanda and making her happy for the rest of her life, I don't have an agenda. I figure you and Karen are part of the package.

"I like your family," he went on. "It feels right being with you. I can see the affection. I envision swing sets in the back yard and family holidays, and dinners where everything's noisy and shared. Things I want for myself, and even more for Norah. The evening we spent with you, she had a wonderful time. We both did.

"But mostly, I love your daughter with all my heart. I promise to cherish her and take care of her—"

"Stop." Colin held up a hand. The belligerence had faded, but Colin still wasn't willing to accept him at face value. He looked him in the eye. "Let's call a spade a spade. You're saying you want to associate yourself with a thief."

Jacob shook his head. "As far as that goes, I'm prepared to tell you I've made mistakes in my life, some of them serious." He paused, then decided that when the stakes were this high, revealing the one thing he never talked about was worth it. He felt heat come into his face. "Amanda knows this, almost no one else does. I was busted for marijuana possession when I was in university. I got lucky, and the charges were dropped, but I went through hell, shamed in front of my family and risking professional disgrace. So I don't cast stones. We all make mistakes. We learn and move on."

Colin frowned at him. After a minute he said, "I see. We'd better get Karen in here." He left the room.

Jacob stood as Karen came in, gave her a polite smile, and repeated his message. "I was just saying that I love your daughter, and I hope to marry her. The one thing I want before I propose is your blessing. That you'll be fine with Norah and me joining your family."

He turned his attention back to Colin. All three of them were still standing, but with everything else going on in his mind Jacob couldn't figure out how to get the older couple to sit down. "The other thing I should say is that my prospects are good. I haven't told Amanda this yet, so I'd be grateful if you wouldn't mention it, but I won't be staying at SI. I don't want to risk complications. I'm marketable, I have skills that will be in demand no matter what the economy does, so we'll be on solid ground, financially."

There. He'd said his piece.

The Sinclairs studied him, puzzled looks on both their faces. Karen said, "Despite everything."

The theft clearly wasn't going to go away. "Despite everything. I'm no paragon, as I've told Colin. It's a reasonable bet I won't always be the perfect husband or father. But I'm willing to give it all I've got."

Amanda's parents looked at each other. Jacob was sure that the last two weeks had left them feeling isolated from the world and uncomfortable with each other. His formal, old-fashioned words probably had thrown them. He hadn't meant to be theatrical, he just wanted them to understand that Colin's crime didn't affect the way he felt about this family.

"Mandy knows you're here?" Karen asked.

He shook his head. "No. I'll tell her when I propose, and that won't be tomorrow. But until then, this is between you two and me."

Karen's puzzled expression cleared. "I'm making tea," she said, addressing her husband. "I think we're likely to have a son-in-law." Her gaze returned to him.

Jacob smiled at her. "Thank you. I'd like that." He held out his hand to Colin. "Sir?"

Colin hesitated, then took Jacob's hand. "There's no reason to stop you. I do want her to be happy, even if—"

"It'll pass. Can we help Karen?" By mutual consent, the two men followed Amanda's mother into the kitchen.

Jacob left the Sinclair home after half an hour of well-intentioned but stilted conversation. He drove home pleased that he'd accomplished what he'd set out to do. He'd shown Colin that the theft wasn't the most important thing, that family trumped everything else, every time.

Plus, he'd received the blessing he wanted.

* * *

"We're here." Jacob let Norah and himself in Amanda's front door. He'd had to hurry home from the senior Sinclairs' house, to have time to change and collect Norah with her paraphernalia; his visit with Colin and Karen had taken time.

"Kitchen," she called back.

Norah pulled up short when she saw Amanda sitting at the kitchen table. "You're still sad." They hadn't told Norah what was going on, but she was too canny not to pick up on the mood, so they'd said it was work stuff and left it at that.

"Not so sad when I see you. Do I get a hug?" Amanda opened her arms to the little girl.

Jacob waited at the kitchen door while his two favorite women embraced, then walked over and dug his fingers into Amanda's neck and shoulders, seeking out the kinks. "You're a wreck," he said.

"Gee, thanks." Amanda leaned back against his hands. "Mmm."

"You're not supposed to say that, Daddy," Norah stated, disapproval dripping from her words. "You're supposed to say how pretty she is."

"And so she is. Sorry, love," he added, dropping a kiss on her head. "So you are."

"And I brought you a present," Norah said, "so you won't be unhappy anymore."

"For me? Did you choose it yourself?"

Norah nodded proudly, then ran out to the entry, returning with a package she'd also, obviously, wrapped herself.

"It was her idea," Jacob explained.

"And you're going to love it." Norah squirmed as she set the gift in front of Amanda. "Go on, open it."

Amanda smiled at the little girl and did as instructed. "Oh, Norah."

"It's a grownup coloring book. Now you can color all you want." Norah danced around Amanda with excitement.

"And markers, too. I've never seen so many colors of markers. This is lovely, Norah. You're right, I'm happier already. And I promise I'll color you a picture as soon as I can."

Once again Norah was in Amanda's arms with a sloppy hug, but not for long; she was too keyed up. She wriggled free and said, "Daddy says he needs to talk about business so I have to go read a book."

"We brought one," Jacob added. In fact they'd brought two, along with pajamas, toothbrush, and Bobo the monkey. Norah was getting used to having her bath and bunking at Amanda's.

Jacob went to settle his daughter in a chair with her books. When he returned to the kitchen, Amanda was on her feet, starting supper preparations. "Leave that," he said. "Come sit for a minute. I do want to talk to you."

Over the table she said, "I talked to Mom this afternoon. They've contacted the place in Arizona about selling the motor home. She's upset. It's a never-ending nightmare." She grasped his hand in both of her own, playing with his fingers. "What is it?" She frowned. "There's nothing going on at SI, is there?"

"No, it's what's happening here. Amanda, consider this. Your family's miserable. I assume Stan is, too. And this is tearing you apart. Why?"

Her reply was prompt. "Because they stole from the company. Because no one can fix it."

He shook his head and leaned across the table. He reversed their hands, so he held hers lightly, chafing with his thumbs. "That's the root cause, but it's not what's making everyone unhappy. Right now it's because they have too much time to stew and no way to make it right. And for you it's because you miss your family and Stan."

She was quiet for a minute, then nodded. "That's the effect anyway, if not the cause. I don't see your point though."

"We can't fix the cause. It happened, and that's that. But I have an idea that might start patching things up. It's way out there, but listen before you laugh at me, okay?" His eyes prompted her for a reply, so she nodded, watching his face. "What might work … Amanda, suppose you hired both of them back?"

"What?" She sat up straighter and pulled her hands free. "I can't do that. After what they've done? I couldn't."

He reclaimed her hand and kissed her palm before speaking. "Don't reject this quite yet. Here's how I see it. They made a mistake that's escalated into this monstrous thing, but perhaps it's not that terrible, when we step back from it. Bad judgment, misplaced loyalty, and battered pride. They're suffering and dragging your mother along with them."

"I'm not so sure about dragging. She's furious that Dad wasn't up front with her about their finances. More than about losing the motor home."

"They both must feel horrible about what they did to you and to SI, and the debt your dad owes to Stan. At least none of this is public knowledge. With any reasonable luck, it never will be."

Jacob squeezed her hand, then was on his feet again, on the move in her little kitchen. He ran his hands through his hair, then turned to her. "So, if you hire them, they redeem themselves. Stan returns to his status in the company and feels useful again. Your dad — you could suggest that he come on as a consultant. He could help with the logistics of moving, for instance, if that's what you decide to do. He earns money, so he can pay Stan back, plus he's doing what he loves. And you have your two father figures working with you."

"I'm not sure I could handle having my dad around, father figure or not."

"I see your point. Where your dad's concerned, you'd have to consider how it'll play out down the road. In the short term though, if you keep him busy enough, let him make a serious contribution, there's a chance things will get back to normal."

Amanda grinned, sending a bolt of relief into his heart. "And it's an absolute certainty that neither of them will do anything like this again." The grin faded. She sighed and stood. "I don't know, Jacob. I'll consider it. It might even be necessary. With moving I'll certainly need a coordinator. Dad could be vice president in charge of change and growth?" She smiled, a real one this time, not forced. "Yes, it might work." She stepped into his arms. "Let me hold onto you a minute. Then we can start supper."

Chapter 37

May had arrived. Jacob woke to a patch of sun leaking around the shade and slanting across the bed. The window was open a few inches, and every bird in Calter Creek was singing in his back yard. The day smelled of spring.

Amanda was still asleep, curled away from him where she'd been spooned all night—all the night they'd slept, anyway. The covers had slipped, so he gently kissed her bare shoulder. It was so ridiculously romantic. The two of them, with Norah once again in Columbus with her grandparents. This perfect morning, the sun, the birds …

You're a guy. You're not supposed to be into sunshine and birdsong.

But the fact remained that at this moment the world couldn't be more right.

Amanda stirred and turned onto her back in the midst of a yawn, stretching her arms up over her head. She opened her eyes and smiled.

He caught her wrists, pinning her. "God, you tempt me," he said.

She chuckled. "When you grin like that, it's hard to take your threats seriously."

"It's not a threat. It's a promise." With his free hand he pulled her closer, released her captive hands to stroke her hair. "I'm so content. I don't want this morning to end."

She yawned and shook her head. "There's a problem with that plan. We'd starve. I suspect it has to do with exercise. Life around you can be strenuous."

"Pancakes, then. But later." Waking up naked in bed with Amanda was a luxury, because of Norah, and there was no way he'd let the moment go without taking advantage of it. Her eyes had a dancing, slightly squinting quality he'd learned to associate with anticipation. All signals go. The hand on her hair shifted to her ribs, his thumb brushing her breast while he began the moves that would drive them to ecstasy.

Later she dozed in the sunlight while he showered. With the water pouring over him and the memory of her in his bed, sleepy and content in the sun, he came up with a plan. A plan that changed the timetable, messed up all he'd gone over in his head so many times. Take her away, somewhere exotic? The romantic restaurant, champagne? Dim lights, soft music … too bad, he'd decided. This was as perfect as it could get.

* * *

Amanda prepared to feast. The table was already set with his blue tablecloth and napkins from their supper the night before, so it was a breakfast with all the trimmings, French press full of coffee, maple syrup in a fancy little pitcher instead of the bottle it came in. Because Jacob made great pancakes; that first bite was pure bliss. She swallowed and said, "What's on the plan for today? We never talked about the weekend, yesterday."

His smile disappeared. He leaned forward, as if proximity would help her hear his words. "I do have an idea." He was serious—and on edge. She understood his moods well by now. "I thought of it this morning. Only it's not new, at least in my head, but this wasn't what I'd planned, I mean, sort of planned, but I don't know if you'll like it. But watching you sleep … anyway, I don't see how it could be any better. So—"

"Jacob, go on. What is it?" She suspected where he was going with this and settled in to enjoy it.

"Give me time. I'm afraid of messing up the moment here. I love you."

"I love you." She put down her fork and watched his face.

He swallowed hard. She had the feeling he was struggling to find words and look at her at the same time. At last he got it out. "I want … I mean … Amanda, will you marry me?"

"Okay."

"The thing is, I want to marry you. I want to live with you and be a husband and do things with you. You're everything I could dream of. I worship the ground you—" He stopped short, and his eyes widened. "Okay?"

"You don't worship the ground I walk on." She tried to suppress a grin and failed.

"Nearly." He produced the thousand-watt smile. "You said okay?"

She nodded.

"You're sure?"

"Yes. Let's get married, Jacob. I want to."

"You saw it on my face, didn't you? How nervous I was."

"You're not the only mind reader. Don't even *dream* you'll be able to keep secrets from me."

"Oh. That's … but we have so much to talk about. There's so much that we have to talk about, to plan … am I grinning like an idiot? I must be." He gave up on the effort and collapsed back in his chair.

"Yes, you are. Calm down, the worst is over." She reached across the table and captured his hand, lying open on the table. Watching his face the whole time, she kissed his knuckles in exact imitation of his habitual gesture, then turned his hand over and kissed the palm, tickling him with her tongue. He groaned quietly; she smiled. "There's lots to talk over, starting with how and when we tell Norah. But you know what? Today, what I'd like to do is go for a walk in the park. Visit a garden center, get ice cream cones."

"Just you and me." He turned his hand over and held onto hers. "We could go to a jewelry store. I have an idea what kind of ring I'd choose for you. I wanted to share choosing it. If you want a ring?"

She nodded. "We could."

"It might have sapphires in it. Or just one, with diamonds around it. Or maybe you'd rather have diamonds alone, or something else?"

She laughed, delighted. "I don't know. I haven't considered it. Don't look now, but your romantic streak's showing."

"You mean it. You'll marry me."

"Yes. Keep asking, I like it. You're so funny when you're off balance. The answer isn't likely to change."

He shook his head, looking a little stunned. Their eyes met.

"There is one thing," she said.

"Don't tell me. I don't want my bubble burst."

She laughed again. "Hold on to your bubble, then. I'm still famished. Can we finish our pancakes?"

"In a minute." He pulled her to her feet and wrapped himself around her, bringing his mouth to hers. His body felt like solidity, comfort, forever. Then he sighed, gave her one final, quick hug, and said, "You'll never get away from me now. Let's eat."

Chapter 38

It was a mild spring day, a week after Jacob's proposal. Amanda and Pat had spent the morning walking in the local state forest, followed by lunch at the picnic area.

Everything began at Fremont Park, at the picnic tables.

"The thing is," Amanda said around a bite of peanut butter sandwich, "I didn't know it could be so much fun."

"What's that? Life? Life can be fun. Haven't we proved it? Of course, that's unless you've just received notice they want to build a mega mall across the street from you."

"You've been moaning about that all morning. They haven't even got planning permission yet. Don't there have to be hearings and things? It's like you to be a social activist," Amanda reflected. "But it's not like you to obsess."

"Trust me, the hearings will come."

Amanda opted to change the subject. "Do you know how long it's been since we headed for the woods? Years. This morning was great."

"Frankly, Mandy, if we're going to spend any more time with mother nature, we need to take you shopping. Your wardrobe's not up to snuff."

Amanda's mouth was gluey with peanut butter. When she'd swallowed she made a purring sort of sound in her throat, then said, "Simple pleasures. I forget how much I like this stuff. And what, you don't approve of my slacks? You want me to get some of those pants with all the pockets, and a compass?"

"GPS. Guaranteed to keep you from getting lost. You need new boots, or at least sneakers that aren't white. We need to keep you in shape, given your desk job. Which reminds me."

Pat took another bite of salami sandwich, then squinted her eyes in Amanda's direction. "You've been strangely silent on the subject of Mister McKinnon today."

"I thought you'd never ask," she responded with every bit of nonchalance she could muster. "There is some news. He asked me to marry him last weekend. I said okay."

Pat put down her sandwich and stared. "Just like that."

Amanda grinned across the picnic table. She didn't catch Pat flat-footed often, and it was fun when she pulled it off. Pat's expression was mixed bewilderment and incredulity. "Just like that. He didn't expect it. He went on trying to tell me why I should, even after I said yes. It took him a few seconds to catch up. We were eating pancakes."

"Mandy!" Pat was on her feet, circling the table to grab her friend in a bear hug. "I'm not surprised about him, but you? Where'd you get so spontaneous? I'm thrilled."

Since Pat had pulled her up anyway, Amanda did a pirouette, then took her friend's hands. "Who said anything about spontaneous? I'd had my answer ready for a while. I didn't expect the question so soon, but he was right." She went dreamy, sank back onto the bench. "You remember last weekend. Perfect weather, sun and flowers and all that. Jeez, when did I get mushy?"

"Ring?"

"Soon. Somehow we never quite got around to it."

"Well." Pat sat, but not still. Excitement buzzed from her; Amanda picked it up all the way across the table. They ate sandwiches for a few minutes, but Pat kept looking at her, grinning for no reason. "That qualifies as fun."

"I agree. I don't kid myself, we both have our share of challenges. And I'm a little overwhelmed by how much have to see to. We haven't told Norah yet, for instance." She sighed, content. "She was at her grandparents' place last weekend, so we took the time and wandered around. We planted petunias." She giggled. "Basic bright pink. Can you imagine me getting into pink petunias?" She took a bite of her sandwich, chewed, and swallowed. "He makes me laugh. Even when—Pat, I never dreamed sex could be so much fun. We'll be, you know, whatever, and then he comes out with some crazy remark, and we're both laughing like loons. I never knew."

"It is kind of a funny thing to do, when you get right down to it."

Amanda's voice shifted from wonder to evil. "I've found all his ticklish spots. He doesn't stand a chance."

Pat laughed. "You're bad. Finish your sandwich, we need to be heading home." She watched while Amanda dutifully took another bite. "Looks like the play therapy worked, doesn't it? Six months ago nothing on earth would get you to laugh about sex. Or get engaged, for that matter."

"The jury's out on whether that's your play therapy or his. It's not only Jacob though. There's so much happening at SI these days with the expansion, and the money mess straightened out, and the buyers are finding incredible stuff right now. It makes me wonder if there's something to that karma thing of yours. Speaking of which, what's really bugging you about this mall business? I get that you don't want it, but there's an undercurrent I can't interpret."

"It's nothing, Mandy. Just an extra annoyance. Past coming back to haunt me."

"You don't have that much of a past—unless you've been keeping secrets. I can't figure out how you could have though."

Pat made a big, open-armed gesture, waving around the last bit of her sandwich. "Consider where I live. Older houses. They roll in and put in one of those modern concrete structures and it'll dominate the landscape, destroy the neighborhood." She collapsed her arms and took a bite.

"You're not answering my question. Out with it, Pat."

She chewed, and swallowed, and said slowly, "Yeah, okay. It's the developers. You don't need imagination to work out that Brandon Caine's involved. He's not the issue. But he's partnered this time with Alan Carmichael. I don't suppose you remember him."

"No. Who's Alan Carmichael and what's he to you? Old mystery lover?"

"Hardly. You've got lovers on the brain. In fact, I was still married to Shawn the Creep back then. Alan dates from my pre-sanity days when I wanted to be an engineer."

"Right age? Good looking?"

"That's not the point. He was my supervisor on my first job out of school. He was one of those patronizing jackasses who treated me like an incompetent ninny because I was a woman. Constant little digs, always needling me, looking for me to make a mistake. His presence did nothing to enhance my love of engineering. In fact, he almost singlehandedly convinced me to go into psychology instead. We loathed each other."

"Has it occurred to you," Amanda asked sweetly, "that you may be protesting too much?"

Pat stared at her. "Trust me. The only pleasure I'd get from seeing him again is so I can stomp on his instep. I'm too ladylike to attack the man parts I really want to destroy."

Amanda laughed. "You're getting yourself worked up. Maybe you should find us both a meditation class. Isn't meditation supposed to keep you in balance? I could meditate with Jacob. Maybe then I'd understand more about your cosmic laws of the universe. And it might help you get over your thing about Alan Carmichael. Face it, Pat, that was, what? Almost twenty years ago? We were kids. He might surprise you and be all grown up. Or most likely you'll never run into him at all."

"You've used up all the positive karma we're entitled to between us. I doubt there's even a crumb of karma left for me. I'm doomed to have to deal with him again, worse luck."

"I'm going to have to learn how to cook. Can I grocery shop at your new mall?" she asked innocently, then shoved the last of her sandwich into her mouth.

Pat groaned. "Next it'll be violins and the twittering of birds. And all I'm seeing on my horizon is bulldozers and bloody Alan Carmichael."

Chapter 39

Using the eraser end of his pencil, Stan traced an imaginary line on the blueprint that blanketed Amanda's conference table. "Well, how about this? If we put the purchasing office here, then we move the viewing rooms around like so ..." More imaginary lines. Sheets of notebook paper covered in drawings, as well as pages and pages of notes, lay scattered over the blueprints.

"Not a chance," Colin said. "Look, you're messing up the traffic flow from reception to the viewing room. We have to move Amanda's office over here ..."

Amanda paid attention, but also watched the two men as they bickered.

Stan had slotted back into SI seamlessly. She missed having regular interactions with Jacob, but it was a comfort to see Stan in fighting form, controlling the finances of her company. She suspected his lost weight wouldn't stay lost, given the quantity of doughnuts consumed on the day he returned to work. Everyone at SI was thrilled. No one except Jacob, Stan, her parents, and herself would ever know the backstory.

Still half following the discussion going on around her, she glanced at her father. He was having a ball. It had required her mother's help to get him to agree, but the new position at SI had revitalized him, and she felt none of the hostility that had marked their interactions for the last eight years. She hadn't fully appreciated how much he'd hated retirement. He was still a vital man in his late sixties, and he had a lot to contribute. Now, he was contributing. From his office down the hall from hers, he reigned over the planning for their move and expansion. No one better, she thought.

Sinclair Imports faced a challenging twelve to eighteen months, because adding product lines meant also adding customers for those lines. An updated web presence, a larger sales team. More trickle-down effects than her brain could handle right now, with her father and Stan in full spate, planning SI's new physical location.

This warehouse had potential. The location, while not as good as they had now, was acceptable, and the options for remodeling to fit their needs were at least possible, if the men ever stopped squabbling. It was a modern, bright building, a requirement in Amanda's mind. The hitch was that the warehouse was for sale, not lease. She, her father, and Stan had spent hours reviewing their cash flow, debating whether the gamble was justified.

She'd talked it over with Jacob, evenings when they were alone, but they'd both agreed it was better to let the two older men control the official discussion.

She forced her attention to the conversation at hand.

"Amanda, have a look. This idiot accountant wants to put you in this corner, but there's no view, but if we move you here—"

"I'm sure you'll figure it out." She turned her gaze to the drawings, but with no desire to resolve the debate. The men would jostle and re-draw and argue with each other for as long as it took, and they'd love every minute. No need for her to get involved.

They left with a plan for an extended visit to the warehouse—tape measures in hand, she thought wryly. Jacob popped in to drop a report on her desk, give her a wink, and disappeared again. And that reminded her they were having supper with her parents that evening. Her dad and Stan both took Jacob's presence at work in their stride, but this added a different, more personal, dimension.

Norah being there would smooth any rough edges when they learned he'd be their son-in-law. She wanted her parents to be happy for her, for them both.

So far, they'd told Pat, Jacob's friend Dave, and Norah. Where Norah was concerned, Jacob had explained that he was marrying Amanda; that meant she would be Norah's new mother. When the little girl had nodded and said, "That's okay, Daddy," he had visibly relaxed. With the caveat that she would call her 'Amanda' instead of 'Mommy', Norah calmly accepted the change in her life. In fact, based on her hugs over the last couple of weeks, Norah was more than happy.

Neither she nor Jacob had wanted their private bubble burst too soon. And Norah had been so, so serious about keeping this Big Secret. Tonight she could let it out.

Tonight's the night.

On the Sunday after the magic Saturday, when they'd been engaged for a whole day, he had told her he'd asked her parents' permission. He didn't elaborate, but in quiet moments she had reflected on his formal, old-fashioned action in this day and age. She still had so much to learn about Jacob, the way his mind worked, the things he believed were important. At least that meant the announcement couldn't be too big a surprise. Still, she was on edge, facing this second family dinner.

* * *

The three of them arrived at the Sinclair residence together. "Hello, we're here," Amanda called out, opening the unlocked door. Norah slipped around her and barreled toward the kitchen. Her father emerged from the living room and hugged his daughter. A perfunctory hug, but at least an acknowledgement. He gave Jacob a small nod and herded them out the back door, where they had the barbecue set up and ready to go on the patio.

"Mandy, you're glowing," her mom said. "I don't remember when you've looked so healthy. Or maybe it's the pink in your shirt? Pink always was a good color on you."

Amanda glanced at Jacob. "I'm feeling good, Mom. And excited. I guess Dad's told you what's going on at SI."

"Interminably," her mother groaned.

"And what with the prospect of a new warehouse and the incredible deals we're finding in Southeast Asia these days, I've never been busier, but it feels good."

Her mother put Norah to work, shaping out hamburger patties on a tray. "It's like play dough," she announced, then grimaced at her hands. "Only it sticks. Yuck."

"An astonishing amount of cooking is yucky," Amanda told her. "Come on indoors, we'll get your hands washed."

"I've got to say it, or I'm going to *explode*," Norah whispered over the sink.

"Then we'd better be quick. I don't want any exploding kids. At least not until you've had your hamburger."

"And cake. Your mom said she made a cake."

"And cake." Amanda led Norah out to the patio. "Ladies and gentlemen," she said, "Norah has an announcement to make. And we have to let her make it now, or she'll blow up right before our eyes."

"Silly."

"Silly back to you. Tell them."

Norah drew herself up. "I have a secret. I've kept it really well, haven't I?"

"You sure have, Pumpkin." Jacob grinned at her.

"So. What I have to say is …" There was a pause, then she screeched, "I'm going to be a bridesmaid! Amanda said I could. And I get to wear a pink dress and lots of ruffles and — oh. That wasn't what I was supposed to say." Norah's dismayed eyes turned from Jacob to Amanda, then back to her father.

They both smiled at her. "I guess we know where your priorities are," Jacob said.

Amanda added, "Now you can tell them *why* you'll be a bridesmaid."

She considered for a moment, then said, the picture of cool, "They're getting married. So Amanda's going to live with us. That's all."

Jacob grinned and said, "Well done, Pumpkin."

Amanda's mother cried, "I'll be your grandmother!" and scooped Norah up into a hug.

Her father remained to one side, his face revealing nothing, but when Norah threw herself at him, he put his arms around the little girl and returned her hug.

Jacob caught Amanda's eye and gestured her over to where he stood a little apart from the others. He took her hand and mouthed, "I love you."

She smiled and met his eyes, and mouthed back, "I love you."

The modest, in-front-of-the-in-laws kiss he gave her sent her heart flying off to the moon.

"Better than perfect," he whispered when he released her.

"Wow," her mother said.

"Wow is right."

Disaster averted. Amanda was almost dizzy with relief. With the secret out and her parents clearly delighted, she felt happier and more relaxed than she had in months. It was as if a warehouse of weight had been lifted from her shoulders, and she was free. Free to be herself, run her business, love her family and make a home with Jacob and Norah.

Free of Brandon and the horrid fears and memories.

She helped her mother and Norah carry hamburger fixings and bowls of potato salad and coleslaw out to the patio table, enjoying the everyday nature of the shared activity, the sight of her father and her fiancé relaxed and chatting.

Later, her father drew her into the living room. He said, "You're sure?"

"Absolutely. Are you concerned?"

"I remember when I first got together with your mother. I thought she walked on water and I was the luckiest guy on earth. After a while I knew she didn't walk on water at all. But there was still something special there that lasted. You see where I'm going with this?"

"I do. We spent a lot of time together before I fell for him. There was plenty of 'like' before the love."

"He's had trouble."

"Well, losing his wife—oh. You mean the marijuana thing? That was a long time ago, Dad. He's grown up. At least most of the time," she added, turning her head toward the whoops and laughter from the kitchen. "He's solid. I know what I'll have when the dream fades into reality. Oh, brother," she groaned. "He's made me go romantic."

"I'm happy for you, Amanda." She didn't expect hearts and flowers from her father, and she didn't get them. But his simple words were a sufficient blessing.

"Thanks, Dad." She wiped her eyes as they went back into the kitchen to join in the hilarity there.

* * *

On the Tuesday after the barbecue at her parents' house, Amanda looked up from a profit/loss spreadsheet as Jacob entered her office and closed the door behind him. She put her fountain pen on the desk and folded her hands. "What's happening? Why the appointment?"

His grin relieved her of the worry that something was wrong. "We're giving Mel a complex, the way we keep closing the door on her." He dropped the grin as he sat across from her. "I'm resigning from SI, Amanda. I thought it would be best to make it formal."

"Oh. But why? Everything's going so smoothly. We told Marcia to stop the search."

"We did, but things have changed. With the missing money you needed me here. Now you don't. More than that though, it's because this is your company. We've done great so far, but I could be a complication one day. And I suppose …" He squirmed. He was uncomfortable, which was unusual. "To be honest, there may be pride involved as well. I'm used to working for myself. I'm not so sure I want to work for my wife."

Their eyes met. She loved the honesty in his, the fearlessness. But then, was there anything about this man she didn't love? For a moment she got lost in the memory of peeling him out of his jacket, his tie, his shirt …

Her mind snapped back to business. "Thanks for telling me. It makes sense, I'm just selfish. I'm used to having you around."

"Don't get me wrong, it's been fine so far. And I'll always be your sounding board if you need one. But it's your company, Amanda. Not ours."

He watched her fiddle with her fountain pen. "How soon?"

"I'll be here until you replace me, and we've been down that road before, so we know it could take a while. I'm not abandoning ship. Then I'll put out feelers. Word of mouth's worked well for me in the past."

"Jacob, it'd be so awkward, writing a recommendation for you."

He grinned. "We'll skip the recommendation thing. If I explain that I'm marrying the head of the company, most people will recognize that nothing you write should be trusted. If I need a reference, I'll get it from Stan."

Her eyes danced. "'To whom it may concern, let Jacob McKinnon get his hands inside your shirt for thirty seconds and you'll see why I hired him'."

He laughed with her. Then stopped. "I'll always be there for you, even when I'm not working for SI. You know that, don't you?"

"I know. You'll talk to Stan? He can notify Marcia to advertise for your position. Best if he coordinates it since he'll be doing the interviews."

"I'll see to it."

"Jacob?"

"What is it?"

"Thanks. For everything."

The grin came back, and the mischief that lit his eyes these days. She wondered fleetingly if his mind had flashed to the memory of peeling her out of *her* suit. "No thanks needed. Accepting the position at SI was arguably the best move I ever made." He stood and gave her the full-wattage smile, then left. She heard him in the outer office joking with Mel for a minute before he disappeared down the corridor.

Chapter 40

Amanda carried the cake she'd made that morning as they walked up to the Carters' house. At least the thing had risen, and had stayed that way, although her red icing had come out closer to pink. She hadn't risked the cake decorating set; she had enough to concern her. It was the Fourth of July, and the fireworks had misplaced themselves. She'd swear they were firing off in her stomach.

Could it be any worse than courting a new client? Merely Jacob's oldest and best friends? This is where you step out of the dream into real life.

The world had already breached their private bubble. SI knew, and she'd had a pleasant online conversation with his parents in Indianapolis. This felt bigger. Scarier.

The woman who appeared on the porch was tall and angular, with chopped-off blond hair and serious muscles in her calves. Nancy smiled and said, "Hey, kid," as Norah barreled into her for a hug. "Joanie's upstairs, Sammy's out back. Take your pick."

By the time Norah was through the screen door, Amanda and Jacob were climbing the steps to the porch.

And right into open arms. Nancy took the cake, shoved it at Jacob, and grasped Amanda's hands in both of hers. "It's taken too long. I've been dying to meet you. Dave's doing male things with the barbecue," she said to Jacob. "Drop the cake in the kitchen."

Amanda returned the smile. "I'm happy to be here. A little nervous."

"Of us? The only reason to be nervous around here is the chaos. I hope your tolerance for bedlam's high. Come on in." She and Nancy followed Jacob into a country kitchen stretching across the back of the house.

Jacob put the cake on the table and caught Nancy in a bear hug. "If manly stuff's going on out there, I'd better make my presence felt." He squeezed Amanda's shoulder and disappeared through the back door.

"Thanks for bringing this. We'll keep little fingers out of it." Nancy stowed the cake on a high shelf while Amanda looked out the picture windows. Norah was with a little boy, presumably Sammy, while Jacob had vanished.

"I think they're in the garage," Nancy said at her elbow. "I'd hoped we could get together long before now, but at least we've managed today. Has it been crazy? New engagements can be. Oh, let me see." She seized Amanda's hand and studied her ring, a simple band of sapphires and diamonds in white gold. "Always knew the man had good taste."

"It was a joint effort." She felt a little breathless from the whirlwind that was Nancy Carter.

"Strikes me as being a good plan. I mean, what if the guy turns up with a ring and you love the guy but you hate the ring?"

"The sapphires were Jacob's idea."

"Now, let's sit for a minute and get to … oh, there they are." Jacob and Dave had emerged from the garage and were standing over the barbecue. "Deep consultation's going on there. I love my kitchen. Never miss a thing, but I'm apart from the hubbub."

So that's Dave. Jacob's height, dark hair, stocky … yes, he looked familiar. "I've met your husband before, but not to say I know him. Chamber of Commerce."

"So that's everyone accounted for except our oldest, but he's almost thirteen now and he's not, under any circumstances, going to have anything to do with a family Fourth of July party. You might see him, might not. How are you getting along with Norah?" Nancy sank into a kitchen chair, pulling Amanda with her by sheer force of enthusiasm.

"I love her. It's possible I'm marrying her father because of her."

"I don't believe that. You're radiant, and so's Jacob. That means so much to us. It's been rough for him since Deb's death."

Amanda looked down. "It's hard, stepping into another woman's shoes—"

"Except you're not. We're talking three years here. And what you've done for Jacob … I'm not sure I've ever seen him so happy. Now, about me. I teach physical education at Northside Middle School. Three kids. My whole story in a nutshell. What about you?"

Amanda told Nancy about SI, how much she enjoyed being with Norah and how unexpected that was. Nancy filled her in on teaching phys ed and the challenges of balancing work and home life. Every once in a while, a shriek from outdoors had both women on their feet, assessing the situation in the back yard. Nancy brought over a pitcher of iced tea. Later they prepped the chicken.

By the time the men came in, hot from badminton with Norah and Sammy, Amanda had forgotten to be nervous. It was natural for Jacob to come up behind her in the Carter kitchen, wrap an arm around her neck, and kiss her there in front of everybody.

Much later, full of barbecued chicken and cake, the adults drove sleepy children to Fremont Park for fireworks. Amanda leaned against Jacob on their blanket, Norah's head cradled in his lap, her hand in Amanda's while she tried to stay awake. The Carters shared a similar blanket next to them, Nancy in Dave's arms while their children sat around them.

Stepped into real life, for sure. But not alone.

Norah's hand tightened on hers whenever there was an especially loud explosion. She stroked the little girl's hair. "It's like being a family, isn't it?" she whispered to Jacob.

He looked at her. It was dark between displays, but that didn't matter; she'd memorized his eyes. "Yes," he whispered back. "I'm pretty sure it's real."

"I think it is." She nodded. "I think it is." Secure next to Jacob, she watched the sky explode in light and color above them.

* * *

Jacob tossed a handful of brochures in Amanda's lap when she settled on his sofa, then dropped down beside her. "I don't know where you've always dreamed of going," he told her. "I was debating Hawaii or the Caribbean, but I'm open to other ideas."

Summer was almost over; soon they'd be caught in back-to-school activities. Amanda had helped him put Norah to bed, and he was ready to have this conversation.

She picked up the brochures and flipped through them. "Are we talking honeymoon?"

"We are."

"We don't even have a wedding date yet."

"And that is relevant how?"

He had refused to consider a date until they found a home. They'd spent most of the summer perusing listings and attending open houses, wandering through places other people lived in. Finally the right place came on the market. "Dream house," Amanda had murmured to him, and he'd nodded and hugged her. A large two-story, old enough to have mature trees and a fenced back yard. Partially updated inside, but room for them to make their own choices, too. Julie, their agent, an enthusiastic friend of Mel's, had produced an accepted offer two days before, so, following his own logic, he'd brought brochures.

"You might consider Europe. I've heard those river cruises are good. We could do fun things in our stateroom all day, come out at night for dinner and dancing ..."

"Suppose I said I didn't want a honeymoon?"

No way. He drew back and looked at her. "Suppose I said I do? I really do, Amanda. I want to romance you and court you and do interesting things with your body and bring you home glowing, cloud nine and all that."

"You're serious."

"Oh, yes."

"I've never traveled much, so I'd rather not go anywhere too exotic. There's enough new to contend with. I want to be comfortable."

"Hence, Hawaii. Tropical, but in the U.S."

"It's a possibility. But Jacob …"

He watched her mull it over, wondering what she was dreaming of. They'd put the wedding on the calendar soon, a simple ceremony in her parents' back yard, followed by a much larger reception in town. All they had to do, from his simple male perspective, was book the hall and finalize the officiant. Amanda had laughed at him when he said that. But one way or another, the honeymoon was front and center in his mind.

"We've planned two weeks," she said. "One week should be enough."

He shook his head. "Nope. You're not going back to SI after a one-week honeymoon. Non-negotiable."

"Just listen." She gave him a gentle punch, then leaned against his outstretched arm. "As for where we go … Hawaii could be fun. But could we try somewhere less adventurous? Closer, anyway, so there'd be less travel involved. Savannah? I've never been into the South."

"We could do that."

"I'm not finished. Here's the rest of the plan. We do the honeymoon thing for a week. Then we come back. We collect Norah and go again, on a family holiday."

He stared at her—not that that was a hardship. Would she ever stop amazing him? "You'd give up a week of your honeymoon to take Norah with us?"

"Of course. We're not starting from scratch. She's your daughter. Soon to be *our* daughter. She's more excited about this wedding than we are. She's not quite seven years old. And we're a family." She leaned into him and began working on the buttons of his shirt.

He felt the beginning of a reaction. No one had ever gotten to him as readily as Amanda did. "I like where this is going."

"You don't know yet where this is going."

He went from near zero to full-blown response in a split second. She must have felt the shudder because she began humming to herself.

Instead of groaning, which was his first idea, he tried to get the conversation back on track. "Disneyland, say?"

She shook her head, but didn't take her eyes off the buttons. "No, that would be too much on top of the wedding. Something simple, like a cabin on a lake, with a beach. We can do Disneyland next year. I'm pretty sure I'd like it."

But by then he'd surrendered. The honeymoon debate would keep. She finished the buttons and trailed her fingers over his chest.

"You're asking for trouble there, lady."

She looked up innocently. "Is trouble synonymous with fun?"

He did groan. And then they didn't talk any more, for quite some time.

Epilogue

On a sunny day in late September, Colin Sinclair sat at his desk at Sinclair Imports, making notes on the pad in front of him. He had a handful of phone calls to make, a man to meet about the move to the larger warehouse, a meeting with IT to review the updated website, and several shipments from new suppliers to view.

He'd never in his life been busier. He loved every minute.

Stan stuck his head in. "What do you hear?"

He set his pen on top of a pile of file folders. "The family McKinnon's having a ball. We got an email postcard from Lake Placid. You'd think they'd been married for years. Norah loves that they pulled her out of school, even if it's for a bunch of nature walks. Amanda says it's a battle to get her to do her homework."

"Let's grab a coffee."

Colin peeled away from his desk, and the two men ambled down the corridor together, stopping at one of the viewing windows to watch the activity on the Floor.

"It's good for the kid," Stan said. "She won't grow up believing that school's a prison. Is Amanda going to change her name?"

"So we hear. She says it's better for family solidarity."

"Any hint she's looking forward to getting back in the saddle?"

"Not so far," Colin said. "She's in wife and mother mode, I'd say."

"She's done a good job. Took what we started and grew it."

"We raised her in this company."

"Sure did. But she's got the knack. A nose for the business. Like her old man."

"Good marketing instincts." In the break room they poured coffee, then propped against the counter.

"You'll be around this winter?" Stan asked. That was the nearest either of them had come to discussing the traumatic events of the previous spring.

"Not all winter. We've sold the RV, but Karen's taken the household finances in hand. Funny that she never had any interest before. She's trimmed the food budget and cut back on some stuff, so we'll be able to manage a month off. Between you and me, a month's plenty. I'd rather be here."

"Like father, like daughter."

"This is the first vacation Amanda's had in years."

"Are they talking more kids? Or is the one she inherited enough?"

"Don't know. She's being quiet on that subject. Norah's great. I'm getting a kick out of the granddad thing."

Stan gulped the last of his coffee and stood. "Gotta run."

"Me, too." They put their mugs in the dishwasher and headed for the door, where Stan turned left and Colin turned right, both of them muttering.

"Month end. Chaos."

"Moving in six weeks. More work than any sane man should take on."

"Stop grumbling." Charlie from the Floor passed them on his way into the break room. "Neither of you would change it for the world."

Nope, Colin thought as he returned to his office. *Not for the world.*

To My Readers

Hello, and thanks for choosing *Amanda*. I hope you'll be inspired to check out what else is happening in Calter Creek, where Pat and Mel both have their own stories of romance and discovery.

If you enjoyed this book, well, I don't need to tell you how much reviews mean to writers.

To keep up with upcoming romances, visit my website, http://lizanncarson.com. There you'll find notices about book events and my musings about life as both a writer and an inhabitant of the real world.

Happy reading,

LizAnn

About LizAnn Carson

It's interesting, trying to condense who you are into a paragraph or two. For openers, there are the basics: husband, three kids, and three kids-in-law, with a shifting grandkid count. I live in Victoria, British Columbia, a smallish city that's large enough to have all modern conveniences, but not so large as to have hours-long traffic jams or heavy duty pollution. I can follow a trail to my local supermarket, or I can be downtown in twenty minutes.

Yes, I spend most of my time writing (and editing, formatting, critiquing for other writers, battling computer problems, and occasionally tearing my hair out). But beyond that, I enjoy a variety of crafts. I draw/paint using oil pastels and colored pencils. I walk a lot and enjoy weight training and yoga. Once, a long time ago, I owned a yarn shop, and for a while I taught English as a Second Language. My career, on the other hand, was in the world of computer systems development.

You can follow some of my explorations on my website, http://lizanncarson.com.